Song Walker

Starseeds One

Ellis Logan

An Earth Lodge® Publication
Roxbury, Connecticut

Also by Ellis Logan

Shades of Valhalla
Fates of Midgard
Gifts of Elysielle
Heart Ward
The Warping
Dream Tracker
Inner Origins: The Box Set

Also from Earth Lodge

Lost and Faerie Found
The Girls Who Could Series
Practical Reiki Symbol Primer
The Comprehensive Vibrational
Healing Guide
Shamans Who Work with the Light
Natural Animal Healing
Grounding and Clearing
Equine Herbs & Healing
The Mudra Book
Eden Is Now
Tarot

Published in the U.S.A. by Earth Lodge®
Cover Design by Maya Cointreau

ISBN 978-1-944396-37-4

"If a man does not keep pace with his companions, perhaps it is because he hears a different drummer. Let him step to the music he hears, however measured or far away...

When I hear music, I fear no danger. I am invulnerable. I see no foe. I am related to the earliest times, and to the latest."

Henry David Thoreau

Chapter 1

The sound of the drums pounded through me, fast and hard, setting the pace for dancers going wild under the lights. Speeding their hearts to racing.

The more furious the dancing became, the slower my own heart pulsed. Relaxing into the rhythm. This was where I was meant to be. This was my home.

If you had told me when I was a kid that I was going to grow up to become a drummer in a rock band, I would have shaken my head and shown you my ballet slippers. If you had told me again when I was a teen, I would have cringed, hating the thought of being on stage. Drumming had just been something to take the edge off, a way of letting loose at the end of the day without hurting anyone, or myself.

Now?

Sitting behind my purple Zildjian drum kit on stage at The Hammer on a Thursday night, a couple hundred people dancing and grinding to the music our band was playing, I was in the zone. I'd answered Nick's flyer for a drummer my second year in college on a whim, and we'd been playing together ever since. Nine years. We'd had several bassists come and go, toyed with a keyboardist or two in the early years, but our band, Molten Requiem, had enjoyed a strong local following throughout all that time. In a rock-and-roll city with over twenty colleges, you couldn't really go wrong. Los Angeles was a musician's haven. Bars and party gigs were practically on every corner. With Nick's head for business and his Irish charm to back it up, the money had been steady and easy. I'd gone to school to be a social worker, but I hadn't worked a day job since graduating.

Which was good, because I wasn't really the office girl type. After almost a decade in a band, I'd come to view stretch vinyl pants and ripped tees as comfort wear. Right now, the music was picking up pace, and I shook my long, sweaty black hair out of my face, hitting the snare and rocketing through the cymbals. My hands became almost a blur, driving the song at breakneck speed, the 122 Ultraviolet lacquer on my nails catching the spotlight.

Nick nodded at me, his pale cheeks brightly flushed from the heat of the stage lights. He backed off to the side of the stage along with Jax, our current bassist, giving me the crowd's attention.

Solo time. I took the beat and pulled it along, flaring the tempo, alternating between speed and a slow, tempting rhythm of need. Girls in the crowd screamed and threw themselves into wild jungle dance, while men bobbed their heads along in appreciation, feeling the music with their feet. Everybody in the band got to rock out a few solos each night, but this one was my favorite, taking me on a crazy ride every time. Passion, longing, dreams – all of mine went into this piece.

I closed my eyes and lost myself in it, the way I always did.

Peace and fulfillment threatened to overwhelm me, even as my arms and feet pushed the beat with a mind of their own. I let my imagination go, dreaming that I ran through the desert in time with the tune, chasing wolves, then leaping and flying through the air, flying free. The sky was dark as pitch, stars twinkling everywhere, and the moon glowed crimson like it was on fire. I rocketed towards the red orb, remembering the weathergirl this morning had mentioned a total lunar eclipse would be occurring. A blood moon, she had called it.

My brain must have fed the fact into my vision, because there it was, in all its gory bloody glory. The sight was beautiful, and I wanted to fly to it, bask in its glow. My mind soared, and I laughed, whether out loud or just in my dream I don't know, and then I heard a man's voice, so deep it made my bones tremble. Like elephant rumbles on the Savannah, the sound traveled through me, into me.

The voice pulled me in, pulled me down, and I plummeted from the sky through layers of clouds, smog, brick and floor. It all happened so fast, and then there I was, standing in a dimly lit office, watching two men in suits argue. One, a middle-aged Asian man, paced back and forth, scowling, while an older white man sat calmly by the desk, not a strand of his snowy hair out of place.

"It's for the best, Kim. You know it is." The seated man said matter-of-factly.

"But we're not ready," Kim practically whined, throwing his hands up in the air before slamming them down on the desk. Chair guy didn't even blink.

"These new warpers aren't going to wait for your people to be ready. We need to keep things under control."

Neither of these guys possessed the voice that had called me here. And what the heck were warpers? This had to be just about the weirdest daydream I'd ever had. But, since it was my dream, I guessed I was free to ask questions and change it up.

"What's a warper?" I said.

The men ignored me.

"Hello, rude much?" I crooned. "Girl with a question here."

Nothing. Kim and Chair Guy were still locked in a staring contest, each one willing the other to break. I was impressed that Kim was holding up under the pressure, because honestly, so far he'd seemed kind of high-strung. And Chair Guy was seriously imposing, with a very conservative, military sort of bearing. If I'd ever had any sort of respect for authority, I probably would have found him intimidating. As it was, the whole scene just made me roll my eyes. Men. So far evolved from Neanderthals, yet still facing off with grunts and staring contests.

A cough on my left surprised all of us. Turning, I saw a third man sitting in a corner chair. Even sitting down, I could tell he was really tall, built with shoulders that made the chair he was in look undersized. He waited for the men to look at him and then propped his hands up behind his head, looking completely relaxed as he nodded in my direction with his chin. We made eye contact then, dark pools locking my amber ones in place, and when his deep voice rolled through the room I felt like I was falling all over again.

"We've got company."

Well, yeah, hello Captain Obvious.

I shook my head and turned back to the other two, still waiting for them to acknowledge me. They looked in my direction, but they weren't looking at me, not really.

"A traveler?" the seated man asked.

"Maybe." The huge man in the corner looked at me, all of me, his gaze slowly roving up my long, lean black vinyl-clad legs, to take in my ripped Social Distortion tee shirt and purple streaked hair. "Why are you here?"

His fingers laced through his warm brown hair, making it stand up in odd directions, the light glinting off of it like copper in wet sand. Unlike the other two, he wasn't wearing a suit. Cargo pants, flip flops and a worn tee shirt fit his laid-back attitude perfectly and showed off the muscles in his arms nicely, but his square jaw was clenched and a vein by his temple was pulsing. He could act however he wanted – the man was anything but relaxed while he waited for my answer. Too bad I didn't have one to give him.

I gave him my sauciest look and shrugged.

"Good question." I had no idea why my mind had taken me here. I wanted to get back to running with my wolves. Drumming was supposed to bring me to my happy place, not uptight office meetings. I was so ready to get out of here.

As if on command, the scene started to break apart, dissolving when a riff of angry guitar jarred me and brought me back to the present moment.

The band had rejoined me on center stage and we were approaching the end of the song. I hadn't lost the beat, but I felt like I might have lost my mind. I always traveled into myself with music, imagining other worlds and places, but my daydreams had never strayed into something so mundane.

Nick's bright blue eyes caught mine, clearly wondering if something was wrong. I shook my head and smiled, following Jax's lead and rolling into the next song. A rock ballad our brown-eyed bassist had written for his new girl, the love song brought the crowd down from their previous high and locked in a few new fangirls for Jax and Nick at the same time. You could practically see the love-hearts popping out of their eyes as they swooned over Jax's surfer bod and raw, husky voice.

I couldn't blame them.

Bassists were hot, and Jax, a recent transplant from Oahu, had it all going on. I would have swooned myself, if I hadn't been sticking to my hard and fast rule never to date in-band since a bad breakup had cost Molten Requiem its first bassist. We played enough gigs with other bands that if I wanted a bassist, I could find another one. Plus, I had my own little horde of fanboys to pick from, if I was really hard up.

The song ended, and so did our last set of the night. We had a regular gig here on Thursday nights, playing our own music mixed in with popular covers. Fridays and Saturdays we usually played after-party gigs, or one-off shows at bigger venues like the Whiskey or Roxy. Compared to some cities, LA bars closed early. Last call was at 1:30am, so after-hour parties were huge. Frank, the owner at The Hammer, liked us to play from nine to midnight, and then he'd finish off the evening with a DJ, claiming the combo made for great sales in booze.

Whatever made Frankie happy, made me happy. We'd been playing here for years, ever since Nick had dated one of the bartenders. The relationship had been short-lived, but lasted long enough for her to hook us up with the gig before she quit town. While some bands struggled to make ends meet, working The Hammer guaranteed rent on my one bedroom in the trendy Los Feliz district. And, bonus, I got to drink and dance for free every Thursday night after we finished playing.

Tonight, though, I wasn't in the mood. The guys helped me load up my beloved van, a 1978 Toyota TownAce Custom Extra that I'd had airbrushed a beautiful shade of turquoise. I pocketed my share of the cash from Nick and waved the guys back inside, promising I'd see them the next afternoon for rehearsal.

Looking up at the sky as I drove home I caught sight of the massive full moon. The eclipse was almost over now, red light waning, covering only a small portion of the orb.

I thought again of my vision, wishing I had made it all the way to the ancient satellite. Remembering the odd run-in with the three men, I frowned. What had made me dream them up, anyways? Maybe I had been watching too many cloak and dagger dramas lately.

They hadn't felt familiar in any way. Though there had been a strange tug in my abdomen when I heard that one man's voice. Like somehow, we were connected by a thread there. Just thinking about it, I could feel the slight pull again, and a pressure began to build in my head.

My favorite Primus song came on over the radio and I resolved to put the whole experience out of my mind. I needed to unwind and get a good night's sleep, I had a full day tomorrow. I made a mental checklist for the rest of the night: walk the dog, drink some water, rest. Tomorrow: birthday lunch, rehearsal, after-party.

Everything was great. Another perfect night in LA.

Then why did I feel so unsettled?

Nervous energy threatening my peace of mind, I turned the music up and drummed along with Herb Alexander on the steering wheel, singing and heading home.

Chapter 2

The next morning I woke up hot and pinned to the bed. My left arm was numb, trapped under the hairy body lying next to me.

"Keeta," I moaned, "come on, up."

Blue eyes opened and stared into mine, tail thumping on the bed, making the mattress quiver and shake.

"Up, Keeta. Move it." I pushed at her with my good arm and she nimbly sprang off the bed, fifty plus pounds of friendly fur. I'd adopted the Husky-Samoyed puppy from a local kill shelter when I'd moved out of the dorms eight years ago at my foster mother's insistence. Even though Kate had no responsibility towards me anymore legally, she had raised me for practically my whole life, and she was as real a mother to me as anyone could have been. Today was Kate's birthday, and I was taking her out with the rest of the family. I was looking forward to it – I hadn't seen my brother or sister in over a month, too long. Again, not my real siblings, but family, all the same.

I sat up, still trying to work some feeling back into my arm when Keeta padded back into the room, leash in mouth. I laughed. At eight years old, she was as feisty and set in her ways as I was at twenty-eight. Single ladies in our prime.

"Alright, two minutes and I'm all yours."

I brushed my teeth and hair, examining myself in the mirror. The early night had done me good, brightening my tawny brown skin and putting a golden glimmer in my honey-colored eyes. I ran a brush through my hair, spritzing it with some fancy hair gloss oil to tame the ever-threatening frizz and went to my closet. After pulling on leggings, a fresh t-shirt and a pair of Chucks, I filled a bottle with water and followed Keeta to the door of the apartment. I put her lead on and opened the door, walking smack into the bright California sunshine. Blinded, I rummaged through my bag for my shades, going by feel and letting Keeta lead me around the small courtyard pool.

Finally, I pulled out the Elvis-style gold frames and put them on like armor. Much better.

Our landlady was sitting by the open gate, something she did most mornings while she drank her coffee and knitted. I think she just liked to keep up with what everyone was doing, though sometimes I could have done without the early morning conversations. Honestly, anyone daring to talk to me before 10am probably deserved a medal for courage.

"Hello, Callie. Good crowd at the bar last night?" Keeta stopped, coaxing Amelia to put down the yarn and pet her instead.

"Yeah, packed as usual." I smiled and patted Keeta on the back.

"Any plans today?"

"Just lunch with Kate." Amelia knew Kate well. My foster mother had co-signed the lease when I had first moved in, making a point of asking Amelia to keep an eye on me at the same time. Numerous follow-up calls to check in with Amelia had cemented the bond.

"Oh, how nice." Amelia beamed up at me. "Tell her I said hello. I haven't seen her in ages."

"I will. She's been busy with a new client." Kate was a personal shopper and dresser, something you could only do in a place like LA.

"Anyone famous?"

"That blonde girl on the new CW show, Hidden Rooms. Have you seen it?"

Amelia shook her head.

"Yeah, me neither. Anyhow, I guess she's fresh in from some tiny town in the Midwest and terrified of making a fashion faux pas, hence, Kate. Bess is the best, you know," I said, winking as I misquoted Kate's surname-derived tag-line, "To Dress Best, Trust Bess."

Keeta whined, looking at the street.

"Well, that's my cue. Duty calls. See you in a little while."

"Have a nice walk, girls."

Keeta pulled me out onto the sidewalk and we turned north on Hillhurst to head towards Griffith Park, the dog's favorite stomping grounds. We walked there almost every day, so Keeta could chase balls and get the exercise her working heritage demanded. Mornings were coolest and safest for exploring the sandy woods at the base of the park hills, so that's when we usually went. Keeta's dense coat wasn't exactly bred for the hot desert climate of LA.

I popped in my earphones and picked the playlist Nick had given me earlier that week of some new covers he wanted to put in rotation. Every six months we'd pick ten new songs to learn and retire some of the more played-out hits. I felt like I must really be starting to get old, because the last six months had literally flown by.

I blissed out on one particularly good drum track. Seriously, with me, it was headphones on, reality gone. When I'd first moved to the area, I'd been blown away by some of the gorgeous houses in the neighborhood but I'd seen them so many times now that they were just bricks and stone. Keeta pulled on the lead, scenting the greener air of the park, and I accommodated her, breaking into a slow jog.

Listening to the beat, the whole time.

For a moment, I felt that tug on my belly again. I had a strange pull to think about the man with the copper-flecked, sun-kissed hair, but I shook it off.

Just enjoying the beat and the rhythm of my feet.

We were almost to the park when the world fell away, and suddenly I was running through the streets of West Hollywood, holding hands with the man as if I'd known him all my life. He squeezed my hand and grinned, his eyes flashing darkly at me, his light brown hair glimmering gold in the sunlight. I didn't know where we were going, or why, but I didn't care. Running around a corner, he stopped without warning and pivoted to face a building, making me crash into him.

I pushed away from him, but his face turned serious and he grasped my shoulders to gently turn me towards the shopfront windows. "Bronzehead Books" was emblazoned on their surface in metallic foil, and a marmalade cat gazed at me serenely through the glass. I'd seen the place before, passed by it more than a few times on my way to The Hammer, but I'd never gone in.

I took a step towards the door and then heard Keeta barking anxiously, drawing my attention away. I turned toward the high-pitched yips, and the city sidewalk morphed into warm sand and clay under rough cedar. The moment was gone, but one word rippled through me, more of a bass tremor reverberating through my head and heart than an actual sound.

"Remember."

Chapter 3

Keeta made sure my mind didn't wander again, playing hide and seek between the trees and making me throw her ball a few hundred thousand times. After over an hour of fun, we headed back home for a shower (me) and a nap (Keeta).

Walking in the door and stripping down to my sports bra and leggings, I contemplated the heavy bag hanging in the corner of the living room. Normally, I tried to get in a little boxing every morning. The exercise helped keep my arms in shape, and stress levels low. I didn't have time, though, not if I was going to meet the rest of the family in Venice Beach at noon. I rolled my shoulders regretfully, fed Keeta and set about getting cleaned up for lunch.

Hair freshly dried and straightened, standing in front of the closet in my standard black cotton undergarments, I contemplated my clothes. Normally I would dress for the gig I was going to later that night, since Keeta came practically everywhere with me most of the time and LA traffic made it difficult sometimes to get home between appointments. But today was Kate's day. There would be plenty of time between rehearsal and the after-hours party to come back and change. Venice would be scorching hot today – Keeta could relax at home in the AC, lucky dog.

Opting for comfort and presentability, I pulled on some lavender stretch capris and a navy blue sleeveless knit top, then slipped into some baby blue Mary Janes from Anthropologie. Keeta settled onto the bed with her favorite plush ducky toy, watching as I lined my eyes in midnight blue liquid liner. Purple and blue were my favorite colors. I found them relaxing. And it didn't hurt that they made my amber irises pop, either. A few coats of mascara, some Polished Purple lip stain, and I was ready to hit the road.

I didn't put on any jewelry, not having pierced ears, and bracelets and rings tended to get in the way when I drummed, so I almost never wore them. The piece around my neck didn't count. I'd worn the gold chain practically my entire life, since Kate had decided I was old enough not to chew on it. It was one of the few things that had come with me through the foster system from my parents, a thick yet delicate twist of links running through a heavy gold ring set with a large purple stone. The ring was an antique, sized for fingers larger than mine and clunky like a class ring. The stone was deep violet, like amethyst, but it had a sort of iridescence to it that reflected rainbows in the light. A woman in a new-age shop had thought perhaps it was an "Indigo Aura" quartz, but when I'd looked the stone up on the net, I'd known that wasn't it. The stone in the ring was too old, and treated quartzes were new technology. If anything, it reminded me of an opal, but I had yet to find an example of one with the rich purple my stone exhibited.

Whatever it was, it made me feel relaxed, and I almost never took it off. I left the chain hanging outside the sweater, since the purple in the ring set off the outfit nicely.

"You'll do, Calliope Winters," I said to my reflection, straightening my shoulders. Kate had always been a stickler for good posture. She was a fashion buyer, but she said the secret most people didn't know was that it hardly mattered what you were wearing, if you didn't know how to stand up straight.

"Stand tall, like you're somebody important, and pretty soon everyone will believe it's true. Including you," she'd reminded me enough times growing up that the admonition had become a personal mantra.

So far, it had worked, too. Oh, Molten Requiem didn't have any kind of record contract, but we had constant gigs and, most importantly, no one ever tried to short us. We made good money, better than most bands I knew, and I knew it was due in part to Nick's business sense and our "don't mess with us" attitude. We walked into every party like we owned it, and by the end of the night, we usually did.

That didn't mean I had iron-clad confidence, though. Being abandoned at a fire station as a baby kind of messes with your mind. And most parents aren't usually too keen on their impressionable angels hanging with kids in the system. But I figured I was about as comfortable in my skin as most people these days. Even if I wasn't sure where that skin came from, I knew everything about the soul inside, and we were on pretty good terms.

I ruffled Keeta's fur, giving her a kiss on the head, and walked outside, locking the door behind me. On a good day, Venice was easily thirty minutes from Los Feliz, and midday traffic on a Friday practically guaranteed it would be more than that. Too many offices these days were giving their workers "summer hours" year round, letting them take off early on Fridays. I'm sure the plebes loved it, but it kind of threw a wrench in my beach time.

Still, I had close to an hour to get there. I backed the van out of the carport and opened the gated parking area, driving out onto Hillhurst Avenue. I picked my way across Los Angeles, sticking to quiet side streets and avoiding the city's chronically clogged freeways.

I barely made it to the restaurant on time. Finding parking near Gjelina's on a Friday in Venice wasn't easy, either, but I did it. Just. I slid into a spot around the corner from Kate's favorite lunch place and hopped out of the van, straightening my clothes before walking quickly down the street.

Inside, I smiled at Sherri, the regular lunch hostess.

"Hi, Calliope. Melissa's already seated outside, table for four on the patio."

"Great, thanks Sherri." Leave it to Mel to be here first. Again. My foster sister could never just be on time. She was chronically early for everything. After being abandoned first by her bi-polar father and then her alcoholic mother, she leaned the other way, finding comfort in predictability and perfectionism. Three years older than me, she'd come to Kate's house when I was just five years old.

At eight, she'd already been prim and proper like an old maid.

My wild side bugged the hell out of her, but she tolerated it like the best of big sisters. I teased her for her color-coded closets and interminably straight edges, fulfilling my duty to be the most annoying of younger siblings.

Back straight, red hair pulled back into a bun at the nape of her neck, Mel sat primly in her chair, hands folded in her lap. Iced tea on the table, already half gone. She'd been here a while, then.

"Mel, hi!" I kissed her freckled cheek and flopped into a chair next to her. "So, we're the first ones here?"

She looked at me wryly. "You know Doug. He just called to say he's on his way. Something about a big case at work, yadda, yadda, yadda. Kate should be here any minute."

"And the cake?"

"Already in the kitchen, double chocolate death with raspberry cream. And I found some pink sparkler candles at this new little party shop in Newport Beach."

Melissa worked as a flight attendant for a private jet company out of John Wayne Airport, and lived in a cute little apartment in nearby Costa Mesa. It was all part of her plan to meet a gainfully employed, preferably rich, and exceedingly normal man. Don't get me wrong, Mel wasn't a gold digger or anything. She just craved stability and security the way I craved sugar and dairy.

Doug, on the other hand, was determined to prove to the world that he was better than his dad, better than a petty thief with repeat convictions who had landed himself in a super-max jail serving a forty year sentence. Since Doug's mom had disappeared, too, probably with a boatload of cash, Doug and his three sisters had been split up. The girls, all young and adorable, had gone to an elderly aunt in Alabama. Doug had been left to the system, twelve years old and angry, rightfully so. After a little over a year and five homes, he'd finally made his way to House Bess, becoming a younger brother to Mel and me.

There had been other kids over the years, but Mel, Doug and I had been the only ones to stick with Kate for the long haul. The only ones that really became family. The other kids had been lucky enough (or unlucky, depending on the case) to be re-claimed by their families or adopted out. Rehabilitated moms and dads. Long-lost grandparents coming out of the woodwork. Cute, rosy cheeked toddlers who won themselves an adoption with their big blue eyes and meager years.

Doug had seen how the law worked, how the system failed kids with dark skin and questionable heritages. Not that we couldn't have been adopted. Kate had offered the option to each of us, more than once. But for our own reasons, we'd each turned her down. I think for Doug, he wanted to prove he could make it on his own. With Kate's encouragement, he threw himself into his studies and graduated school a year early, enrolling in a Naval ROTC program at college and then enlisting after graduation, fast-tracking for officer status. At 27, he was one of the youngest naval JAG officers, a military lawyer who worked on cases he couldn't and wouldn't share with us. Client privilege took on a whole new level of meaning when your client was the US government.

The waitress came by and I ordered a bottle of Kate's favorite wine, a refreshing Sancerre from Oregon. Mel and I made small talk, and when the waitress arrived to uncork the chilled white wine, I saw Doug and Kate walk in together.

I sipped the wine, nodding my approval to the waitress, and stood to hug Kate. Her blonde hair was styled in short waves around her head, perfectly accentuating her cheekbones and wide, innocent, cornflower blue eyes.

"Your timing is perfect, as always. Happy birthday, Kate," I smiled. Doug was dressed in his crisp officer's uniform, the white linen casting setting his flawless ebony skin aglow, so I just had to give him a big, shirt-wrinkling hug, too. "Hey there, big guy. Looking handsome, as always."

Doug looked down at me from his 6'4" height and laughed, the hard angles of his face softening with amusement. "And you're not wearing leather. Feeling okay, Callie?"

"Today was a special occasion, I'm pulling out all the stops. Don't worry, tonight I'll be back in uniform." I winked and handed Kate a glass of wine. "Shall we toast? To everyone being here, together, and to Kate, the best Bess a boy or girl could ever hope to meet."

"Here, here," Doug and Mel cheered. Kate blushed and we all clinked glasses, Doug sticking to water and Mel her iced tea, both of them with work demands to return to later that afternoon. Kate and I had no such constraints. The entertainment industry was quite forgiving. Not only was wine at lunch tolerated, it was encouraged.

Everybody got down to the important business of checking out their menus. Once the waitress had taken our orders, Kate broke out her usual set of questions. When we were children, she would ask us each day after school, "What was the best thing that happened today" and "What was the worst part of your day?" Between those two questions, she pretty much always knew everything about us that she needed to. She still asked the same thing whenever we talked, except now it was usually "your week" instead of "day." And she broadened the scope sometimes, so instead of "best" it might be "most fulfilling" or "most exciting."

I chewed on a bread stick while Melissa practically glowed, telling us about a new pilot the company she worked for had hired. He was her age, not married, and from a family of crop dusters in Iowa. She said he had the bluest eyes, and the most perfect country manners. I hadn't seen her talk about a guy like this in years.

"Sound like you've found a keeper," I said.

"I know, right?"

"Yeah, I can practically hear that clock of yours ticking, tick tock, tick tock," I teased.

"Shut it, you," she laughed, blushing as she stirred her iced tea with her straw and took a sip. I was teasing, but honestly? I'd seen her "life plan," a total map of her adult life that she'd drawn out when we were in middle school, and I knew "married" had been penciled into her 30th birthday. I also knew she still had that drawing folded inside her nightstand drawer, and she was a whole year past the big three-oh. Relaxed as she might try to appear, her desire to conform and control life had to be kicking in big time.

I wondered if she'd listened to the "Staying Present and Mindful" CD I'd given her for the car last month. Probably not.

Kate turned to Doug. "What about you? Any gorgeous young men on the horizon?"

"Are you kidding? I'm surrounded by hot guys. But work has me so busy, and you know I don't date anyone on base."

The Navy may have allowed homosexuals to come out of the closet, but they weren't exactly welcoming of it. Doug kept his sexual preferences close to the vest, like pretty much everything else in his life.

"Have you even had a real boyfriend since college?" I asked.

"I date, don't worry about me. You're not exactly a poster child for relationships yourself, you know."

"Yeah, yeah, I know. That's why I want to hear about you, little brother. So I can live vicariously through your dashing exploits."

Doug rolled his big, dark eyes.

"So, what's all this business at work?" Kate broke in. "What has you so busy?"

"I can't really say-"

"Big surprise there," I muttered and he glared at me.

"But," he continued, "they've moved me to a special research division. As you can imagine, the Navy always has to make sure everything is done legally and above board, even when we're dealing with things that are top secret."

"Wow, that almost sounds exciting," I said, intrigued.

"It is. Maybe when I retire someday and everyone who worked on the project is dead, I'll be able to tell you all about it," he joked, making Mel almost choke on her tea in surprise.

"We can't wait," Kate said drily. "So, Calliope, that leaves you. I won't bother asking about the men in your life. What was the most surprising thing that happened to you all week?"

"Hmm." I thought about it. "Well, Nick booked us a gig opening for The Rooks next month, so that's pretty big. Other than that..." I remembered the guy with the copper hair. "You know how I always sort of trance out when I get really into a song?"

Everybody nodded, and Doug rolled his eyes, looking bored.

"Yeah, okay, so last night I was playing and instead of the usual daydreams, I saw these guys, talking, except it was like they couldn't really see me. Then one of them did see me, and he asked who I was. It was the weirdest thing I've ever imagined."

"That is weird," Kate said, looking intrigued. "Maybe it was a message from your subconscious? What were the guys talking about?"

"Nothing interesting, not that I could tell. Something about needing to get things under control and not being ready, and something about 'warping'." I shrugged. "Mean anything to you? Because the whole thing made no sense to me. And then I found myself thinking about the guy again today, too. He showed me a bookstore I've always wanted to go into."

"Ah well, then, there you go," Kate said, leaning back in her chair looking satisfied. "Your subconscious is trying to give you the help you need. If I were you, I would check out that bookstore and pick up the first few books that call to you."

Kate was a big believer in following your intuition, so this advice wasn't really surprising.

"Call to me, huh?"

"Yeah, you know. Whatever looks the most interesting, whatever catches your eye. It's what I always tell people to do when they don't know how to pick a new outfit. Of course, with clothes you do have to try them on, too, and make sure they fit."

Melissa nodded in agreement and I shrugged. "Alright, guess I will be getting some new books."

Doug stared into his water for a moment and then looked up at me, his face confused.

"And the people, you say they were talking about warping?"

"Yeah, weird, right?"

"What does that even mean?" Mel asked.

"I have no idea. I think I even said the same thing. Not that I got an answer." I looked at Doug. "Why, does that mean something to you?"

"No, never heard the word before," Doug said, taking a big drink of water. "Just thought it sounded weird. That's why I asked."

"Yeah, you sure it's not from one of your super-secret cases?" I teased him.

"Absolutely," he said, laughing uncomfortably. "When the Navy puts me on an x-file, I'll be sure to let you know."

Our food came out, and everyone dug in. But I couldn't help thinking that the truth was closer to what he'd said before, and he'd tell us when we were all old and gray.

Chapter 4

After too much cake and several promises to put everyone on the VIP list for our show with the Rooks, I'd managed to get out of the restaurant before three, and made it to rehearsal at Nick's warehouse space in West Hollywood just before four. So, only half an hour late. Not entirely terrible.

The guys had already warmed up and were going over the song order for the evening when I arrived.

"Were you body snatched?" Jax drawled, looking over my outfit. "Is that why you're so late?"

"Ha, ha. No. I was having lunch with my family."

"Ah, right. Kate's birthday." Nick nodded, remembering. "Well, now that you're here, why don't we rehearse some of the newer songs?"

"Sounds good to me," I shrugged. I sat down behind the older set of drums I kept at the studio, a silver-sparkled kit. Having two sets had become an obvious choice after a few years, once it was clear that we would have steady gigs. Schlepping drums in and out of a van four times a day gets old fast.

Nick started playing the intro to a song by the Black Stripes and I tapped my foot in concert with the melody, getting ready to come in at just the right moment.

Timing was everything.

I stomped on the kick pedal and glided across the cymbals, leading us in. Jax joined with a blast of bass, and then we were away.

We played for more than an hour, tightening up new songs. Still, something was off. I was having a hard time concentrating. My mind kept drifting over random details from the last twenty-four hours, and finally Jax stopped playing mid-stream.

"Dude, what is up with you?" he asked me, pulling the strap for his bass over his head and leaning the instrument against the couch nearby.

"What do you mean?" I said, knowing what he was asking but not having an answer.

"I don't know, you just sound like you're somewhere else." He cracked his neck, looking frustrated.

Nick spoke up. "Jax is right. Maybe you should head home early, get some rest before tonight. There are supposed to be some big names at the party. I'm hoping to lock in some new gigs. Can't have everyone's favorite drummer sounding like she's on cough meds."

"That bad?" I grimaced.

"Dude, you sucked," Jax grinned at me.

"Awesome, thanks, J." I tossed my empty water bottle at his head and repressed a smile as he caught it neatly in one hand.

Bassists.

"Anytime, Calliope," he winked.

Still, they had a point. I hadn't realized I was that out of it, but I knew I'd had a hard time keeping up. If I played the party like that, we'd be out of work in no time. The rumor mill in LA was a fast and unforgiving machine.

I promised to catch some Z's and climbed back into my van. The guys might practice a little more on their own, but somehow I had a feeling they would be chowing down on takeout and playing Call of Duty within the hour, so I didn't feel too guilty. I'd seen the way they were eyeing the PlayStation as I left.

Back at home, after I'd taken Keeta for a quick walk, I stripped down to my underwear and crawled into bed for a nap. I didn't have to leave for our gig until after eleven, so I set my alarm for ten and wrapped myself around Keeta, allowing myself to drift off to sleep.

I always had pretty vivid dreams when I napped, and today was no exception. Dressed like a student, complete with a backpack, I walked into the back of a lecture hall at some big official looking building. The ceilings were tall and decorated with thick crown molding, and the walls were hung with traditional landscapes and hunt scenes in gilded frames. It reminded me of the time we'd visited D.C. and toured Washington's estate at Mount Vernon.

Not impressed, I dropped my backpack on the floor and collapsed into a hard black plastic chair, pulling another towards me to prop my feet on. I noticed a guy on my right who had already done the same, a real tough looking soldier-type with close-trimmed hair, green cargo pants and a tight black tee-shirt that did nothing to hide the muscles underneath. He grinned at me appreciatively and I smiled back before I turned back to the front, where the speaker was about to begin. Someone shifted on my left and I saw the same guy from my earlier visions, except this time there was nothing relaxed about him.

He was dressed almost identically to the man on the right, his hair damp now as if he had showered earlier. There were others nearby wearing similar clothes, though the rest of the people looked more like me – students – or like office professionals in drab suits and skirts.

The man up front was wearing a suit, too, and as he started welcoming everyone in the room, my mind drifted, bored already. I zoned out, and for a moment found myself out in the hallway, watching men in black tactical uniforms sneaking up the stairs. Then I flashed to another part of the building, and another. In each instance, I could see men converging on the building like ants. I didn't know why they were here, but I'd seen the guns and ammo they carried and everything in my mind screamed "Danger!"

And then I was back in my seat, feeling shocked and scared. I sat up, stuffing my notebook and pen back into my pack and getting ready to get the hell out of there.

"Ethan. They're here." The man on my right spoke, his low voice laced with warning, and the guy on my left looked at him, nodding. We stood up at almost the same time and recognition flashed over his face.

"You again. Come on." He started to go towards the door nearest us, and I stopped.

"No. We can't go that way. There are men out there. This way." I turned and ran towards the exit at the back of the room, flinging open the door and rushing out into the hall.

"Ethan, who the hell is this?" The other guy sounded annoyed. "How do we know she's not one of them?"

"Not now, Tag. We've got to get to Kipner." Shots rang out in the room behind us and people started screaming.

We took off down the hall, Tag pushing past me and breaking into a room three doors down. A uniformed man, the same white-haired one I'd seen talking to Kim, whoever the heck "Kim" was, was standing next to a desk, three men in black surrounding him. They didn't even look at us, just continued staring at the white-haired man, and then it was like something broke inside him and blood burst from his ears and eyes with a horrible popping sound and he collapsed to the floor.

Before I could scream, Tag pulled a gun out of his waistband and shot all three men in an instant, even as Ethan was hauling me out of the room, backwards, back into the hall.

"Go, run! There's nothing we can do. Tag, come on!" Ethan pushed me and we took off in a dead sprint, dashing into a stairwell.

I was too choked up to argue. Even as we ran, my mind seemed to stretch out and I could *see* where the other intruders were in the building. The stairs were clear, and the way outside, too. The men in black were swarming the front of the building, shooting people as they fled indiscriminately, but somehow, I knew their target had been the man in the uniform. The rest was a distraction. A deadly one.

The stairs came out in a small hall, and I knew which way to go. I ran through a laundry room, an empty kitchen decked out with industrial grade appliances and steel countertops. At the far end, I careened into a heavy fire door, the push bar giving way under my arm as the door opened into the sun.

There, a van, not my van but a commercial looking plain white deal, idled ten feet away. A small Latina woman, thin with short curly hair, crouched on the opposite side of me, in front of a gate that led to the front grounds. This would have been a bit odd on its own, but she was surrounded by at least twenty dogs of all shapes and sizes, and even as I watched two more came running around the van to stand next to the pack, panting. She patted the newcomer on the head and then opened the gate.

"Run, perritos, and help the others get to safety."

The dogs took off like hounds on a hunt, streaming around to the front of the building. In my mind's eye I could see them distracting the men in black, giving those who fled time to run, time to hide.

I hoped the dogs would be okay.

The girl stood up, dusting her hands off on her shorts, and smiled at the rest of us. "Okay, we better take off. Where's Kipner?"

"Dead," Tag said.

The girl frowned but didn't miss a beat. "Who's this?"

"I don't know, ask him." They both looked at Ethan, who just shook his head.

"Not now. Come on. We've got to get back to HQ."

"Not with her, we don't," Tag argued, pointing at me.

"Yes, with her." Ethan gently prodded me to get in the van, and I did, shock starting to freeze my limbs and my mind.

The woman got in the front, backing up the van to turn around and head out to the service entrance, Ethan taking the passenger seat next to her. Tag spread out in the row behind me, and I could feel his glare on my shoulders.

I looked down at my hands, focusing on a tiny spot of blood on one of them. Not my blood.

Kipner's blood.

I woke up with a start, feeling stunned and full of adrenaline still, like I'd just been in Jason Bourne movie.

I stretched and looked at the clock. I'd only been asleep for an hour, and the sun was still shining, just like in my dream. No way was I going to fall back asleep now. I reached out to turn off the alarm.

And froze.

On my hand, like a ghost, my skin bore a small red mark. I held it up to my face to inspect it.

Not blood.

A raw red splotch, no bigger than the drop of blood had been, as if I had marked myself with the tip of a marker.

As if my mind was trying to make sure I wouldn't forget.

Chapter 5

I tapped my fingers nervously against the wheel of my van, waiting to get buzzed in the gates of a Hollywood Hills home. In less than an hour, the gates would be open, valets waiting to park guests' cars for them on the narrow hill streets, but for now, they were locked. Nick and Jax were already inside, wondering what was taking me so long.

I knew that because of the ten-odd texts I'd received in the last fifteen minutes, wondering if I was okay. I hadn't responded, since I knew better than to text and drive at the same time, especially when it was nearing closing time for all the bars.

It wasn't like me to be late.

The dream I'd had during my nap had really thrown me for a loop. I'd taken a long shower, trying to wash off the red mark on my hand, but it hadn't budged. Only now, hours later, was it starting to fade slightly.

It shouldn't have bothered me. I mean, it was probably just some ink I hadn't noticed earlier in the day. Not consciously anyway. Maybe my mind had picked up on it, and worked it into a whole dream scenario.

Yeah, a dream with the same guy, for the third time in less than twenty-four hours.

If I told anyone, I was sure they would tell me to call their therapist. Everyone in LA had one. At least, it seemed that way.

But I'd avoided therapy my whole life, I wasn't going to start now. In the system, I'd seen what happened to people who got slapped with a mental label. No way was I going to let that happen to me. Sure, I had issues. But didn't everybody?

Finally, someone pushed the right button and the gates began to slowly swing open. The extra moments ticked by, upping my tension until there was an opening large enough to squeak through. All-nighter, here I come, I thought.

I was really looking forward to some dream-free time.

The massive post-modern monstrosity gleamed white under enough landscape lighting to illuminate Dodger Stadium. The people who lived here probably drank smoothies and ate organic vegetables, but God forbid they point their mood lighting downwards. Wouldn't want the rest of us plebes to see the night sky or anything.

A rent-a-cop directed me to unload at the main entrance, where the rest of the band was waiting to help me carry things inside. When we'd finished, one of the newly arrived valets took my keys and told me she'd park it around back by the servants' entrance. Relieved to have something constructive to do, I settled into the rhythm of setting up, helping the guys hook up the amps and lining up my kit just the way I liked it. We were just finishing our sound check when the first guests started arriving.

It was your typical Hills party, with a lot of starlet wannabes cozying up to under-dressed, unshaved hipsters. Lots of booze and a few exhibitionist swimmers. Hard drugs and cigarettes had become more of a taboo, so those things were kept out of sight, but you could see a lot of vapes being passed around, with who knew what inside.

As a drummer, I didn't need to work the crowd, not the way Nick and Jax did. My job was to keep everything together, and I did it well. Concentrating on the beat, letting my body relax into the flow of the music, I knew I was smiling. Drumming took me into my own little world, just where I liked to be. This time, though, I made sure not to let myself go completely. No flying with owls or running with wolves in my imagination today. I don't know why I had been having these strange interruptions to my usual dreams and drumming meditations, but I wasn't in the mood to have any more tonight.

Our first set flew by, over an hour of current indie hits that were guaranteed to warm up the audience. Our second set would have more of our own music, along with a few audience requests if we felt like it. Now, though, Nick popped on a half-hour playlist the client had sent us, allowing the music to stream out through the speakers while we headed to the bar for some much-needed refreshment.

Jax popped the top on a large bottle of water, chatting up the bartender while she poured us each a beer and we guzzled our waters. Playing to a crowd was hard work, and we all had slightly damp hair and glistening skins.

I was just about to try my beer, some farmhouse micro-brew from San Diego, when I saw Nick's eyebrows rise at something behind me. I had a moment to process his low warning of "incoming," before I heard one of my least favorite voices by my ear.

"Hello there, Calliope." A large, soft hand came down on my shoulder in ownership. "Nick, Jax."

Nick scowled and Jax continued on with the bartender, oblivious. I shrugged off the offending hand and turned, sneering up at my least favorite ex-boyfriend.

"Tommy. Still prowling the Hills for fresh young talent, I see?" I put extra emphasis on the words "fresh" and "talent." Tommy liked his girls young and impressionable – otherwise known as clueless and too naïve to know better. As a top agent, he had no problem luring in new faces every week, to his office and his bed. I'd made the mistake, years ago, of believing he really cared about me. Finding him in bed with three of his "clients" had been an instant cure for my innocence and trust.

"Now, now, sweetheart, don't be like that. You know I never mix business with pleasure." His words slurred a bit, betraying the number of drinks he'd already had.

"Yes, I know. You don't actually bother to sign any your conquests."

"I'd sign you."

"Not a chance," Nick growled.

Tommy lurched forward with a threat in his eyes, and I reached a hand out to stop him, planting myself squarely in front of him, my palm on his chest.

"Like the man said, thanks, but no thanks. We manage quite well on our own, as you know."

Tommy snorted, at least, I think that's what he meant to do. It came out more like something between a gurgle and a parrot losing its tail.

"Oh, come on." Tommy breathed heavily down in my face, his own cheeks flushed with anger and alcohol.

"After parties? That crappy gig at The Hammer? You know you could do better with me."

I laughed. "You mean you could do so much better with us. We're making good money. We have a loyal fan base, and we're respected by a lot of people for not taking any crap from industry tools like you. We play on our terms, not yours or anyone else's."

I could feel Nick standing several inches behind me, heat pulsing off of him. I thought I heard him whisper in my ear, "And the concert next month, tell him about that," but maybe I just imagined it.

"And we're opening for The Rooks next month, not that it's any of your business. People trust Nick. They like him. I can't say the same about you."

I wouldn't have thought it possible, but Tommy actually turned an even darker shade of red. I remembered the last time I'd seen him like this, the night I'd dumped him seven years ago.

Not good.

That was all I could think. I felt a frisson of fear go through me, a cold chill, and my stomach clenched reflexively. For just one moment, I felt like a victim all over again and something deep inside me cried out for help.

Not something. Someone. The old me. Young, innocent, weak me.

Stress wasn't the only reason I'd taken up boxing.

Guys like Tommy, they'd made me want to be able to hit back. He'd been the second boyfriend to push me around, and the last. Years of drumming and training had me reasonably sure no one would ever get the drop on me again, but I wasn't stupid. I knew that look. He wanted to ruin someone's face, and if we weren't careful, he might even wreck the party and our gig.

"You can't talk to me like that."

Right, I thought, never tell a narcissist he doesn't matter. I'd forgotten Tommy's number one unwritten rule.

I felt, more than heard, Nick's growl behind me. Even Jax, usually oblivious to anything but the ladies, had noticed the tension brewing and swiveled around in his seat to observe.

I opened my mouth to speak, but someone else beat me to it.

"Hey, love, sorry I'm late." An arm draped around me, and a kiss whispered across my cheek. I looked up, ready to tell the guy he'd made a mistake. My gaze traveled upwards longer than I was used to. Damn, this guy was tall. And built.

And familiar.

"Ethan?"

"Don't look so surprised. I had a feeling I should swing by to check in on you tonight, so here I am." We locked eyes for a moment, his so brown and deep I thought maybe I could dive into them and hide forever. I didn't understand how a guy could drop into the real world from a dream, but at the moment, I found I didn't really care. Any other guy, putting an uninvited arm around me like he owned me, the hair on the back of my neck would be standing up. But this guy? I didn't feel owned. I felt safe.

He swung his gaze forward, back to Tommy. "Hi there, name's Ethan Hale. And you are?"

Tommy frowned, clearly flustered. "Tommy Fein," he put on a fake smile and stuck out his hand. Tommy may have been an abusive scumbag, but he'd always known when to put on a good face. In Tommy's world, every conversation was a potential deal, every moment money.

"Pleasure to meet you," Ethan nodded at Tommy, but didn't remove his arm from around my shoulders. Tommy pulled his hand back, the skin around his eyes going tight at the slight, and Jax smothered a smile behind his beer. Nick didn't bother, clapping his hands together with a laugh.

"We're always happy to meet a friend of Callie's. I'm Nick, and this here's Jax. Can we get you a beer?"

"Maybe later, thanks. I actually need to borrow Callie for a moment, if you all don't mind," Ethan said, somehow making the request sound both friendly and non-negotiable. The iron authority behind the easy smile made me think of my dream that afternoon.

Ethan, working with that guy Tag. The shootings. The blood.

It all came back in a rush, and a flash of real, true fear came over me. Who was this guy? How could he even be here?

Was I losing my mind?

I started to ease away from him, thinking I would just slip away, but I made the mistake of looking up before I went. Our eyes met, and I felt caught, like a possum in the road. Should I just play dead?

"Okay?" This time, his voice held more invitation than command, and like an idiot, I found myself nodding. He let out a breath, as if he'd been holding it, and without another word steered me away through the crowd, towards the back terraces overlooking the city. I turned my head to peer over my shoulder, watching Tommy storm off angrily in the other direction. Nick and Jax grinned and gave me two thumbs up.

Just another hot, desert night in Los Angeles, without a cloud in the sky.

And I felt like I was drowning.

Chapter 6

Outside, Ethan led me past the pool, past the revelers and the hookups and the people having quiet arguments. He led me away from all of them, away from the lights and the noise. Into the quiet darkness.

Only then did he remove his hand from my back, putting his hands in his pockets and taking a step back.

Too late, I realized we were entirely alone and out of sight, standing by a rosemary hedgerow, hidden behind some outlandish dolphin topiaries, where no one could see us.

"Who are you?" we said at the same time.

"You first," I said.

"I already told you, I'm Ethan Hale. And I think you know that. What I don't know, is who you are, or why I'm here."

"You're kidding, right?"

"No." He said it calmly, slowly, which made me pause.

"Oh. Okay, I'll go along. I'm Calliope Winters. Cal or Callie for short."

He stared at me, like he was expecting me to say something more.

"Well, um, sorry about the drama back there. Tommy can be a real jerk when he wants to be. Or, just, pretty much all the time."

"Do you know how I got here?"

"How you-? What do you mean? Don't you know?" I cocked my head to the side. I'd seen plenty of people get so loaded they couldn't remember getting to a party, but this guy seemed pretty sober. "Do you remember who drove you?"

"No one drove me. You brought me here."

"Seriously? Look, dude, I don't know you, I've never met you before," I said, pushing the weird dreams I'd had before out of my mind. I mean, those didn't exactly count. Not in real life. And it definitely wasn't the sort of thing a girl would go around saying to guys she's just met.

Like, ooh, hey, you're so cute. I had a dream about you. You're my soul mate. Let's hook up.

Ugh.

No.

I was definitely not going to let that cat out of the bag.

"I don't know who you are, or who you think you are, but I am not some damsel in distress, and I don't need your white ass saving me. Cute as it might be. And I most definitely did not bring you here, unless you were hiding in the back of my van." I raised one eyebrow at him. "Which I hope you weren't, because that would be seriously stalker-like, just so you know."

He grimaced, looked up at the sky and closed his eyes for a moment, almost like he was silently counting to ten. I'd seen Kate do that enough times to know the signs.

"Callie," he said, opening his eyes. "Back there, when I showed up, you said my name. How did you know my name?"

Ah. Well, now, that sort of stumped me. What was I supposed to say to that, without sounding like a total lunatic?

I really had no idea, and found myself shaking my head. I crossed my arms and backed up a step.

"Who are you, really?" I asked.

"I think you know," he said.

"I don't, I swear, I don't."

"Okay, well here is what I think. I think I met you last night." I swallowed, surprised, and his eyes narrowed. He took a step toward me, and then another. "I saw you again this morning, and then this afternoon. I think you've been following me, and pulled me to jump here, and I want to know why." He'd backed me up into the rosemary, and the leaves surrounded me with their scent as I brushed against them. "After this afternoon, I have a couple ideas, but I can't say I really like any of them. So I'm going to ask you one more question. Who are you with?"

He wasn't touching me, and there was only the barest hint of a threat in his voice.

But it was there. I knew I should do something, push him away, use my training, something.

Yet I didn't. I couldn't. Because what he was saying didn't make any sense.

"Those were just dreams," I whispered.

"Dreams?" He grasped my shoulders in my hands. "You think you were just dreaming?"

"Wasn't I?"

Face grim, he released me, digging his phone out of his pocket. He tapped on the screen for a minute, and then handed the phone to me.

The media headline shone brightly in the darkness, but I couldn't process the words. Bodies on the floor of a room, blood everywhere. The image was burned into my brain, familiar, even though I had seen it from a different angle than the photographer.

"Kipner?" I asked.

"So you do remember," he said in clipped tones.

"I remember. But I thought...I was sleeping. Napping. With Keeta. I didn't think any of it was real."

I looked up at him, crossing my arms over my chest, feeling more vulnerable than ever.

"You're real? It's all real?"

"Yes, it's real. I'll explain everything, I will. But I'm running out of time. I need to-" He closed his eyes and nodded, as if he was listening to someone else, someone I couldn't see. "I'll be right there, I need one more minute." Then he turned back to me. "Look, I can't stay. I'm needed somewhere else right now. I want to believe you, I do. Come find me tomorrow at the place I showed you. The bookstore. Do you remember?"

I nodded, not quite able to speak.

"I'll be there at noon. Promise me you'll come."

"I..."

"Promise me, Calliope."

"I promise." My oath came out sounding more like a question than anything else, but he seemed satisfied.

"Good," he said, stepping towards me again. "And stay away from that guy Tommy."

He gazed into my eyes, like he wanted to say something more. For a moment, I thought he might even try to kiss me.

And then, he disappeared.

Chapter 7

Yeah, like vanished. There one minute, gone the next. He literally winked out of existence.

Crap.

I really was going crazy.

I mean, there was no way that I had actually dreamed about someone real. I couldn't have talked with someone while I was trancing out playing drums. Real people didn't teleport or disappear into thin air or whatever.

No, that kind of thing just didn't happen.

Except it had.

So after looking behind every tiny tree in the vicinity for a tall, sandy-haired man, I could only come to one conclusion.

I'd been hanging out with a ghost.

Because, yeah, why not, right?

Somehow, it seemed better than the lunatic theory. Even if it was still a full moon.

I was being haunted, in my dreams, in life, by a seriously studly poltergeist. It had to be a poltergeist because I had felt his touch, right? I'd read somewhere that most ghosts couldn't interact with the physical world, but the ones who could, they were usually trouble. I couldn't explain a ghost having a phone, but then, I couldn't explain any of it.

And he wanted me to go to some bookstore and say hi? Maybe get sucked into the haunting even further? Screw that. I went inside, determined to forget the whole thing, slammed a few shots and rode out the second set. Tommy seemed to have left for the night, so that was a plus. The bad news? When we finished playing, Jax and Nick couldn't stop talking about how awesome Ethan had been.

"I mean, come on, Callie, did you see Tommy's face?" Nick said as he snapped the latches shut on his guitar case.

"Oh wow, that was priceless," Jax laughed.

"You've gotta bring him to more gigs. When did you meet him, anyway?"

I concentrated on putting away my cymbals, letting my hair hide my face like a veil. "Oh, um...just a few days ago. It's not serious."

How could it be? I thought.

On the bright side, it meant I wasn't imagining things, or if I was I wasn't the only one.

Somehow, that didn't make me feel much better.

"So I guess now we know the real reason you were so spacey at practice this afternoon, eh?" Jax grinned at me as he knelt down and started spooling speaker wires.

"What? No, not at all. I told you, I was just tired."

"If you say so." Jax winked at Nick, who looked at me.

"Well, anyone who can get under Tommy's skin's got our vote. You don't have to hide him away anymore." Nick sounded a bit wounded. Which would make sense if I actually had been dating Ethan, since I always told Nick everything. He was one of my closest friends. But there hadn't been anything to tell.

I sighed, putting my last drum away and tapping out a frustrated beat on my hand with my drumsticks.

"Look, I haven't been hiding him, I swear. I barely know the guy. I don't even remember telling him about the gig tonight." That last part was true, at least.

"Whatever you say, Cal-gal," Jax shrugged. "Still seems like a cool dude to me. Anyone who can get rid of that loser ex of yours so quickly is alright in my book."

I grunted non-committedly, picking up some of my gear. Nick followed me out to the van, opening the back doors and helping me load up.

"You know, you haven't really dated anyone in a while."

"I date," I protested.

"Scratching an itch after a gig isn't dating."

"I had coffee with that guy two weeks ago. That was a date."

"You mean the time you called me while the guy was in the bathroom, and then you pretended I had called you so you could leave and give me a ride to fix a non-existent flat-tire?"

"So, what's your point? I go on dates. That one just sucked."

"Please. You are a poster girl for commitment issues. And I get it, I do, trust me. I mean, it's not like I've had a lot of luck lately dating, either. All I'm saying is, this guy seems okay. Just, think about it. Give him a chance."

"You want me to give Ethan a chance," I repeated back slowly, climbing out of the van to walk back towards the house.

"Seems like you could do a whole lot worse."

Oh, he had no idea. How could you do worse than dating a ghost?

I might not be crazy, but I was pretty sure that was the kind of thing that landed you in the psych ward.

"I don't know. I'm not sure he's really my type," I said, unable to hold back a nervous chuckle.

"I'm no expert on guys, but you're kidding, right? He seems like he'd be pretty much anyone's type."

"Who's this?" Jax asked, passing by with an amp in his arms.

"Callie's guy, Ethan."

"I'd do him," Jax tossed back.

"There, see?" Nick grinned, bending down to pick up more equipment.

"Who hasn't he done?" I laughed for real this time.

"True enough," Nick agreed.

We walked back to the van. Jax looked up from his phone, where he'd been checking his messages.

"Where did he disappear to, anyway? I didn't see him leave," Jax asked.

"Who?"

"Your dude."

"Ugh, he is not my dude, I told you." I slammed my kick drum into the van with more force than I meant to. "I don't know. One minute he was there, the next minute he wasn't." If only they really knew. For all I knew, Ethan could be floating behind me, invisible, watching.

Haunting.

Perfect. I had my very own ghost stalker. Like Tommy hadn't been annoying enough.

This was why I didn't date. I was a serial jerk magnet.

"You should invite him to the show tomorrow night," Nick nudged me. We'd have a small show at the Satellite, another one of our regular gigs. We played there at least one Saturday a month, which I loved since it was pretty close to home and usually meant an earlier night for me. The shows there were free, and we had enough of a following that our share of the bar tab was always more than generous, too.

Invite a ghost to haunt my little oasis on Silver Lake?

Not happening, I thought. Out loud, I simply said, "We'll see."

The guys let the subject drop. We finished packing up and got paid, which included two bonus trays of leftover food as a tip. Back outside, Jax waved Nick off, saying he had a ride home. Nick and I divvied up the trays between us and went our separate ways. As I backed out of my spot, I saw Jax heading to a small Honda, his arm around the cute bartender. Score another one for Jax. I guessed his new relationship wasn't exclusive yet. Or wouldn't be anytime soon.

I couldn't wait to get home to Keeta and my bed. At least we'd had a long run right before I left late that evening, so she'd probably let me sleep in a bit in the morning.

Not that you could call what I did sleeping when I finally did get home.

I took a quick shower and crawled into my bed with the dog, willing myself to fall asleep. And failing.

If my eyes ever closed, it didn't last long.

I watched the moon track across the night sky through my window, and ran over the evening in my mind a thousand and one times. Whenever I remembered the look on Tommy's face when Ethan had refused to shake his hand, I smiled. I couldn't help it. Maybe having a ghost wouldn't be such a bad thing.

I thought about Ethan's body, and how warm it had felt against me.

Definitely not all bad.

But that brought up another point – weren't ghosts supposed to be cold?

How could I feel him so strongly? I was pretty sure ghosts were supposed to be wispy. Insubstantial. Weak.

Ethan seemed anything but weak.

The biggest question I kept coming back to was: why come to me? I'd never even really believed in ghosts, and horror movies usually just made me laugh. Surely Hollywood had some new age psychic peddlers better suited to the task of helping this guy cross over, or whatever.

By the time the sun came up, I wasn't feeling any wiser. No answers had come to me during the night. Still, something about the ever-lightening sky soothed me, lulled me to sleep.

If I dreamed, I didn't remember it when I woke up. I felt rested and relaxed. I stretched and Keeta nuzzled me, tail thumping. I looked at the clock. Almost noon. I had slept for six hours, not bad for a Friday night.

I stretched and Keeta whined, jumping off the bed. I knew where she was headed – getting her leash, I was sure. Husky-Samoyeds were too smart. I was surprised she hadn't figured out how to unlock the door and the gate to take herself on a walk yet.

Sure enough, she pranced back into the room with her leash in her mouth. Oh, who was I kidding? You know I thought it was cute, or else I would keep the leash on the coat rack by the door, instead of in her toy basket where she could get it anytime she wanted.

I rolled out of bed and slipped into a pair of sweats, some sneakers and a hoodie. Time for a nice, long walk. I hadn't really eaten the night before, so I decided to take Keeta down to House of Pies on Vermont and treat us both to some chicken-fried steak and eggs. Breakfast and pie were all-day affairs at the old diner, and they had no problem with giving Keeta her own plate and water bowl when we sat out on the patio.

Fifteen hundred calories and two hours later, Keeta and I were both feeling lazy and full. I spent the day reading and relaxing in the apartment.

I managed to think about Bronzehead Books only three times.

I didn't go.

Instead, I took a short nap followed by a nice jog at twilight through Griffith Park with Keeta. After that, it was time to eat, shower and go. Keeta whined to come with, so she sat up front in the passenger seat, panting happily out the window as I drove.

She loved coming along on night gigs and guarding the van, even though all she really did was sleep while I was gone. Maybe she enjoyed the change of scenery, or maybe it was just feeling like she had a job to do. Either way, if she was happy, so was I. Plus, it was nice knowing no stalker would ever be lurking in the back of the cavernous vehicle when I returned. The last guy who had tried breaking into the van had almost lost a hand to my sweet fluffy snowball. He'd had the nerve to try and get her put down, calling her vicious. The judge had laughed him out of court, and sentenced him to two years for attempted theft.

Satellite was only a short drive from my apartment, and I wound up getting there before the guys. Ed, my favorite bartender, helped me unload so I could find a parking spot before the revelers started arriving. Lucky me, there was one right around the corner. The street was well lit, lamps blazing in the night and the semi-full moon casting a fair amount of its own light, even though it was waning. I patted Keeta on the head, promised I'd be back soon, and headed back to the bar.

Jax had arrived, but still no Nick. We had plenty of time – I was always kind of an early bird – so we sat at the bar and had a beer with Ed.

Nick walked in just as the bar was starting to fill up, and our beers were dry.

"Perfect timing," I said, smiling as I swiveled around to greet him. I noted the short length of his old-school buzz cut, and reached up, running my hand through the newly shorn dark fuzz.

"Ah, soft as a newborn duck," I sighed.

"Cut that out," he said, swatting my hand away.

"I can't help it," I smirked. "You know this is my favorite time in your monthly hair cycle. It's just. So. Soft." I reached up again and he body blocked me, turning and leaning to heft me over his back and drag me over to the stage.

"Come on, forget your duck fetish and get those drums set up."

I laughed as he set me down and got to work. It wasn't until we'd finished our sound check that Ethan came to mind.

I blamed Nick.

He's the one who had the nerve to bring him up again.

"So, did you call him?"

"Call who?" I asked, not really paying attention as I pushed my hair back out of my face. Today it seemed to be everywhere. I reached into my bag and pulled out a French clip, securing the offending strands in a messy half-updo on top of my head.

"That guy, Ethan. Is he coming?"

"What, here?"

"Yes, here. You said you'd call him."

"No, I said I'd see. And hey, look." I gazed around the bar, searching. "Nope. No Ethan."

"You're hopeless."

"Nah. Just a girl, standing in front of a guy, waiting for him to shut up and play some music."

He crossed his arms over his lean chest, not moving.

"What?"

"You can't chase every guy away, Cal."

"Who's chasing? I told you, I barely know the guy. Maybe I'm old fashioned. Maybe I'm waiting for him to call me."

He snorted and shook his head, walking back to pick up his guitar, pull the strap over his head, and grab the mike towards his face.

Jax scrambled to get in position and I adjusted myself in my seat.

"Welcome to the Satellite!" Nick's voice rumbled out over the crowd. "We're Molten Requiem, and this is a song about love."

The uptempo punk rhythm of Alkaline Trio's "Love, Love, Kiss, Kiss" blasted out the speakers. He threw me a kiss and started singing while I rolled my eyes.

I picked up the beat, matching the fast pace he was setting, speeding up the original song with pure punk-rock adrenaline. We'd played the song enough times that I didn't miss it when Nick turned around and gave me the eye as he sang, making his point. The lyrics sarcastically outlined disgust with romance and all public displays of affection.

It was a sentiment our whole band could normally get behind.

Yeah, yeah, I nodded at him. I got the point. I knew I had some commitment issues but could you blame me when you coupled it with a history of abandonment, and a small dose of PTSD? Whatever. I was a work in progress, and I thought I was doing pretty damn good.

We could wrap this song up anytime. When it finally ended, I gave as good as I got, segueing into Fall Out Boy's "I Don't Care." Take that, Cupid, I thought.

53

After that, we just played. Three shorts sets of hard, fast music, the kind that helped all the good little worker bees release some frustration so they could get back to their cubicles on Monday without killing anyone. I liked to think our band served a greater purpose, reducing road rage and saving the greater Los Angeles area from the angst of many an errant postal worker.

The night rolled on, and I didn't give Ethan another thought.

I went home, I went to bed, and life got back to normal.

Until it all went to hell.

Chapter 8

Most people hate Mondays, but for me, it's the start of my weekend. No gigs. No rehearsals. Just two blessed days of relaxation and quiet. Sometimes I'd go hang with Kate while she shopped for her clients. Sometimes I'd go to the beach and read, play ball with Keeta. It was my time to recharge, and it was sacred.

Everyone knew better than to bug me on a Monday or Tuesday.

Which is why, when I heard knocking at my door at 9am on Tuesday, I ignored it. It could only be political canvassers or Jehovah's Witnesses. Anyone else would have rung my cell first. Hell, anyone else I knew would still be in bed.

I turned around at my desk, making out two blurry shadows of men through the layers of vermillion gauze and plum lace over my living room windows.

Mormons, for sure. They always traveled in pairs.

The knocking stopped, and I went back playing with my Audible software, laying down some new drum tracks for a song I'd been working on.

Low barking made me turn around again, removing my headphones.

"Keeta, what-"

"Open the door, Callie." Ethan was standing in my living room.

"What the hell?" I asked. Keeta's barks grew louder, more frantic.

"The door," he repeated.

"Open it yourself," I dared.

He took a step toward me and I bristled. Keeta didn't like it, either, and launched herself at him. The blood drained from my face when she went right through his leg, and his image flickered.

"Fine, have it your way," he said, sounding resigned. He faded away, leaving Keeta sniffing an empty space. She shifted her eyes to mine, whining.

"I don't know, girl, I-"

With a crack, the door flew open, splintering the frame where it had been bolted. Keeta squared off in front of me, growling now, and I sprang up from my chair, heart pounding.

Tag strode into the room and shot something at Keeta, and she dropped silently to the floor.

"You bastard! You shot my dog!"

"You really should have answered your door." He shrugged and pointed the gun at me.

Ethan stepped into the room, making a face of regret when he looked down at Keeta.

"I'm sorry, Callie. I really had hoped to do this the easy way."

"Do what the easy way?" I shouted. "What is going on?"

"I think you already know," he answered cryptically, and nodded at Tag. I looked at him, too, and only had a moment to process the fact that something blue was shooting towards me before it struck me in the neck, stinging sharply, like a bee. I reached up, feeling the protrusion. A dart, then.

I heard a soft sigh leaving my lips and my legs gave out. The last thing I saw, as the room went dark, was Ethan standing over me and Tag lifting Keeta in his arms.

Chapter 9

A pounding headache brought me back to consciousness. I opened my eyes and quickly closed them again against the harsh glare of bright overhead lights. Gently cradling my head in my hands, I sat up. A moan escaped me, the small sound hurting my head further.

A warm hand tried to soothe me, callouses rubbing over my bare skinned shoulder above my tank top, easing the pain. And reminding me.

Squinting against the light, I opened my eyes and looked around. I was sitting on a white-linened bed among four plain, pale grey walls. A window showed only a dark, empty night sky. No buildings. No clue to where I was being held. A wooden dresser stood between an uncomfortable-looking chair and a narrow closet on one wall. It didn't look like a hospital room, or a prison cell. A dorm room?

"Here, drink this." A man handed me a paper cup filled with water. I looked up into his face.

Ethan.

I glared at him, and then the cup.

"It's not drugged. I swear. It'll help with the headache."

"Thanks, really, but I think I'll pass."

"Fair enough." He drank the water himself in one gulp and moved to pull the chair closer to the bed. He sat down and leaned back, putting his hands behind his head like he had that first night, the first time I'd seen him.

"So."

"So," I echoed.

"Are you ready to talk?" he asked.

"Are you freaking kidding me?" My headache was receding, anger quickly taking its place, driving it back. "What the heck is this place? Where am I? Where's my dog? And who the hell do you think you are, kicking down my door like that? You're going to have to pay for that, you know. After I have you arrested for illegal entry and assault."

"Already done. Your door has been repaired, and your dog is fine. She's quite happy, actually, making friends with Evie."

"Evie?"

"Yes, Evie Garcia, one of ours. She's good with animals."

My mind flashed back to that day at the estate, the fighting, Kipner, and the Latina woman with the pack of dogs.

"Why am I here?"

"You tell me. You've walked to me more than once, and pulled me to you. You were there Friday. Are you working with the warpers? What's their plan?"

"Dude, I have no idea who you are, or what you are talking about, but I do know my rights, and you can't just kidnap a person like this. I'm leaving."

I swung my legs over the side of the bed and tried to stand, but succeeded in only falling back on the bed. My legs wouldn't support my weight.

"What have you done to me?" I asked, fear creeping into my voice. Unwanted visions of scenes from every bad serial killer flick I'd ever seen paraded themselves through my head.

Ethan grimaced. "Not what you're imagining. Muscle weakness is normal after you've been sedated."

"You mean shot."

"I meant sedated. If we'd wanted to shoot you, we would have. You'll be fine in ten or twenty minutes. We're not holding you hostage, but we do need to talk."

He paused, examining me like I was book he couldn't read.

"Who do you think I am?"

I snorted in a most unladylike way. "Well, I thought you were a ghost, or some weird dream, until you broke down my door with your friend."

His lips quirked up. "A ghost?"

"Well, yeah." I flushed, realizing how stupid that sounded now.

"Well, I have to say that is the most original story I've heard all year. Alright. I'll play along. Here's what I know. Your name is Calliope Winters," he said, and began ticking off my personal details like a shopping list. "You entered the foster system at age two, grew up with one Kate Bess, finished school for social work, but the only job you've ever held, officially, is as a drummer. You've lived at the same apartment since you finished school, with the same dog, the same van, and the same job, all of which indicates you crave stability and hate change, despite appearances."

"Excuse me?" I said, bristling.

He continued on, ignoring me.

"Your hair, your clothes, even the music you play, it all suggests you have a wild personality. But, I think it's the opposite. I think that everything you do, down to pounding that worn out heavy bag hanging in your apartment, makes you feel safe. You seek security, and you have trust issues, an awkward combination."

"Gee, thanks Dr. Phil. I guess you have me all figured out," I drawled sarcastically, trying to hide just how close he'd come on every count.

"Not everything. I can't figure out who you're really working for, and what your agenda is." He leaned forward in his chair, an earnest expression on his face. "Look, if you're in trouble, we can help you. You're obviously not in too deep, or you wouldn't have helped us out on Friday. But you need to come clean. Can the act, Callie. You need to tell me who you're working with."

I let out a small scream of frustration. "I told you, I'm not working with anyone. How about instead of grilling me, you tell me who you are, really, and what this is all about? How were you able to be in my place, before your muscle kicked in the door? How did you disappear from the garden on Friday night?"

He slumped back in his seat, an odd look on his face.

"You really don't know, do you?"

"That's kind of what I've been trying to tell you."

He swore under his breath. "If you're telling the truth, and I'm still not sure I believe you, then I guess I owe you an explanation. You're a traveler, like me. Some people call us walkers."

I just stared at him blankly.

"Have you heard of people who have out of body experiences? Astral travel?"

"No."

"Okay, well, short story, anybody's soul can leave its body when it dreams, or through really deep meditation. But only some people have the natural ability to travel anywhere they want, anytime, as if they are really there. We can even alter the energy around us enough to interact physically with our environment, given enough practice."

"Okay, now who's the crazy one," I muttered.

"I'm not crazy. And neither are you. We're travelers."

"And Tag? Kipner? Lemme guess. You're all part of some secret government spy group made up of travelers?"

"Not quite," he said patiently. "Tag and I work with a private organization that occasionally consults with the United States government. And we're not all travelers, there are...other skills."

"I'm sorry, this is all a bit too much for me. Can we back up to the astral travel thing again?"

"Actually, I'm probably not the best person to be explaining all this. How're your legs? Are you up for a walk?"

"Yeah." I stood up carefully. "I think so."

"Okay, great." He got up and walked to the door. "Come on."

"I still don't trust you," I said, following him.

"Then we have another thing in common."

Chapter 10

The hall outside was just boring, empty and gray as my room had been. We walked past several closed doors before stopping at an elevator. Ethan reached out and pressed the down button, then rocked back on his heels while we waited.

"Cheery place," I said, making conversation without really knowing why. I mean, this guy had abducted me from my own home. I shouldn't trust him. I shouldn't talk to him. But part of me felt like I'd known him for years.

"It's better downstairs, you'll see. This floor is for the newly awakened. Sometimes too much color can be...overwhelming. Some people do better with less stimulation."

"Well then, your interior decorator did a really good job. So, you guys tranq a lot of people, huh?"

"What?"

"You said newly awakened, I figured-"

The elevator dinged, the doors sliding open, and we stepped inside. He punched the second floor button lightly, and leaned against the wall while we began our descent. We were on the fifth floor, the highest number on the panel.

"I'm gonna let someone else handle that answer, okay?"

"No," I said, flicking my hair over my shoulder, and facing the doors. "But I guess it'll have to do."

The doors opened. I stepped out and waited for Ethan to lead the way. We walked down a nicer hallway, just as quiet but this one was carpeted with a beautiful blue on blue pattern that meshed really nicely with the creamy beige walls. Copper and brass scrollwork sconces lit the walls. We took a few turns, emerging into a sort of common area, done in the same colors but furnished with tables, chairs, and few sofas. A pool table stood in one corner, and a TV played some reality show above a dormant fireplace. On one sofa, a girl lay sacked out, watching the TV, with her arm around a sleeping white dog.

"Keeta?" I stepped forward. The trio playing pool paused, looking my way, but I ignored them. I only had eyes for the white ball of fur flying towards me.

I knelt down to the floor, letting Keeta lick my face happily while I buried my head in her neck. "Mmm, I missed you girl." Tears pricked my eyes, and I remembered the sight of her lying prone on the floor of my apartment. I never would have thought I'd be grateful to be tranqed, but there it was. I'd take a dart over a bullet any day.

"So, you must be Calliope," a girl's voice said.

I looked up, recognizing the woman I'd seen on Friday in my vision. She looked street-tough today, her short curls

65

mostly hidden under a grinning skull bandana. I would have gauged her age right around mine, although I was sure people probably treated her like she was younger, since she was so petite. "I prefer Callie, actually."

"Okay, Callie." She gave me an artless smile, putting me at ease. "Great dog you've got there. She really likes you."

"The feeling's mutual," I laughed as Keeta licked my ear and almost knocked me over.

"Yeah, she really appreciates everything you do for her. Sounds like she's got a great life with you. That makes you all right, in my book."

"Um, sure, okay," I said. Who was the crazy one now, I thought. "What are you, some kind of dog whisperer?"

She laughed like I'd said something really funny, but at a look from Ethan, she sobered up.

"Something like that," she said, eyeing me strangely. "Ethan?"

"I'm taking her to Kim now. He's better at this sort of thing than I am."

"Good plan," she said seriously. She knelt down next to me and gave Keeta a pat on the head. "See you later, beauty." She looked at me. "Good luck."

And then Evie sprang over the couch and settled back in among the pillows.

Ethan moved away and I scrambled to follow, Keeta close on my heels. We walked down another hall, and stepped through a set of double doors. I'd been expecting some sort of office, maybe a weird lab or, well, I don't know what I was expecting. But it wasn't this. We'd walked into a room full of sleeping people, everyone lying on elevated cots, hooked up to monitors. Several more people were walking between the beds, checking charts against the machines.

Ethan stalked over to a familiar and slender Asian man. "Dr. Kim," he said and tapped the man's shoulder. "You got a minute? We need the talk."

The doctor nodded and handed his chart to a nurse nearby, then followed us out of the room. We walked across the hall, this time into the kind of office I had envisioned.

Big wooden table. Several chairs. Large window behind the desk.

It was the room from my first vision, the one where I'd first seen Ethan, Kipner and Kim. Except now, Kim moved to sit behind the desk, and Kipner wouldn't be joining us.

Ethan motioned for me to take the seat next to him, and I did, feeling overwhelmed.

The room was real. Ethan was real. Kim was real.

I wasn't going crazy.

But then what the hell was happening to me? Was it possible that this was all just some big hallucination and I had nodded off at my desk at home?

Keeta moved in front of me and sat, leaning against my legs protectively. I fisted a hand in her fur, comforted, strengthened by her very real presence. I spread my legs slightly and she eased back between my knees, merging into me like a spirit animal. My dog. My totem.

"So, Ms. Winters. Allow me to introduce myself. I am Henry Kim. I understand you have some questions?"

"More than you know. How about we start with who you are, and why your people have brought me here. Wherever here is."

He removed his glasses and clasped his hands before him on the desk. "My family has worked with people like you and Ethan for generations. Guided them. Shielded them. Trained them."

"People like me?"

Somehow, this took him off guard. Kim glanced at Ethan.

"She doesn't know?"

"As far as I can tell, she doesn't know a thing. My read's never great, but everything comes up blank."

"Mmm. Okay. I'd better start at the beginning, then. Ms. Winters, any chance you are a history buff?"

"Not especially."

"Have you ever heard of the Dogon tribe in Mali?"

"As in Africa?"

"Yes."

"Nope."

The doctor's lips compressed into a thin line.

"Well, the Dogon tribe, they have an interesting story about how humans were created long ago. Like many oral traditions, it's not a hundred percent accurate. But it does hold seeds of the truth, seeds sown by the ancient people of Mesopotamia, particularly those from the regions of Syria, Turkey and Iraq. These ancient stories, they all share a common thread, a story about Star Walkers, or Soul Travelers, beings from another world who came here with greater abilities and intellects than our own. People who intermarried with humans and passed on their own special powers. The Dogon also tell of the Nommo, or Star Walkers, guardians who traveled to earth as pure consciousness, taking over the minds of men and giving special powers to humans while they used their bodies. Some, they aligned with the energy of the sun using copper wires. These enhanced humans had the powers of telekinesis, mind control through speech, and could create illusions or glamours that would fool the keenest eyes. Others were aligned with the energy of the moon using bands of bronze, gaining the power of telepathy and astral travel like the Nommo themselves. Sumerian stories call the visitors the Annunaki. In the Bible, they are the Nephilim. New Age authors call such travelers walk-ins. The names don't matter. The powers do."

He paused. "Are you following so far?"

"Oh, yes. Please, go on." I felt like I was watching an episode of Ancient Aliens. Amused, and wondering how anyone could ever believe all the nonsense.

"So, as you can imagine, some of the people abused their new powers, went wild with greed and madness. A great war ensued among men, the Nommo and the new breed of star children. The Nommo left, and their children, the starseeds, were forced to hide, forced to get their powers under control or be wiped out."

"What does any of this have to do with me?"

"Well, I would have thought that was obvious. You, dear girl, are a traveler."

"Ethan mentioned that before. I'm sorry, but it doesn't sound any more believable coming from you, especially when you start talking about all this alien walk-in nonsense."

"It's not nonsense. Astral travel, or soul travel, happens to all humans when we are asleep. It's a sort of bodiless, freeform exploration through the astral planes that we sometimes remember as dreams, and can be quite difficult to recall since the conscious, physical mind of the body remains completely uninvolved during this time. Children also experience astral travel while they are sleeping (at which time many parents often feel compelled to check on their sleeping infants, intuitively sensing that their child's spirit has left its body and is no longer present in the house.) In fact, many people who have early childhood memories have visual clues for this, remembering observing their surroundings both with the eyes of their bodies and from across the room or up high near the ceiling. As children age and grow more accustomed to the earthly plane, they tend to become more and more tied to their bodies, spending fewer waking moments in astral form."

"Humans have these abilities naturally, which is why the Nommo were attracted to our planet in the first place. But descendants of the starseeds still carry the genetic mutations of the Nommo. In those families, the powers of the Nommo live on. Young adults awaken around their twenty-eighth year to their powers, when Saturn returns to its original place in the sky to match the position it held when they were born. The return acts as a catalyst, activating an innate cellular susceptibility in our body to other astronomical influences. Once this happens, disturbances in solar and lunar cycles have the ability to awaken our full potential."

He looked at me expectantly.

"I'm not sure I'm following you."

"Let me put it another way. Powers of the sun are triggered by solar eclipses-"

"And lunar eclipses can trigger astral travel," I interrupted, the answer coming to me all at once. "Thursday night, the blood moon. That was my first trip."

"I presume so, yes."

"So, I'm not crazy."

"No."

"You're not a ghost," I pointed an accusing finger at Ethan.

"No," he laughed and I glared at him. "Sorry?"

"Damn. This is some crazy stuff you're laying on me, you know that? Anything else you want to throw at me?" I asked, looking back at Dr. Kim. "What are warpers?"

"Well, like I said, those who can travel are called walkers, or travelers. Telepaths are readers; people who move things, which you might know as telekinesis or psychokinesis, are lifters. Bards, or speakers, have the power to influence people with their voice, and grammers use illusions or holograms to shift the appearance of reality. Every ability is powerful in its own right, but the last two...They tend to offer the most temptation for abuse. Bards and grammers are the ones who most often become twisted by their power, greedy. Dark. But really, any of us could choose to use our powers to warp the minds and realities of others, and in the process, become warped ourselves. When that happens, a person becomes a warper."

"Ah," I said, as if it all made sense. In reality, it was all a bit much to process.

"Our greatest task as star children is to protect the legacy the Nommo created, our families, along with humanity. We are all connected. It is my people's most central belief. We work together, teaching the newly awakened of their gifts and helping them adapt so that they do not become twisted."

"So, the men who killed Kipner, those were warpers?"

"Yes. There has always been a small, but vocal, group of us who believe we are better than other humans, that we should be the ones in power. It's been the same story since the Nommo first created us, since the great wars. Some of us are working within the government to make sure that never happens again. Unfortunately, the warpers sometimes try to do the same, but to alternate ends. Kipner was a great ally, and our work will be tougher without him, but it isn't anything you should be worried about. Good always prevails."

"So Ethan and Tag, you guys are what, psychic soldiers?"

"No," Ethan shifted uncomfortably in his seat. "We both left the military a long time ago."

"Ethan is a scout," Kim explained. "He has a special ability to sense newly awakened, and helps find people like us, people like you, who need help. Usually, gifts run in families. Many adepts are sent to us the year before their awakening, so we can prepare them. Train them. But the gift can sometimes skip many generations, or even be activated out of cycle, and not everyone understands what is happening to them. You, for instance..."

"Have no family."

"Not in the conventional sense, no. I am sorry. Do you know what happened to your birth parents?"

"No. I was left on the steps of a firehouse. My name, Calliope Winters, was stitched in my jacket, and I wore this chain around my neck. Other than that, I have no idea. I have no memory of anything from those years."

"A pity. But knowing that Winters may be your real birth name, that is something. We'll put calls in to other facilities. The name Winters is not uncommon. Someone will know something, I am sure. In the meantime, I think you should stay here."

"Here? But I can't. I have things to do." Or, at least, I would eventually. Did I really want to stay here with these people? Could I trust them?

Kim looked at me like he knew what I was thinking. And maybe he did.

"Please, at least stay for the night. This way, you can meet some of our people, learn a bit more about us. About you. Think of it as a vacation."

"I don't know. I don't even know where this is. Where are we?"

"Two hours outside the city, near Joshua Tree. Most of us find the desert environment a welcome escape from the city noise."

"Do I have to stay in that gray room?"

"No, not at all. We have plenty of open rooms, people come and go all the time. Ethan, why don't you show Callie a room on level four?"

"Actually," I spoke up before Ethan could answer, "I'm starving. Before I make any decisions, do you think I could get something to eat?"

Chapter 11

I walked out of Kim's office with Ethan, following him down the hallway, but not really paying attention to where we were going. We rode the elevator down to the first floor, where a bunch of people were waiting to ride back up, covered in sweat and laughing as they passed us.

"The first floor is where we do all our physical training – running, fighting, weapons," Ethan volunteered, watching me evaluate the group.

"I thought you weren't soldiers."

"We aren't. But training the body helps train the mind. The two go hand in hand. You can learn to control your mind without the physical work, but it goes a lot faster when you combine the two. Plus, it helps people let off steam. Most people find they enjoy it."

"Boxing helps with that. Letting off steam, I mean."

"Yeah, I saw your equipment," he said.

I tensed, remembering how and when he'd been in my apartment, and Keeta moved closer to my side in response.

Ethan walked on, not saying anything more, and we entered a large room with tables and a cafeteria. Most of the tables were empty, but there were a few people hanging out, chatting, reading, lingering over their food.

"So, this is the main cafeteria," Said Ethan with a grand wave of one hand.

"I don't suppose you remembered to kidnap my wallet, did you?" I joked.

"No, but don't worry, everything here is free. One of the perks of working with Gregory."

"Who's Gregory?"

"It's not a who, it's a what. Gregory started off as a group of watchers, also called guardians, of the starseeds. Egregors, in Greek. Eventually, the watchers evolved into a guiding council of sorts, run democratically by all the top families – both watchers and walkers. Fiscally, it operates in a lot of ways as a trust. Financing is not a problem, working with Gregory."

"Wait a minute, you're not talking about Gregory Bank?" I stopped in my tracks, halfway through the room.

Gregory was a huge multi-national investment firm, controlling billions of dollars in mortgages, stocks and bonds. It was one of the only banks that hadn't been linked to causing the national recession back in 2007, and had a reputation for actually caring about its customers.

"One and the same. Of course, the banking part of the company is kept separate from operations at facilities like this one."

"Of course," I said, shaking my head. "Are you sure you guys aren't involved with the Illuminati? New World Order?"

Ethan chuckled. "Definitely not. Although regular people have feared our abilities enough over the centuries that certainly it could feel like that to an outsider. But I assure you, none of us have any desire to take over the world. We just want to co-exist peacefully. Maybe use our powers for good, when we can."

"No conspiracy theories hatching upstairs?" I grinned as if I was kidding, but I was interested in his answer, too.

Ethan looked at me seriously. "No, definitely not. I promise, Callie, we're the good guys. Now, the warpers, on the other hand...well, a lot of stories about the New World Order and the Illuminati are based on them, or at least people who have worked with them. Warpers are usually willing to work with just about any lowlife, if it will help them gain more power or disrupt the peace we are trying to maintain."

"Sounds kind of dangerous."

"It can be. As you've seen."

I bit my lip, thinking of Kipner.

"But it doesn't have to be for you," he went on. "You can be as involved as you want. Or don't want."

"Okay," I sighed.

"I know, this is a lot to take in. Personally, when life gets to me, food always helps me relax. Come on."

We threaded our way through the rest of the tables, dark wooden circles gleaming above pale industrial carpeting. A few people looked up, waving and smiling at Ethan, looking curiously at me. No one gave me the stink eye, as if I didn't belong, so that was nice. I wasn't sure exactly what my heritage was, having never had a DNA test or anything, but I was dark enough to have received more than my fair share of unwanted attention from overzealous shopkeepers and bored police. Of course, my sister Mel liked to point out that my hippie van and punk-rock clothes probably didn't help. She may have had a point, but I didn't see how it was my responsibility to dress up just to make other people feel more comfortable around me. I was comfortable in my body, in my skin. Kate said I had an artist's temperament. I thought I was just exercising my God-given American right to live free.

Who knows, maybe Kim would really be able to track down some of my birth family. I'd never looked, myself. I hadn't ever been interested in knowing who would leave their baby for other people to take care of. When I cared about someone, they were family, blood or not. And family never got left behind. But, knowing more about my family might help fill in some worthwhile blanks. Maybe.

I followed Ethan up to a deli-style counter, complete with ready-made salads behind glass. Sandwiches, soups and warm menu items were listed above on the wall. I placed an order for some broccoli-cheddar soup, a grilled cheese sandwich on rye, and a plain hamburger for Keeta. After taking my number, I walked over to grab a lemon seltzer from a cooler nearby.

"Everything is made fresh, so we might as well grab a seat. It'll be a few minutes at least," Ethan said.

"Will they call our numbers?"

"Nah. They flash it on the sign there." He pointed at a news-style LED ticker hanging on the far wall. At the moment, it was scrolling headlines and random inspirational quotes. A number went by several times, and I saw a girl head to the kitchen pass-through window and come back with a rich looking chocolate lava cake.

Oh yeah, a girl could get used to this place, assuming the food was as good as it looked.

I leaned back in my chair, petting Keeta absently beside me, and looked at Ethan.

"So, you seem to know a lot about me. What's your story? You said you were in the military?"

"Yeah, a long time ago." He locked his dark eyes on mine, smiling, but the gesture didn't quite reach past his mouth. "I grew up in Maryland, outside of DC. My father worked with the State Department. My mom was your typical homemaker, taking care of my brothers and me. Or at least she put on a good act. Once we were all in school she started working with another center like this one, north of Silver Spring. She still teaches there, from time to time."

"And your dad?"

"He passed."

"Oh, wow, I'm sorry."

"Don't be. He had a good life." Again, a quick smile, not reaching his eyes. There was clearly more to the story, but I couldn't exactly ask. Even I knew when to employ some tact. Kate had tried really hard to teach me manners, and from time to time her lessons had stuck.

"So, brothers? How many?"

"Two, both older. Frank is a carpenter down in Asheville, married to another reader who works as a psychic. The other, I haven't seen in a few years, he's overseas."

"With the army?"

"No. Warpers."

"Oh, crap. I'm just asking all the wrong questions tonight."

"No." He exhaled a whoosh of weighted breath, and tugged on one ear. "It's not your fault. My family's complicated. My mom's a reader, a scout like me, and my dad is a traveler. I was the only one to inherit both gifts, although my reading isn't that great. My oldest brother, he and my dad never really got along. I guess it took three of us to kind of mellow him out. When it was just him and Colin...well, Dad was always stricter with him. Tougher on him. I was the baby, so I always had it easy. Anyway, Colin started using his powers to read our dad, and sold some secrets to the warpers. I think in the beginning he just did it to get attention, or maybe to feel like he could get one over on my dad. But when my dad found out and confronted him, things got really ugly. They had a huge fight, and my dad collapsed. He died in the hospital two days later. Colin never forgave himself. Sometimes I think he went full warper after that so he could be as bad as he felt. I don't know. Frank says I'm always making excuses for Colin."

"I get it. He's your big brother."

"I guess." He watched the ticker behind me for a moment, then stood. "Orders up. I'll get them."

I sighed as I watched him walk stiffly to the counter. Somehow, no matter what angle I came at a conversation from, I always managed to make it awkward. Why should this be any different?

I slipped off one shoe, more of a slipper really, something they'd given me in the gray room, and used my foot to rub Keeta where she lay under the table. I closed my eyes, imagining I was back home, relaxing at my desk. Not in some secret psyops facility. Life had definitely gotten strange, and I wasn't sure I wanted any of it. Ethan said I had a choice, but I wondered. People who kidnapped other people weren't usually big believers in freedom of choice. Though, to be fair, after seeing what the other side was capable of, I could understand their reasoning. I supposed that in his shoes, I wouldn't have believed I was innocent either. Not when I'd kept popping in on him and Kipner.

Keeta huffed and stretched, and I opened my eyes to see an older woman approaching the table. Without smiling, she sat down across from me.

"So, you're the girl that Tag dragged in today." It was a statement, not a question. She had the same military bearing that Tag and Ethan had. My eyes darted to Ethan, where he was gathering silverware and condiments.

"Don't worry, you're safe from me. For now, anyways," she smirked. There was nothing soft about her, and I made a mental note to never get on her bad side. Not my greatest skill, but I'd make an effort, at least.

"I get that you don't want to say the wrong thing, but you do remember how to talk, right?" she asked.

"Oh, um, right, sorry. I'm Callie. And you are?"

"Marnie." The word cut the air between us like a knife.

Gee, and I was the bad conversationalist?

"You're right," she said. "My bad. I'm not the best talker, doesn't always make for a great first impression."

"I never said-"

She waved my words away. "I hear better than I listen sometimes. You'll get used to it."

"Marnie, I hope you are behaving yourself," Ethan said in a gentle teasing voice, setting down our trays of food. His was piled high with a huge platter of fish-and-chips, mozzarella sticks, a bowl of creamed spinach, and dipping cups of tartar sauce and ketchup.

"Of course." She winked up at him, her tough exterior relaxing with the softness of friendship.

"Marnie is one of our best teachers, she trains all the readers that come through here."

"Readers, you mean telepaths? Wait, were you reading my mind before?"

Marnie put her hands up in mock defense. "Sorry, occupational hazard. Right now you are broadcasting so loudly, anyone with half an ounce of ability can hear what you are thinking."

Crap, that couldn't be a good thing. I had some pretty outrageous thoughts. I didn't want anyone in my head except me. Before I could say just that, Marnie continued.

"Don't worry, I'll teach you how to stop. Some people are better at it than others, but eventually, everyone learns."

"But, what if I'm not a telepath?"

"Doesn't matter. Anyone can learn how to block a reader, with enough practice. You'll get there. Come see me in the morning, and we'll get started."

I was about to ask where, when Ethan spoke up. "I'll bring you. Consider me your own personal tour guide for the time being."

"Can everyone here read minds?" I grumbled.

They both laughed.

"No, not even close. My skills are rudimentary at best," Ethan said biting into a large piece of fried fish.

"Oh, so you're saying I just think really loud?" Marnie laughed even harder. "Nice. Really nice."

I raised an eyebrow at her, and couldn't help it. The whole thing was just too absurd, and I joined in, giggling along with her.

After a bit more small talk, Marnie left us to our dinner, and then Ethan showed me some lit paths outside where I could take Keeta on a walk. Town lights glittered in the distance to the west, but in every other direction all I could see was black desert and night sky.

Beside me, Ethan walked in silence, hands in his pockets. For a long time, I was content like that. Watching the stars, letting Keeta explore. Not talking. But after a while, questions I had couldn't be ignored.

"So," I began. "You can sense people when they come into their powers? How does that work, exactly?"

He tugged on his ear as we walked, considering. When he answered me, it was in a quiet tone of voice, perfectly aligned with the still of the night.

"It's a mutation of the reading gene. Like I said, I'm not the best reader. Not of thoughts, anyway. But I can sense powers when they are used within any reasonable distance. The further away they are, the quieter it feels to me, like an echo. Like thoughts, powers have signatures, so I can tell who is using the power, and if it is wild, or new, or precise, controlled."

"How can you tell the difference between thoughts or powers?"

"Thoughts come like voices. They all have their own signature energy patterns, like sound waves. It's hard to explain, but you'll see. It's something everyone picks up on. Some thoughts will hit you in your ears, like a conversation, but others will come to the frontal lobe, or above your ear, or behind your neck in your brain. Your own thoughts are full brain. You *feel* it everywhere."

I looked at him skeptically.

"No really. You'll see, if you can read," he promised. "Anyway, powers are the same. I can recognize powers I know, and sense when a power is newly awakened."

"How?"

"They feel wild. Young. I just know."

"Then why did you think I was a spy or whatever? Couldn't you tell I was new to all this?"

"That's the thing. You don't feel new to me. You feel...familiar. Like I know you from somewhere. And your powers, you might not have control over them yet, but they aren't wild. It's more like they are playing." He shook his head, rubbing the back of his neck. "I don't know how to explain it, really. Usually, I just sort of know."

"Reader's intuition?" I smirked.

"Something like that."

"So, you said reasonable distance. How far do your super senses reach?"

"Five hundred miles, give or take."

I stopped short.

"Five hundred miles? Is that normal?"

"Well, it's not a common mutation, being confined to only a handful of families. But yes, among us, it's pretty normal."

"And readers? Can they read minds at that distance?"

"Some can. Most are limited to under a hundred miles, or even fifty. And that's only through using advanced mental targeting and focus techniques. Normally, a reader will only hear what is in her general vicinity, in a room or a building."

I let out a breath I didn't know I'd been holding. "Well, that's a relief. At least I'm not bugging every reader in LA with my thoughts. Do you think I will be able to learn to read, too?"

"I would say that's a definite possibility, based on your signature. And there's something else, something I can't put a finger on, like a dissonant chord playing behind the music."

"Flattering."

"No, not like that. I'm sure there's nothing wrong with you. There's just something different about your energy patterns."

"Before, you kept asking me why I'd pulled you to me. Could that have been why?"

"No, that was something else. It's like your energy sent out a beacon of distress at that party, and I couldn't ignore it. I had to be there, right then. Tag wasn't too happy when I traveled out in the middle of a strategic planning session, I can tell you." He smiled at the memory, like a kid remembering putting salt in his brother's pudding.

"Anyway, we should head inside. I've got some other work I need to catch up on. I'll show you where your room is, and mine in case you need anything."

Turns out, my room was just a few doors down from his.

Cozy.

The room wasn't bad, either. Decorated in classic hotel colors, it had all the basic amenities, including its own small bathroom. A queen bed with attractive chocolate colored linens across from a television, which excited me until I saw there was no cable, only a handful of local

84

access channels. A BBC period drama was on PBS, so I snuggled in with Keeta and before I knew it, I was fast asleep, dreaming I was flying above the desert sands.

Chapter 12

Berlin. Cinder blocks.

Thorny hedges.

Barbed wire.

"Wire and hedges? Come on. Try again."

Marnie looked at me sternly across the table, sitting stiffly. I hated how she'd been able to sit in one position for over an hour without moving a muscle. I slumped back in my chair and let out a small scream of frustration.

"I can't do this."

"Sure you can. Everyone succeeds eventually. You need to learn to build a mental wall. The chances that you will learn to make an impenetrable defense are slim, but you have to at least be able to stop broadcasting your every thought."

"But how?"

"Try something else. You're a drummer, right? What if you imagine your thoughts are like a song, and the beat of a drum keeps them contained? Do you have a theme song?"

"Theme song?" I asked, quirking an eyebrow.

"Yeah, you know, something you love to hum more than others. The song you come back to again and again. Everybody's got one."

I tried to imagine what song Marnie would hum in the shower, and came up at a loss.

"Focus," she smirked. "When you get this, maybe I'll tell you."

My cheeks heated, knowing she'd heard my thoughts again.

"God, I suck at this."

"Just try. Think of a song."

I closed my eyes and thought of some of my favorite songs. I ran through Molten Requiem's current playlist, then some golden oldies, like Zeppelin's Immigrant Song and Metallica's Ride the Lightning. Then, it came to me. The first song I'd learned on the drums, Green Day's American Idiot. I remembered what it had felt like to master the beat, to match the CD on the stereo perfectly, syncing up seamlessly with the song. It had been such a rush. I allowed the feeling to permeate my entire being, that pure adrenaline of achievement and joy. The beat took over my body, blocking out my own heartbeat, and wrapped around me like a glove. This was why I played the drums. This was the feeling I sought out night after night.

A voice broke into my reverie.

"You have a song?

I opened my eyes and nodded.

"Good, what is it?" Marnie asked.

"You tell me," I shrugged with a grin.

She bowed her head for a moment, then looked back up at me, smiling.

"Green Day, American Idiot."

My smile faded, and the song got a bit quieter, but it kept playing.

"Don't lose the song. Keep it going. Good. Now think about what you had for breakfast today."

I remembered the chocolate waffles and whipped cream I'd eaten with a side of fresh squeezed orange juice. It'd probably been enough sugar to doom me to a mid-day coma, but I'd enjoyed every bite.

I looked at Marnie, and she looked at me.

I thought about the syrup I'd poured on my plate, the butter that hadn't melted before I'd had my first taste.

"Congratulations," she smiled. "I can't read you anymore. You did it. In pretty good time, too."

"I did? But you heard my song." Green Day tapered off into silence, and I leaned forward, confused.

"That's alright. It's nothing you don't want me to see, so it's okay. With practice, you can even learn to create a thought loop that will play and mask your real thoughts, the way it masked your breakfast. But this was a great start."

"So, I have to do this all the time? I'm not sure I can do that."

"No, not all the time. The more you practice, the more your wall will lock into place. Eventually it will always be up. The subconscious mind is an amazing thing. We all have a sort of "robot" in our mind that can be programmed to automate mundane tasks. Haven't you ever been driving, and suddenly you arrive at your destination with no memory of even watching the road?"

"All the time."

"Well, that's your autopilot. Your body is hard-wired to have autonomic responses. You breathe without meaning to. Your heart pumps on its own. Your body regulates its temperature. Pretty soon, your wall will be one of your brain's basic functions, and you won't have to worry about it. Some people are lucky, they are born with naturally strong walls already in place. But the rest of us, we have to work at it."

"Even you?"

"Especially me."

"That's hard to believe."

"Let's just say I started out a lot more innocent than you, and almost as clueless."

"Gee, thanks."

Marnie laughed. "You know what I mean. I knew people in my family had powers, but I didn't know about warpers, or any of the other big bads in the world." For a moment, her face became haunted, before a mask of seriousness slid into place. "Anyway, that's another story for another time. Why don't you spend the rest of the morning practicing what you've learned here today, then come back with Ethan after lunch? We'll see if we can work on those involuntary trips you've been taking."

"Alright. But does it have to be with Ethan?"

"Why, don't you like him?" She sounded surprised, as if everyone liked Ethan. I imagined they did.

"No, it's not that," I brought up the strains of Green Day again, so she wouldn't hear what I was really thinking. That maybe I liked him just a little too much. And if I didn't date guys in my band, what did that mean about dating guys I shared psychic powers with? Somehow, just the idea of it made me feel a bit too open and exposed. There was some kind of attraction there, but maybe it was just that tug he had, his scout sonar or whatever. I don't know. Truth is, I'd never felt so safe, and so off balance, around anyone before.

And I wasn't sure I liked it.

"It's just, I figured he must be sick of babysitting me. Doesn't he have a bookstore to run?"

Marnie smiled. She had to know there was something I didn't want her to *hear* but she didn't press me on it.

"Don't worry about Ethan. This is part of his job, helping newbies settle in. He's a great trainer, too. You're lucky, actually – between the two of us you've got some of the best support in the United States. So get on out there, and try to keep your theme song going. Feel free to go mingle and make some friends, or get some rest."

"I was thinking I might explore the trails outside a little more with Keeta, if that's okay?"

"It's fine, of course. Everyone here is free to come and go as they please, including you." Her chair squeaked as Marnie pushed away from the table, metal scraping against linoleum, and I stood, too. "Just remember to practice holding your mind shield."

"Thanks, Marnie."

"Anytime, kid. And Callie?"

I turned at the door.

"Yeah?"

She paused, and seemed to reconsider. "Never mind. I'll see you in a couple hours."

I shrugged. Whatever she was going to say, apparently it could wait.

I headed back to my room and collected Keeta. It was unusual to be somewhere with so many strangers and have her off leash, but she did great, staying by my side and barely sparing anyone a glance. That is, until she saw Evie heading across the lobby towards us with a couple of guys.

Keeta barked happily and loped towards the woman, running around her in a circle before she stood on her hind legs to lick her face. If I hadn't been a more secure person, I might have been jealous.

Oh, who was I kidding?

Keeta had never greeted anyone like that, other than me. Not even Kate. Husky-mixes were notorious one-person dogs.

"You've got some serious mojo, girl," I said, shaking my head as I approached the group. Evie was giggling, petting Keeta and pushing her down gently at the same time.

"Almost as special as your girl here," she said, smiling. "Calliope, this is Cliff and Toby. They're newbies, like you, just came in last month."

"Nice to meet you." We shook hands, and I concentrated on keeping the music going in my head. "I was just headed out for a hike. Want to come?"

Toby, a thin, wiry man with glasses, stuffed his hands in his pockets, looking disinterested, but Cliff perked up.

"I'd love to. I've been dying to check out the desert some more while I'm here. Evie?"

"You two go ahead. Toby and I have some more work to do." Toby looked at Evie with something between worship and gratitude, and right away I knew someone had a schoolboy crush.

Cliff snorted. "Suit yourselves. You ready, new girl?" He took off his baseball cap, ran his hand through the thick dark hair and stuck the cap back on, backwards.

"Yep. See you later, Evie. Nice meeting you, Toby."

Evie beamed as she waved goodbye, and Toby said something I couldn't quite catch, although I thought it might have been "good riddance." Maybe he thought Cliff was running the same game, giving him competition with his new mentor. Or maybe he wasn't as harmless as he seemed. Cliff was certainly the friendlier of the two, but first impressions could be deceiving, and he did have the whole 1990s backwards cap thing going on.

I decided to withhold any judgments for now.

At least Toby had good taste in women. Evie seemed to be completely natural, genuine in her general enthusiasm. Plus, Keeta approved of her.

I supposed that would have to be good enough for me, too.

Chapter 13

"So then, after that solar eclipse a few months ago, weird things started happening. I was just starting to realize that I wasn't crazy, that I really was making things happen, when some people showed up and invited me to come visit here."

"What kinds of things are we talking about?" I asked Cliff.

"Oh, you know. I-"

We walked around a group of boulders, Keeta trailing behind us sniffing every rock in the dirt, searching for lizards and mice. A dry, rasping rattle cut through the air, and I glanced down.

"Snake!" I cried, pushing Cliff sideways before he could step forward. Just then Keeta ran forward, yipping. "Keeta, no!" Off leash, I had no way to stop her as she went bounding toward the lethal serpent. I tried to grab her, but caught nothing but air as she raced off, straight past the snake, chasing after a mouse as it streaked towards its burrow.

I held my breath, hoping against all odds that the snake wouldn't strike, or that it wasn't as poisonous as it seemed.

The snake hadn't shifted its attention off of me and Cliff, which was good for Keeta, and bad for us. I stared at it, not sure what to do next, and watched as a ripple went through the animal and it faded from view like a bad afterimage. Like a hologram.

Cliff started laughing, leaning against one of the boulders while he cracked up.

"Oh my God, you should have seen your face," he said, eyes gleaming with amusement. "That was priceless."

"You did that?"

"You asked what I could do." He shrugged. "I figured I'd just show you."

"Dammit, Cliff. I thought my dog was going to die." I glared at him. "That was a really crappy thing to do."

He stood up, the smile gone from his face. "Geez, sorry. I didn't mean anything by it. I thought you could take a joke. Guess you're no more fun than Toby. My bad."

The words formed an apology, but his tone didn't fit.

"This was your idea of a joke? A word of advice? Don't go into stand-up. You suck at it."

"Alright, alright. Look, I'm sorry, okay? I'll behave." He held his hands up in a gesture of truce. I lifted one eyebrow and narrowed my eyes at him.

"Fine. But come clean. You're a grammer?"

"I prefer the term 'glammer'. Grammer just sounds so, so boring. Reminds me too much of school."

"Can you do anything else?"

"Nah. But my holos are pretty good, I can hold them for ten minutes or more. As long as I don't lose focus, and start laughing, that is." He grinned at me, an aged, charming frat boy. Luckily, those kinds of smiles had never held any sway over me.

"Of course. And I suppose you've been practicing on Toby?"

"Oh yeah, he's a prime subject. Falls for my holos every time."

I thought about what I'd been told, how abilities could corrupt kindness and empathy with the lure of power. Listening to Cliff, it was easier than ever to imagine. Part of me wanted to call Keeta and stalk back to the Center. But I could hear Kate in my head, reminding me that tough exteriors usually masked pain. Reminding me that the surest way to doom a child in the system was to give them the poisoned gift of another rejection. If Kate were here, she would give him her time and courtesy. I'd seen her build up torn down children time and again with kind words and some attentive friendship. Magic took time, she liked to say, just like baking cake. But the results were almost always worth waiting for.

Instead of walking away, I forced a smile. "So, your powers are tied to the sun, right?"

"Yeah, or at least, that's what activated them. You're a walker, right?"

"Yeah."

"Well, you're lucky. Solar powers work a little differently, sometimes you have to experience a few eclipses to get triggered. I was almost thirty-one when my power finally activated. My mom had given me some stupid line about how my father had promised a special gift for me when I grew up, that I'd see when I turned twenty-eight or twenty-nine, but nothing ever happened. She didn't really know what to expect, though, so I don't really blame her."

He scuffed the earth with one toe and kicked a stone ahead of us as we walked.

"What about your dad?"

"Never met him," he said, sticking his hands in his pockets and looking down. "He disappeared before I was born. My mom always thought he ditched us. Kim looked into it and found a file that says he was killed by warpers. The Gregors had no clue about my mom and me, or else Kim says they would have helped us out. As it was, my mom was stuck raising me all alone. She still thinks he left us. I haven't figured out how to tell her the truth yet."

"Wow, that really sucks. I'm sorry, Cliff."

"Yeah, well. At least now I know he wasn't just some loser pretending to be better than he was. So it's not all bad. Silver linings and all that." He gave me a lopsided grin.

"Heh, right." I chuckled and shook my head. "At least you had some kind warning. I didn't have a clue. In fact, until yesterday, I was pretty sure I was going crazy."

Cliff huffed. "Warning? I thought I was going to get some inheritance, a big fat trust fund or maybe some cushy property. I wasn't expecting to look in the mirror one day, wish for a better hairline, and then see it all grow back in."

"You're balding?"

"Like an eagle, baby."

I giggled, thinking Cliff really wasn't so bad after all, and we shared a conspiratorial smile.

Score another one for Kate.

"That must have been a big shock. What about Toby? What can he do?"

"Ah, he's solar, he can move things a little with his mind. Not far, but still, it's pretty cool. And he's a speaker."

"Really? Like one of those inspirational gurus?" He seemed way to shy for that, but maybe on stage he opened up. I'd known more than my fair share of entertainers like that.

Cliff let out a bark of amusement. "Toby? No, no, nothing like that. I think he works from home as a computer programmer or IT manager, something like that. No, he's a speaker, a bard. He can use his voice to control people, you know, like in Star Wars?" He lowered his voice and put on a semi-decent Brit accent as he waved two fingers in front of me. "'This is not the guy you're looking for.'"

I chuckled. "Right. Classic. So that's really a thing? Mind control?"

"Well, the jury's still out on that one. Personally, I think what I do is more mind control than what Toby does. I mean, you really believed you saw that snake. When Toby speaks, it's more like he's hijacking your free will. Even if you don't want to do something, when he pushes you to, you'll do it." He frowned.

"Sounds like you're speaking from experience."

"Yeah. I pulled a little prank on Toby once, too. Let's just say he gives better than he gets." He made a face and spit on the ground, like he was trying to get the taste of something bad out of his mouth. Whatever Toby had told him to do, I got the impression it hadn't been too pleasant.

I guess Toby had more backbone than I'd given him credit for.

"So what's his story, then? Was he just as clueless as us about his powers?"

"Nah. Kid's got a platinum pedigree. Parents are both bards. His mom's a hostage negotiator with the LAPD. Dad is a top-shelf corporate lawyer."

"So why's he even here? Couldn't his parents have taught him whatever he needs to know?"

"Could've, and probably should've. Kid doesn't talk much about his parents, but I got the impression they don't have much use for him. Too busy with work, fundraisers, blah, blah, blah. Besides, Gregory's makes it their business to keep a close eye on the newly awakened – especially the sun kids."

"Sounds like you don't like the Gregors too much."

"They're okay. It's just kind of crappy sometimes, the way some people here look at me. Like any moment I might bug out on them, turn into a warper."

"But any of us could do that, right? I mean, it's not just you guys."

"I overheard some guy talking to Evie a few weeks ago. He said forty percent of sunseeds go bad. More, if they're speakers. Sounds like pretty crappy odds to me." He kicked another rock ahead of us and stopped, staring up at the sky. "I don't know. I probably shouldn't be telling you any of this. Can't be making the best impression."

I put my hand on his shoulder and turned him to face me.

"Hey, don't talk like that. I'm glad you told me. Frankly, I think if you're telling me this kind of stuff, you must be one of the good ones. So don't sweat it, okay?"

"Yeah, alright." He took a deep breath. "You're pretty cool, you know that? So what's your story?"

I filled him in on the last several days, and the bare bones of my childhood.

"So you're a drummer? Seriously?"

"Yeah, what do you do?"

"Not much, according to my mom. I'm a prep cook at a place in Malibu. I've been working on a few screenplays since college, you know, the old Hollywood dream. I never really thought I'd have to work for a living, I was sort of banking on that trust fund." He gave me a lop-sided grin. "Maybe now I'll take a job with Gregory's."

"Are there a lot of those?"

"Enough. And from what I hear, they're going to need more of us than ever. The Warpers are planning something big. Some bad stuff has been going down. I heard they even took out one of the Gregors' main leaders last weekend."

I knew he had to be talking about Kipner.

"Yeah. I hear that was pretty awful," I said hollowly, and changed the subject as soon as I could without being too obvious.

We spent the rest of the walk talking about music. The longer we were together, the more comfortable I felt with Cliff, like I'd made a real friend. He didn't always make the most appropriate jokes, but he was genuine, and a good guy. I'd always liked people who didn't filter everything that came out of their mouth. I felt guilty, not telling him what I knew about Kipner, but a part of me still wasn't ready to acknowledge what I had seen. The violence that the warpers were capable of.

As far as I knew, the power they'd used to kill him wasn't even a regular ability. How had they done it? And more to the point, why?

I wasn't sure I really even wanted to know. I'd never missed my drums so much. The desire to pound out a steady beat called to me like a siren song, but part of me wanted answers even more.

And I knew just who was going to give them to me.

Chapter 14

When we got back to the garden entrance, Ethan was sitting on one of the benches under a small, gnarled Joshua Tree. The strange, prickly form didn't offer much in the way of shade, but it seemed to suit Ethan, whose head was propped up against his arms, as usual, while he let the sun's rays hit his face.

He opened his eyes as we approached, no doubt alerted by the crunch of sand and gravel under our feet – that, and Keeta's wet nose, pressed against his neck as she stood on the bench to sniff him. He laughed and petted her, letting her kiss him.

When had she decided to forgive him for busting into our apartment, I wondered? What kind of guard dog was she, anyway?

Then again, I had pretty much forgiven him already, too. Even without having all my questions answered.

Still, watching my dog lick his face left me conflicted. Part of me felt reassured – after all, weren't dogs the best judge of character?

The other part felt betrayed.

"Hey, Cliff. Callie." He gave us both a lazy smile.

"Ethan," Cliff nodded, sticking his hands in his pockets.

"Hey," I said.

"You guys have a good walk? Evie told me you went out."

"Is that why you're out here? Checking up on the newbies? I promise, I behaved," Cliff joked. I could see now that he liked to test people, push their buttons. Given his history, it wasn't surprising. I'd seen his kind a hundred times before in the system. Not knowing why you'd been left behind by a parent, always wondering if you were good enough – those things tended to weigh on a person.

"Not at all. I'm sure you were the perfect guide," Ethan said easily.

"Just catching some rays, then?" I teased.

"Actually, I was waiting for you."

I pushed my hair back behind one ear. "Did you need to see me?"

He gave me a wry grin. "I think it's more the other way around, but sure, we'll go with that."

Cliff shuffled his feet uncomfortably. "Okay, well, I'll just leave you two to chit chat. Callie, maybe I'll catch you at dinner?"

"Oh, um, sure. That sounds great."

He tipped his cap to us both and retreated indoors.

Ethan turned back to look at me, and I cocked my head to one side, examining him in consternation.

"What?"

"I think it's more the other way around?" I threw his words back at him.

He shrugged. "I call it like I see it."

"And what gives you the idea that I wanted to see you?"

He laughed and shook his head.

"You really have no idea what you're doing, do you?"

I raised an eyebrow in response. "Huh?"

"You pulled me again. I didn't travel this time, but I felt the pull, so I decided to ditch the paperwork and wait here." He stood up and approached me. "So what gives? What do you need from me, Callie?"

I stared up into his face, the sun casting it in shadow and setting his hair alight. I couldn't read his expression, blinded as I was by the brightness that surrounded him, and I couldn't tell just what he was asking me, simply by his words.

So I took him at face value, and kept my own passive.

"I have some more questions."

"Why am I not surprised?" He sighed, but without rancor. "You want to sit and talk?"

"I could walk some more. I think better on my feet."

"Alright then. Lead the way."

We walked quietly for a while, allowing Keeta to take point.

Finally, I opened up. "I guess, my biggest question now is, what the hell is going on with the warpers? I know you said that I don't need to worry about it, but I have to be honest – I'm worried. I saw three guys explode a man from the inside out with his own blood. How? And why? Why not just use guns, or poison, or something a little less, I don't know, obvious? Why like that, out in the open? It wasn't exactly discreet."

"You do realize that was more than one question, right?"

"Like you said, I have needs."

He coughed, hiding a smile. "Right. Okay. I'll start with the easiest question first. The warpers you saw were telekinetics, lifters. They used their minds to force the blood out of his body all at once. The amount of power such an act requires goes beyond regular telekinesis. Each one of those men could probably lift that boulder over there over your head and twirl it around for an hour without breaking a sweat. But counteracting the innate will that directs living tissue is something that is beyond even the best of lifters. There is a magic to life that negates coercion of that kind. The human brain, the nervous system, the body – it has powers of its own. Before this year, I would have told you that what they did to Kipner was impossible. Now? I don't know what limits these new warpers have, if any."

"But how? Why are they so strong?"

"As best we can gather, a branch of the government has been working behind our backs to enhance our powers, combine them with new technologies to create the ultimate warriors. Much of their focus seems to be on sonar."

"Like the navy uses for navigation?"

"Yes. Sound waves never end, they travel forever. All matter has unique frequencies, and if you can find the right frequency, you can destroy anything. You can also use sound to strengthen cells, speed healing. We believe they are using sonar to boost the destructive capabilities of the lifters, among other things."

I swore. "That sounds bad."

"It is."

"Okay, so you answered one question. What about why? Why Kipner? And why like that?"

"The working theory is that they're testing us. Seeing how strong we are, if we have secret techs of our own, that sort of thing."

"Do you?"

"Not really."

I noted how he didn't quite say no, but decided to save that discussion for another day.

"But," he continued, "we think their main motive was to send a message. The government has worked with Gregory's a long time, but they have always feared us. More than that, they fear a return of the star walkers, the ones who made us what we are today. It's an arms race, Callie, pure and simple. Except instead of trying to make the first nuclear bomb-"

"They're making super killers capable of fighting off aliens," I finished for him.

"Yes. That's the theory."

"Sounds about right." Something I'd learned growing up, the state liked to be in charge. Organization and control kept it strong and alive. More than anything, it hungered for unending power.

"The Gregors have always watched over us as a ruling council without borders," Ethan explained. "We have no affiliations to nations, to cultures. That makes governments nervous."

"But you said you just want to maintain the peace."

"We do." He shrugged. "But try explaining that to the Pentagon. We're a threat, Callie, and we always have been.

In their mind, threats must be contained, neutralized, and then weaponized. It's standard operating procedure," he said bitterly.

"Is that why you left the army?"

"I served my full time."

"You make it sound like it was a jail sentence."

"Sometimes I felt like it was. The army wasn't for me. I knew I wasn't interested in fighting on the front lines, where I might have to kill some innocent kid or something, so I joined military police. It seemed noble. But it wasn't. The army was full of rules that made no sense, other than to beat a soul down. I hated it. As soon as my opportunity came up for reserve duty, I took it. But the fact that I've served, it comes in handy. Norms like Kipner, they prefer working with ex-military, they feel like they can trust us, since we all sort of speak the same language."

"Okay, but still. Why kill one of their own leaders, a military man? And why do it so openly? It's gotta be raising questions at the morgue."

"Sure. It wasn't just a message. It was a threat. They've come far enough to let us know that they aren't afraid of us anymore. More than that, they don't need us. Incidents like this can be used to incriminate the innocent, or worse, incite a new war based on fear. This program is not being run with the government's full knowledge, so who do you think people will blame when they realize it was warpers?"

"Oh," I said, a knot forming in my stomach. "But you said not to worry." My voice rose. "Are you crazy? What if they decide to take us all out?"

"Shh." He stopped and took me by my arms. "Don't worry. We're not gonna let it get that far, I swear. We're on it. Everything is going to be okay."

I looked at him doubtfully. "Sorry, but it's gonna take more than just pretty words to reassure me. You need help. A lot of help."

"Are you offering?" He cocked his head.

"I-" Was I?

"I think I am." I don't know what possessed me, but I couldn't let him, them, do this alone. The part of me that had always yearned for social justice, to work on behalf of the kids set adrift in the system, cried out with purpose. I needed to do this. Needed to serve.

"Well then," Ethan's face broke into a grin, "we'd better get you back to Marnie. You've got some training to do."

Chapter 15

Green Day had been playing in my head for two hours while I practiced traveling with Marnie and Ethan. She'd put him in a room next door, and I was supposed to travel to him on command. For the first hour, I kept pulling him to me instead.

Ethan described the pull to come to me as irresistible, a gentle tug that bordered on painful if he tried to ignore it. Every time I tried to focus on him, to travel there like Marnie wanted, I tugged instead. After the first few times, Ethan looked annoyed, but I didn't know what to do. Marnie just laughed and called the problem "interesting." Finally, we put Keeta in the room with Ethan, and had me focus on her, instead.

I traveled there without any problem. Keeta sniffed me, concerned that I seemed to be there but had no odor, and Ethan and Marnie just gave each other high fives and then made me do it again. And again. And again. Then they had me try traveling to other people I knew – Tag, Evie, Cliff. Tag was fun, since I surprised him and made him spill his coffee a bit. I have to admit, it gave me a little shiver of amusement to upset the big, grumpy lug. I wasn't stupid, though – I shimmered back out before he could see my smile.

Finally, after another hour, traveling was coming so easily that I was able to find Ethan in another office down the hall. This time, he said, there was no tug, and Marnie told me I'd done enough for the day.

Which was good, because I was exhausted. I called the band to let them know I'd be missing practice that evening, and asked Ethan to take me home. We had practice and a gig the next night, and I needed to rest. More than that, I missed my own bed. The facility was comfortable enough, but it wasn't mine. Independent to a fault, I needed that sanctity to truly unwind.

We grabbed an early dinner, timing the drive back so that we would miss the worst of rush hour traffic, and headed back in Ethan's car, a gold Oldsmobile 442 from the 70's.

"This is a pretty sweet ride," I said, trailing my hand over the chocolate leather-lined door. "Another perk of working with Gregory's?"

We were heading west over the mountains towards the city lights and the last rays of the red sun in the sky, listening to Creedence Clearwater. I felt thankful to finally have Green Day out of my head.

"I do have a job, remember?" he laughed.

"Oh, right, the bookstore. What is it called again?"

"Bronzehead Books."

"That's an interesting name."

"It's a nod to our ancestry. As moonseeds, our powers are strengthened by the lunar metal, bronze. Plus, it sounded better than copperhead. I'm not a big fan of snakes."

"Ah." I looked at his hair, the way it reflected gold and copper in the light and thought it was just the right name, after all. He coughed, blushing, and I realized suddenly he must have heard my thoughts.

"I thought you can't read well?"

"I can't. But you broadcast better than Norad."

"Right. Sorry." Feeling put out, I put Green Day back on repeat in my head. Could I help it if he had nice hair? I'd never liked blondes much, having been teased by too many mean Barbies in my days at school, but the gold in his light brown hair was mesmerizing sometimes. I was a sucker for shiny things. Always had been. "Better?"

"Sure. You really like that band, huh?" He reached over and turned off the stereo, relieving me of the conflicting beats.

"First song I ever learned on the drums. Something like that, I guess it sticks with you."

"Tell me about it," he grinned, and I realized he must be just as sick of the song I was, after the day we'd had.

"Everybody at HQ must be relieved to have me gone," I said.

"Not everyone. Only the readers," he teased. I must have looked offended, because he changed tack. "It's not so bad, really. White noise, that's what we call it, it blocks your thoughts and it doesn't read nearly so loud as a broadcast. Trust me, Green Day is good."

"Good, because it's the only thing that's worked so far. Speaking of which – I haven't heard any thoughts, at least I don't think I have. Is it possible I'm not actually a reader?"

"You've probably been picking up on some thoughts without realizing it. Plus, when your walls are up, you're not going to hear anything unless you want to – it works both ways. The easiest way to practice is with a partner. Why don't you come by the bookstore on Friday and we can do some drills? I'm not a great reader, but I know how to project well enough. The Bronzehead is a local hangout for a lot of the other starseeds, since HQ can be a bit of a hike."

"Sounds like a plan." Since he was inviting me into his world, I thought it only polite to reciprocate. "My band, we have a regular gig at the Hammer on Thursdays, you know, if you're not doing anything."

"Sounds fun. I still haven't gotten to see you play. You guys do a lot of Green Day?"

"Not lately, no," I laughed.

"Alright then. I'm in."

"Great, you can get to know Nick and Jax a little better, my bandmates. They think we're dating, you know, after that show you put on at the party."

"Sorry about that. I thought I was being kind of smooth, especially since I had no idea at first why you'd pulled me there."

"It's okay. It's a good cover. If I'm going to be doing double duty, training with you guys and playing with the band, there'll be less questions about my schedule if they think we're dating. Besides, they already have man-crushes on you, after the way you handled Tommy."

"They're not really my type," he winked.

"Keep your eyes on the road, Romeo," I scolded with a grin.

"Yeah, yeah, okay. About that guy, Tommy. He bother you often?"

"No, not really. We used to date, and he's been wanting to sign us since forever. But he's kind of a jerk, and Nick does well enough."

Ethan exhaled. "I got the impression he'd been...unkind. When I showed up, you were broadcasting pretty hard. I made you feel safe. Do you remember that?"

"Yeah," I said, shifting uncomfortably. I turned up the volume on my "American Idiot" loop and stared out the window, trying to school my features.

"I just, I hope you'll remember that. I want you to know that you can trust me, Callie. I'll do whatever I can to keep you safe."

"Like tranq me?" I smirked.

"If I have to," he said seriously.

"Yuck. You just totally upped your creep factor, you know."

"You know what I mean. We did that because you were an unknown threat and you weren't cooperating. It was the safest way to bring you in – don't forget, we were pretty sure you were a warper. I think that's pretty nice treatment for someone who could potentially blow me up from the inside with her mind, don't you?"

"Point taken. Just don't do it again."

"I'm not planning on it," he promised with a smile.

"Good."

"So, about that guy-"

I groaned and slumped down in the bucket seat. Keeta stuck her head between our seats and nuzzled my hair, warm breath tickling my ear.

"Okay, Keeta, okay!" I giggled. "I'm good." I sat up and pushed her back into her own seat.

"So?"

"He's an ass. I dated him when I was starting out with Molten Requiem. Nick hated him on sight, but I thought he was great, a real gentleman. Tommy can be really charming when he wants to be," I explained.

"And then?"

"And then he's not, okay?" I crossed my arms over my chest. "Let's just say he likes to scout out young talent."

"He cheated on you?" Ethan sounded like he couldn't believe it, and I snorted.

"Yeah." I thought back to that night, finding him in bed with those girls. The way he'd tried to get me to join in, the fury on his face when I'd stormed away, calling him every bad name I could think of. The sudden yank on my arm, just as I was leaving his villa, and the smack that had rattled my teeth together.

"Crap, Callie. He hit you?" Ethan's angry voice broke into my reverie.

Uh-oh. I'd let my personal soundtrack slip, apparently.

"Just once."

Ethan swore, and swerved around a car on our right.

"Jesus, Ethan, watch out! What are you doing?"

He pulled over into the breakdown lane and turned the car off, not moving.

"Ethan?" His eyes were closed, and his hands were tight on the wheel, but otherwise, he was still.

A minute. I just need a minute.

I gasped. I'd heard him clearly, but it had been in my head. Like Marnie had said, the voice was clearly defined, building strongly in my frontal lobe like a gentle palm strike to the forehead. And it wasn't my own.

Oh my God. I thought I had been accustomed to believing, but I guess part of me had still been in doubt. Now, experiencing being a reader, faced with the undeniable experience of it, my last thread of doubt slipped away.

Ethan, can you hear me? I asked silently.

"I hear you," he breathed, not whispered.

"Are you okay?"

"Yeah, I just- I kind of have a thing about women getting pushed around. My parents raised me to be a good ole Southern boy. I was taught to open doors for women, not slam their heads into them."

"That's not exactly what-"

"I saw what happened Callie. Don't tell me how it went down, because I might as well have been there. God help the bastard if I ever see him again," he vowed in a low voice.

"Sorry," I whispered.

Don't you dare apologize, his voice whipped through my forehead in sharp rebuke, at the same time he said, "Don't. Not to me. Not for him."

"Okay, I won't. But you can't hurt Tommy. He's not worth it. He's just a loser. Ignore him. I do."

"Does Nick know what happened?"

"Not all of it."

He grunted, and we both knew why. Nick would never have allowed Tommy to get away with smacking me around, either. He was like an older brother, like blood.

"I don't need anyone's protection. I can take care of myself," I protested.

"And I'm glad that's true, but I'm still going to look out for you. I don't know what this pull is you have on me, but I do know I can use it to keep you safe. Next time you're in trouble, I'll be there. I promise. Dammit, Callie. A woman shouldn't have to know how to throw a punch, just so she can go on a date."

"No. But I do, so stop worrying about me, okay?" I said with an edge to my voice. I'd worked hard to be self-sufficient. I wasn't about to let him take that from me.

If I was honest, I wasn't ready to depend on him, or any man.

I had that thought, and he swore again, reminding me to turn the music in my mind back on. And I did. Full volume.

He winced and turned the key. "Point taken."

And then he let off the clutch and roared back onto the highway.

Chapter 16

We didn't talk much after that. Suited me fine. I'd had enough drama and excitement in my life for the week. Ethan was a long tall drink of a man, but not one that I was ready to try. Turning that drink frosty wasn't the worst thing that could have happened. If we were going to work together, it was better that we just stay friends. Comrades at arms.

That's what I told myself.

After he let me out at my apartment, I took Keeta for a quick walk and returned home to do what I do best. I put on my headphones and got back to work, mixing up some new tracks. Right away, I relaxed. Head phones on, troubles gone.

It didn't hurt that I had a nice little following on BandShare.com, where people could download my songs and pay what they liked. I'd bought myself a new set of tires with last month's proceeds. Contrary to what most folks would tell you, art does pay. The donation atmosphere of the music site actually encouraged people to pay double or triple what you could usually get for an mp3 single, which more than made up for the people who downloaded songs for free. And sometimes, people contacted me with barter arrangements. I'd gotten some gorgeous album covers and t-shirt designs out of deals I'd made, both for me and Molten Requiem, which had a sister page linked to my own.

My own songs ran the style gamut, bouncing from bass heavy electronica and dubstep to old school grunge metal, whereas Molten Requiem played strictly alternative punk rock designed to set your pulse racing. Having my own site gave me the freedom to indulge in whatever genre fit my mood. The one common thread all my songs had were driving bass lines and raging beats.

And right now? Sorting melodies and shifting harmonies was just what I needed to help organize my thoughts and soothe my nerves.

I stayed up half the night finishing two new songs, uploaded them, sent out a social media blast to my followers and crawled into bed, curling myself around Keeta. When I woke up ten hours later, lunch was calling my name and Keeta was standing over me with a leash between her teeth.

Some things never changed.

Outside, Amelia was at her post. I couldn't help wondering where she'd been when the guys had blasted through my door. Maybe they'd knocked her out too.

"Hello, Callie. Did you have a nice trip?"

"Um, yes, I did, thanks."

"The workers did a really nice job installing the new security door you ordered. Next time, though, you should check with me. Any exteriors changes are supposed to be approved through the association."

"Oh, sorry about that. I didn't think." I sent an insincere prayer of thanks to Ethan for causing the issue in the first place.

"That's alright, dear. I imagine you get a lot of strange young men trying to follow you home in your line of work. A girl can never be too safe."

"Tell me about it." Thinking about the warpers, and what they could do, I had a sudden spark of inspiration. "If you ever see anyone unusual hanging around, please make sure to tell me."

"Oh, of course, dear. I do try to keep an eye on things, you know."

"I do, and I appreciate it. Well, have a nice day, Ames."

"Thanks, dear, you too."

I took Keeta for a walk, then came back and changed into more appropriate clothes for The Hammer. I hadn't seen the guys in days, and I figured I'd have to make up for it.

I wasn't wrong.

After rehearsal, Nick and Jax guilted me into ordering a couple of pizzas. I played them my new tracks while we waited for the delivery guy, enduring a fair amount of ribbing over the second one, a slow trance piece with some haunting flute melodies that I'd pieced together in the dead of night. Even I had to admit that it wasn't my usual fare. But my fans seemed to like it – it'd already had eighty-six downloads, fifty of which had paid an average fee of a fancy iced coffee.

That eased the sting of my bandmate's barbs.

We played a couple of hours of video games, mostly an alien civil war game. Jax and Nick took turns saving my character from some evil Martian monsters, and then we headed out for our gig. The way traffic could be in LA, you always wanted to give yourself plenty of time to get where you were going. This time, the highways were pretty clear, and we made it to the club in record time, leapfrogging on the way, passing time passing each other.

The club was dead when we got there, we were so early, but Frank was happy to see us and treated us all to some free beer. Before long, customers started shuffling in, and we got down to the business of setting up our gear.

We were deep into our first set when I noticed two men leaning against the bar, both a head taller than most of the crowd.

Tag and Ethan.

Nick must have noticed them, too, because he grinned at me when he introduced our next song: Alkaline Trio, again. I rolled my eyes and shook my head, accommodating the change in our playlist with a roll of my drumsticks.

A couple more songs and it was break time.

I laid down my sticks and hopped off the stage, hoping to head off Nick, but somehow he beat me there. Jax, too. They were shaking hands with Ethan, Nick clapping him on the back, when I walked up. Tag gave me a terse nod, and I saw Toby, Marnie and Evie were there, too.

I slipped into the crowd and flagged the bartender before anyone could notice me. I needed rehydration, and I needed liquid courage, though not necessarily in that order. I couldn't believe he'd actually come, after the way we'd left things. I mean, sure, I was planning to check out the Bronzehead the next day, but that was different. Did we really need to merge worlds right now? I knew we had talked about making a cover story, but surely now wasn't the best time?

I downed my beer in a couple long gulps, signaled Jody for another and made my way over to the group.

"Ah, here's my girl," Ethan said with a smile, slipping an arm around me.

I stood up on my toes as if I was giving him a kiss, and whispered in his ear instead. "Laying it on a bit thick, aren't you?"

He just laughed and squeezed my side. Jerk.

I thought it loudly enough that he heard me, and Evie and Marnie, too, judging by the way they started laughing.

Crap. Theme song. Right.

I put Green Day back in rotation and forced a smile.

"It's great to see you again." Evie came forward with genuine enthusiasm.

"You, too," I said, sliding away from Ethan to give her a quick hug.

"How's our girl?"

It took me a minute, but then I realized she meant Keeta. "She's good. Hanging out in the van, guarding her turf out back."

"That's perfect. She likes being useful. She takes her job as your caretaker very seriously."

"My caretaker?" I scoffed. "I don't remember her feeding me anytime lately."

Evie gave me a disapproving look. "Nevertheless, she considers you pack, and pack means she is responsible for your safety and happiness. It's important to her."

"Okay," I said slowly. "I'll remember that, thanks."

"Sure thing." She grinned, and transformed back into the light, bouncy girl I remembered from before.

"So, no Cliff?" I asked.

"Nah. He decided he wanted to stay in, something about catching up on the Walking Dead."

"Really? Doesn't sound like him, passing up on a group hangout to watch TV," I mused.

Toby stepped up next to Evie and handed her a fresh drink. "He's like that. Changes his mind a lot. Not the most reliable person I've met," Toby said.

His words didn't add up to what I knew about Cliff, and yet, I found myself nodding in agreement with Toby before I could stop myself.

"I'll drink to that," Evie said, tipping back her beer and linking her arm through Toby's. Toby flushed and pushed his glasses up his nose, grinning down at her like a kid with a new puppy.

I heard someone snort, and looked around to see Tag frowning into his beer. No shock there. I was surprised they'd managed to coerce him into coming along. I found it hard to imagine the tough, gruff man doing anything for fun.

"What's the matter, Tag?" I called over to him. "Bug in your beer?"

He looked at me impassively, finished his beer and went over to the bar for a refill, slamming the glass down on the counter.

Okay then.

Someone grabbed my hand and I looked down, taken off guard. I couldn't remember the last time someone had done that. A large, calloused thumb rubbed over my palm, and I looked up into Ethan's black eyes.

"We're on a mission, remember?" He smiled down at me. "We're supposed to be working on your cover story."

"Right," I said, pulling my hand out of his. "I think we're good. Excuse me, I'll be right back."

I needed a moment, and a bathroom break was in order, anyway.

I brushed past Marnie, who'd been chatting with Nick and Jax, and headed through the thick crowd of dancers.

In the bathroom, a short line of girls was waiting. There were five stalls, and as with every LA bar, one was destroyed in a mess of toilet paper and filth, which left four for use. I joined the queue and leaned back against the wall, running a hand through my hair to smooth the knots while I waited.

I was one person closer to relief when the door opened with force and Marnie strode in. She took her place next to me and pulled her hair out of its ponytail, shaking it loose around her shoulders.

"Woo, girl, you've got quite the life, I gotta say. You do this every week?"

"Yeah," I laughed.

"Pretty cool. You've got some great bandmates, too."

Ah, I thought. There it is. I'd seldom had a friend meet the guys without them falling for one of them. Too bad Nick was a serial loner. Jax liked women, but in the year I'd known him, I hadn't seen him keep any for long. Too many choices, he said. He needed to sample them all. I wondered which of the boys Marnie was eyeing.

"They're good guys," I said easily. It was true. Maybe not stellar boyfriend material, but definitely great friends and decent people.

"Nick says you've been playing together for almost a decade?" Ah. And there it was. The object of her interest.

"Yep, he recruited me in college. Never thought I'd play in a band, but here I am." I lifted one shoulder.

"It's great you guys have stuck together for so long. So, you and Ethan, huh?"

"What? No! Didn't he tell you? We're just showing off so that the guys won't ask too many questions when I'm off working with you all."

"Uh-huh. If you say so." She grinned and gave me a little push. "Your turn."

A stall had opened up, and I was next in line. I entered the sharpie-decorated closet gratefully, happy to escape Marnie and her assumptions. Ethan and I were not a thing. We were not going to be a thing. End of story.

I flushed the toilet with a vengeance, using my booted foot to stomp on the handle, and exited the stall.

I was soaping my hands diligently when Marnie came up next to me.

"Hey, I hope I didn't overstep earlier. It's just, you guys seem pretty cozy. And it's hard to hide this kind of thing when you're around a bunch of readers."

"Yeah, well, you read us wrong. There's nothing to talk about."

"Okay, that's cool." She rinsed her hands and I passed her a paper towel to dry off.

"Cool," I said, letting out a puff of air with the word in relief. The door opened and I heard a guitar riff cut over the music.

"That's my cue." I gestured at the door. "Better get back on stage."

"Sure, no problem. Just one thing, first."

"Yeah?" I sighed. I had a feeling this wasn't about borrowing lip gloss.

"Ethan's a good guy. Like, a really, really good guy. And he's had some bad luck with the people he cares about. A lot of us have. Which is what makes us family."

"Okay, so?"

"So, try not to mix him up too bad, okay?"

"I told you, we're not doing any of that. He's just...like you. He's my mentor. Nothing more."

"You keep telling yourself that. You might even convince the rest of us, too." She laughed.

I threw up my hands in frustration and blasted her with a heavy dose of Green Day. "I gotta go," I said, and stalked out of the room, her laughter following me out the door.

Back on stage, I slammed into my seat at the drums. Nick raised an eyebrow at me in question and I shook my head. Second set always led off with lady's choice, so I started in on an amped up intro to "Shake It Off." Jax loved this song, and the ladies loved him singing it.

We played, and I started to relax. By the fourth song, it was time for my drum solo, and I let loose, feeding it all my frustration and releasing the drama. What did it matter what people thought? Nothing had changed. I was free. If anything, I was freer now than I had ever been.

And with that thought I was up and out of my body, running with my wolves in the desert.

No restrictions. No boundaries. I laughed, hearing the drums distantly, our feet pounding the hard packed sand in time with the rhythm.

Evie had spoken about pack, and now I was with mine. Keeta ran with us, too. I felt the joy of companionship, and an empty tug in the pit of my stomach. And then, he was there.

Running with me.

Hand in hand.

Dammit. Somehow I had pulled Ethan in again.

"It's okay, Callie. Just run." Somehow, he'd known what I was thinking. Well, not somehow. I knew how. I'd let my song slip, and now he wasn't just hearing my thoughts, he was in my head, in my journey.

"Don't think so much. Just see if you can keep up," he dared. He dropped my hand and picked up his pace, pushing the lead wolf, outpacing the rest of the pack.

So I did. I stopped thinking. And I ran.

Chapter 17

The song ended and I came back to myself, back to my body. Like Marnie said, I'd been on autopilot, playing the drums without conscious thought or direction, as I had so often in the past. But now, I knew I wasn't daydreaming. I wasn't trancing out.

I was traveling.

The music didn't bring me home. It set me free.

I locked eyes with Ethan across the crowd, sinking into his gaze for a moment. And then Jax was exploding into a new bass line and I closed my eyes and drove it home, filling the room with the crashing beat of one our original signature songs. Old-time fans on the floor started jumping and singing, joining in with Nick to belt out "The Reckoning."

"Cry as you might,

There are no tears.

No fears to hold you down, cold in the night.

Because you're free, and it's time to let go.

Let go, and set that ice on fire.

Try as you might

We're in the night,

And the reckoning is near."

Evie had dragged Marnie and Toby out on the floor, Marnie swaying gently, sipping her drink and watching Nick. I wouldn't have thought she could soften that tough exterior, but in a tight black tank and jeans, smiling over her drink with a come hither stare, Marnie was doing alright for herself. Silently, I wished her the best of luck.

If she got her way, Nick was really in for it. After all, he wasn't a loner because he didn't like dating – he was single because he'd had his kind, gentlemanly heart broken too many times. There was a reason we got on so well; we both had walls of iron around our hearts. Someone like Marnie'd eat Nick for breakfast. Maybe it was about time.

Evie was jumping around, catching on to the lyrics quickly and shouting the chorus out with the rest of our fans. I wondered if she used her reading abilities to get the lyrics on tap. Toby was at her side, watching her with an adoring look on his face. For his sake, I was glad he was standing slightly behind her. That boy really could not dance, and would have been better off not trying. It was like watching an octopus have a seizure.

I focused on the music. The last thing I needed was the guys ribbing me about being distracted because "my guy" was here. Ugh. So I played, and I played hard. By the end of the set, sweat was dripping down my back between my shoulder blades and I'd pegged up my hair in a messy topknot.

I stood, stretching, and blew away an annoying strand of purple that'd come loose to tease my nose. Water was good. Water was life. I guzzled the last of my bottle and set to breaking down my drum kit. The guys were already one step ahead of me, unplugging their instruments and stacking amps on the side of the stage.

Frank's DJ started up, easing into the evening with a downbeat pop song, giving people time to get new drinks and cool down before throwing themselves back on the dance floor.

I was just bending down to grab the first load for a trip to the car when someone behind me asked, "Need a hand?"

Ethan's deep voice surprised me, made me jump a little, and I tried to hide it.

"No, I'm good, thanks."

"What, you don't trust me? Think I'll drop a drum?"

I sighed. "Fine, you can carry. Come on up." I waved at the stairs on the other side of the stage, but Ethan just put one hand on the stage and vaulted up like a five-foot jump was nothing. Which apparently, for him, was true.

I grunted, handed him the kick drum and picked up a few smaller items.

"You might want to use the stairs this time," I said in a fresh tone as I headed for the door.

He laughed. "Oh, I was just planning on rolling the drum out the door," he teased. "Was that wrong?"

I stifled a laugh and didn't bother answering. Nick had propped open the back exit, so we headed out without pausing, straight to the van where Jax was taking a break and petting Keeta.

"She doesn't get lonely out here?" Ethan asked, fluffing up the fur around her neck.

"She likes guarding the van. Makes her feel useful," I quoted Evie.

"Good. I'm glad you've got someone looking out for you."

I groaned and Jax watched our exchange with amusement.

"Careful, brah, too much of that and you're gonna set off Miss Independent over here."

Ethan laughed in surprise and nodded. "You're probably right."

"Jackholes," I muttered, and hopped out of the van, walking back inside without another word to either of them.

Onstage, Nick helped me grab the last of the gear and we walked out together.

"So, not your guy, huh?" he taunted.

"Shut up."

"What's the matter, is that cold dead heart of yours pumping again?"

"I don't know. Are you ready for yours to stop?" I retorted.

"Ouch. You wound me, Cal."

I walked faster, leaving him behind and reaching the van first. Ethan and Jax were laughing at something, looking like the best of friends, completely at ease. Together, they looked like a couple of surfers waiting for the morning waves, not a care in the world.

If only Jax knew the kind of night crawlers Ethan had to deal with on a regular basis, he might not be looking so relaxed. I envied him that ignorance.

I missed that ignorance.

Had it really been only one week since the lunar eclipse?

I hopped in the van and pushed my cargo into place, making room for the large cases Nick was placing at the door before sliding those home, too.

Finished, I backed out of the van and dusted off my navy blue pleather pants.

"So, Ethan here says you're going to be helping him out at his bookstore a few days a week?"

Somehow, Jax managed to make the innocuous words sound naughty.

"Yep." The less I said, the better. I wasn't sure what would come out of my mouth if I got going.

"What, you not making enough money? I can book more gigs if you want. JoJo's called me a few weeks ago about playing two Wednesdays a month, but I figured-"

"No, no, it's not that," I reassured Nick. "I just thought it'd be fun."

"Fun." Jax waggled his eyebrows at me. "I bet."

I stuck out my tongue at him, and Ethan had enough wisdom not to laugh.

"Truth is," Ethan said, standing up and drawing me close, "I begged her to come. The Bronzehead has been really short-staffed lately."

Nick and Jax burst out laughing that time, and I shoved Ethan away.

"You all suck," I declared, trying not to laugh myself, and went back inside with what little dignity I could muster. "And make sure you lock up the van," I called over my shoulder.

Frank was nowhere in sight, so I headed to the bar to wait, knowing he'd be out soon with our pay for the night. Tag was leaning back on his stool, watching the dancers with a stony expression. I signaled Jody for two beers, seeing Tag was running on empty, and took the seat next to him.

"What's got your panties in a twist?" I asked.

"What do you mean?"

"You. That look on your face. Not that you seem like the happy go lucky type, but you're grumpier than usual tonight."

"Hmphf," he answered.

"Whatever. Here. Maybe this'll help." I handed him the fresh beer and pried the empty glass from his grip.

"So," I said, looking around to make sure no one was nearby, "I know you were in the army, like Ethan, but that's about it. What's your superpower, besides turning people to stone with your glare?"

He let out a little laugh, in spite of himself. "I'm a lifter."

"Oh, cool! You're the first one I've met. Well, besides..." I trailed off, thinking about the three men who had surrounded Kipner. "Well, you're the first one," I finished brightly.

"Lucky you."

"I always wanted to do what you do, you know. Well, that and make lightning or fire with my mind, like Drew Barrymore in Firestarter. Oh, and teleport. That would be so cool. But I guess I sort of can now, huh? Wow. I never thought of it that way," I rambled. "Cool."

I took a drink of my beer to stop the flow of words, and this time, Tag did actually smile.

"Hey, look, there you go. Maybe next time I can make you smile without having to be a complete idiot, first."

He laughed and drained half his beer in one go. "Easier said than done."

"Whatever, loser," I said, elbowing him in the ribs, and hopped down off my stool. "I'm gonna go get paid."

I walked off in search of Frank, deciding I'd waited around long enough. In the hallway by the office, I found Nick and Marnie laughing and whispering. As I approached, Marnie slipped Nick a piece of paper and gave him a quick kiss on the cheek, followed by a gentle pat in the same spot with her hand before she sashayed past me.

Marnie. Sashaying. Who woulda thunk?

I stepped up to Nick and eyed the piece of paper in his hand.

"You got digits?"

"Yeah," he said, sounding a bit dazed.

"Good for you. Marnie's nice."

"She scares the crap out of me," he admitted.

I laughed. "Good. She should. Real women tend to do that." I stepped around him to rap on Frank's door and waited.

I heard Frank yell "Yeah?" and put my hand on the doorknob. I tipped my head to one side and grinned at Nick.

"Now let's go get paid."

Chapter 18

The next day I walked into Bronzehead Books determined to focus on honing my psychic gifts. Since it was almost lunchtime, I'd stopped at the local bakery and picked up an assortment of bagels and doughnuts. Yeah, I know. Too many carbs. So many additives.

What can I say?

I'm a grownup. I get to eat what I want.

A quaint golden bell tinkled about my head, announcing my arrival. The orange tabby I'd seen in the window in my vision curled itself around my legs, purring as it walked a figure eight between my calves.

Careful not to step on the friendly animal, I moved forward between shelves holding books, candles, crystals, and assorted statuary. The shop had a cozy, vintage feel, like something out of the late 1800s. Everything was made of dark wood and golden brass. Or maybe it was actually bronze. The lights were Tiffany style, gorgeous stained glass pieces that cast a warm, inviting glow over the room. The shop had a definite esoteric vibe, though nothing actually shouted witchcraft at me. I stopped to admire a large sculpture of a dragon-like bird. Or was it a bird-like dragon? I couldn't tell. But the chimera appealed to me. I glanced at the price tag.

Three hundred dollars?

Maybe I did need a second job after all.

"That's a replica of a twenty-first century Akkadian piece. Beautiful, isn't it?" A young, nicely rounded girl spoke from behind the counter. Piled high with books and a massive, century-old cash register, it was easy to see how I'd missed her.

"Yes, it is. Aren't we in the twenty-first century now?"

"Yes, of course. I should have specified, BCE, before common era."

"Thanks. I'm actually here to see Ethan Hale. Is he around?"

"Sure thing, let me page him for you." She ignored the vintage intercom system on the wall and tapped on an earpiece. "Ethan, you have a visitor...Okay." She tapped the piece again. "He'll be right down. I'm Laura, by the way."

I walked forward to shake her hand. "Calliope Winters. Want a doughnut? Bagel? I brought plenty."

I showed her the box and she shook her head. "I don't dare. I just started this new juice cleanse, anything in that box would set me back a whole week."

"Suit yourself," I said, smiling. "I totally get the juicing. I get tons of energy whenever I do it."

"Energy would be nice, but I'm actually trying to lose a few pounds."

"Oh," I said, biting my lip. "But why? You're gorgeous."

135

She blushed. "Thanks, that's really nice of you to say, but my boyfriend thinks I'm not healthy enough."

"What does he know? You look great to me. My motto is, eat happy. Calories only stick when you're sad. If you eat happy, your body will always find its optimum weight, whatever that is."

"Sounds like some pretty magical thinking," she laughed.

"Hey, whatever lets me eat doughnuts," I winked.

"Did I hear someone say doughnuts? Ah, Callie, I see you've met our resident librarian, Miss Laura," he grinned down at her.

"Mr. Hale," she beamed, curtsying. "We were just discussing the Akkadian replica there."

"Anzu? She's known to most historians as a storm bird, but we know better don't we?" Ethan grinned and went on to explain, "Anzu originated as a Sumerian legend of a powerful starseed who held the powers of both moon and sun, and took on this glamour to prove it. She was a major player in the great war."

"Oh. Is it wrong that I kind of love it?" I asked, trailing my fingers over the shining metal.

"Not at all. Why do you think I have it here? She's a gorgeous display of power and grace. Unfortunately, legend has it Anzu could be as capricious and destructive as she was generous. But who knows? Maybe that's just history painting the picture they preferred to remember. Come on, I'll give you the full tour."

He took the box of pastries from me, opening it as we excused ourselves and walked down the stairs in the back. He chose a strawberry jelly and talked as we descended.

"So, down here we have a training area for defense and combat. We focus mainly on defense – like I said, we're not soldiers. But anyone who wants to learn, or just let off some steam, is welcome to train here. There's almost always someone working out."

And there was. Two guys were at a weight station, one spotting the other, and a woman was kickboxing against a humanoid dummy in the corner. Five more people were doing yoga in the middle, holding an impossible pose for longer than seemed comfortable.

The cozy atmosphere of the store above had been deceiving. The lower level was one massive, open space. The ceiling had been painted sky blue, with a yin-yang symbol made from a sun and moon in the middle. Seeing the sun and moon reminded me to keep my mental block in place, so I wouldn't disrupt anyone's workout with my loud thoughts.

"We've got UV-rated lights down here," Ethan continued, "so no one misses the lack of a view too much. Plus, the houseplants keep it cheery."

By houseplants, I assumed he meant the large-leaved fig trees dotting the walls at intervals.

"Nice," I said. "Definitely beats my local gym."

"Thanks. I try to make it comfortable for everyone."

"So, this whole place is yours?"

"Pretty much. I own the building. Gregory's helps foot some of the monthly bills, since we started using it as an official training center a few years ago. Before that it was just me and some buddies, letting off steam. But word spread and it grew pretty fast. People would rather come here than fight traffic all the way to Joshua Tree."

"Sure, who wouldn't? You've done a great job here. And the bookstore? Is that just a front?"

"No, I've always had an interest in history, and how so much of myth and legend is actually based on fact. More than most people know. I found this place cheap during the recession, and the bookstore was an easy way to cover the mortgage. Plus, you can't beat the commute."

"Must have been nice to take it easy after your time in the army."

"Definitely," he agreed.

The yoga group must have seen the box in Ethan's arms, because pretty soon we were surrounded by happy eaters. Ethan introduced me all around, and then we continued the tour by heading upstairs.

The second floor had several smaller classroom sized rooms for small groups and one-on-one work, plus two larger conference rooms. Like the bookstore, the rooms were decorated in dark, soothing colors with antique furniture and an array of items to help with relaxation and meditation. One room even had an entire wall of singing bowls and a large pow-wow style drum in one corner.

"Wow, look at that! I've never seen one of those up close."

"The drum was made for me by a Navajo friend from Keet Seel."

"Another starseed?"

"No, I met him when we were serving together. Taini actually saved my life in basic training."

"What happened?"

"We were out doing field training at night. They'd warned us to watch out for rattlers and copperheads, but most us of thought they were just messing with us. Wouldn't have been the first time." He shook his head in disgust. "But they weren't kidding. There I was, sneaking up on the other team, crawling in the dirt, and all of a sudden I was face to face with a really pissed off copperhead."

"No way! What did you do?"

"I froze. Probably would have been snake bait, but Taini reached over my shoulder and grabbed the damn thing right behind the neck."

"Shut. Up."

"Seriously. He flung it over his shoulder and kept crawling, went right past me like nothing had even happened. Him, me and Tag were all assigned together as MPs, we were inseparable."

"So I guess that's why you don't like snakes?"

"I can think of more than one reason." he said in a tone I'd come to recognize. It was the way his voice changed when he was reminded of something he didn't want to think about. Something painful to remember.

I didn't push for the memory, content instead to settle down in one of the chairs by the drum. I picked up a long-handled drum stick and began beating out a slow steady rhythm. A wordless song rose in me, and I let it out. It was sad and mournful, and it filled me with longing. For what, I don't know.

After a couple of minutes, I stopped, remembering I wasn't alone in the room. I opened my eyes. Ethan was leaning against the wall, just watching me.

My cheeks heated. "Sorry, I get taken away sometimes."

"Don't apologize. You have a beautiful voice. How come you don't sing? With your band, I mean."

"Oh, I don't know. I'm not much of a stage person. I just love to play. I do sing sometimes on the stuff I record at home. Just songs for fun that I upload to BandShare."

"I'll have to check it out. Looks like you're a song walker." He held out a hand to help me up, leading me from the room.

"Song walker?"

"That's what the old shamans called people who could travel like us, journey to other places through song and dance. A lot of them, of course, were starseeds. But most humans can journey, with enough practice."

"You say humans, like it's something we're not," I said as we climbed the stairs to another floor.

"Oh, we're human alright. But we're also something more. And, according to a lot of people in the government," he said, holding a fire door at the third floor landing open, "we're just a bunch of dangerous aliens, people to be feared, corralled and studied, in that order."

"Sounds like a bad sci-fi movie."

"Sometimes, it feels like one," he said gravely. "But we're working on that."

We entered a large common area, complete with an open kitchen, fireplace, some tables, couches and a huge TV on the wall.

"Another dorm?"

"Sort of. Sometimes people need a place to stay, especially when their powers first emerge. Not everyone can make the daily commute to HQ. So, I made this."

"You're a real mother hen, aren't you?" I joked.

"I like to think of myself as more of a Foghorn Leghorn," he said easily.

"You know, if we hadn't had that conversation in the car before, I would think it was impossible to ruffle your feathers."

He scowled, eyes darkening. "Don't remind me. There aren't many things that piss me off, but misogynists and bigots rank pretty damn high on the list. Right under abusive sons of-"

"Alright, alright," I stopped him, putting my hands up in peace. "Sorry I brought it up."

He ran a hand through his hair, messing it up more than anything else. "I'm sorry, too. I promised myself I wouldn't do that again."

"Do what?" I batted my eyelashes naively and laughed. "So you live here, dorm-style?"

"No, my place is on the fourth floor. Want to see it?"

"Um, no, not today," I hedged. That seemed like the last place I should be checking out, unless I wanted to push past the friendship barrier I'd erected around Ethan. "I have a gig tonight in Burbank, and some errands to run, so maybe I should get some training in now?"

"Yeah, okay, no problem." He put the box of doughnuts down on a table. "You want to eat some of this first?"

"Definitely." We poured some drinks from the kitchen, sweet tea for Ethan, milk for me, and proceeded to devour half the box.

Don't worry, there were scallions in the cream cheese. That's a vegetable, right?

Chapter 19

In a small room, sitting on two couches facing each other, Ethan and I alternated between practicing traveling and blocking. We visited the beach, the park, Double Rainbow Ice Cream on Melrose. All my favorite places. Then we tried a few places I didn't want to go to, like the strip in Vegas, the mall, and Alcatraz. We went together, and I went alone.

After three hours, I felt strong enough to try something different.

"Let's practice reading."

"I don't think that's a good idea," he said. "You've done a lot today. More than most people can do their first month. Why don't we take a break?"

"Aw, come one. Just a little bit of listening in? How about we do a test like in the movies, you pick a card, and I'll guess the color? Or think of a number, one to a hundred."

"Fine," he sighed, lying back on the couch with his feet up. "What did I have for breakfast today?"

I tried to open my mind.

Nothing.

Then I thought, maybe it's the opposite of a wall, and imagined I was tunneling into his head. Didn't work. I envisioned one of the water slides, and rode that toward his brain. Still nothing.

"What am I supposed to be doing, exactly?"

"Reading requires both power and skill. Mostly, you just have to be good at listening, at least, if I'm projecting. If you want to read someone who is protecting their thoughts, that's a whole other story – it's like cracking a safe. For now, just imagine you can hear everything. Listen to your breath. Reach for the sound of your own heartbeat. Extend your ears both inward, and outward. Relax. And listen."

Nothing.

I suck at this. Just another crappy day in a string of crappy days.

I felt so sad. So defeated. So... wait a minute. I was feeling good. Strong. Those other thoughts, they weren't mine. But I didn't think they were Ethan's either.

I took another shot at hearing Ethan's thoughts. What the heck did a body like that eat for breakfast?

Cornflakes.

Really? "Cornflakes?"

"Nope, sorry." He grinned.

"I could have sworn I heard cornflakes. What did you have?"

"Trick question. I didn't eat breakfast. That doughnut was my first food all day."

"Argh! You suck." I swiped a pillow off the couch and tossed it at his head.

Maybe I should just kill myself.

"Really, Ethan? I hardly think killing yourself is the answer," I laughed. "Even if you're dead, you'll still suck. You'll just be a jerk that's dead."

"Excuse me?" He sat up and looked at me, confused.

"Didn't you just say you should kill yourself?"

"No. I'm pretty sure I'd remember that."

"Oh no." Realization dawned over me. "I think I'm hearing someone else. It's definitely a guy; someone who had cornflakes for breakfast? They're having a really bad day. I think they might actually do it, kill themselves."

"Are you sure?"

"Do I look like I'm sure? But I did hear someone, I swear. I thought it was you, messing with me."

"Alright, well, readers hear best at close range. Let's see if anyone's around."

We got up and went out into the hallway. Empty. Ethan started opening doors, one after the other. Finally, at the end of the hall, we found Cliff, standing in front of a mirror in a room. His cap was off, and half his hair was just gone, showing a heavily receding hairline fading into a buzz cut on one side.

"Cliff? Everything okay?" Ethan asked.

"Yeah, sure. I guess." He jammed his hat over his head, looking embarrassed, and sat down.

"Cliff, what did you have for breakfast today?" I asked, watching his face for a reaction.

"Cornflakes. Why?"

Ethan swore. "Callie, you stay here. I have to make a call." And like that, he'd left me alone with Cliff. Seriously, I thought? Did I look like a crisis counselor? Damn and double damn. Time to put my degree to work.

I went over to Cliff and took his hand, dragging him over to the table to sit.

"Cliff, you have to tell me, what's going on? I heard you thinking about what a rough couple days you've been having."

He blushed. "You heard that? I guess I'm just feeling sorry for myself. Sorry I missed your show, by the way. I really wanted to go."

"Really? Then why'd you miss it?"

"I- I'm not sure, actually. I was planning on going, I was going to meet up with Toby and Evie, but then Toby called and told me I sounded sick and should stay home. I did feel kind of crappy, so I did. I didn't go to work today, either. My boss was so mad, he called a little while ago to fire me from the kitchen." He looked at me, sad and confused. "What am I going to do? I need that money, Callie. And I've been trying to practice glamming all day, and nothing's happening. Maybe it's like Toby said, I'm totally useless."

"Seriously? You are awesome. Your snake the other day scared the life out of me. Something else is going on. What else could make your power stop working? Walk me through everything again."

He ran through the whole story, bit by bit.

"Even my powers aren't working right," he said as he finished. "You saw my hair, I can't even maintain that small glamour now. Lately, any holo I try for is messed up. I'm telling you, it's like I'm cursed or something. Or I just really suck at life."

"Holy mother!" I exclaimed, everything clicking into place. "I think you've been warped!"

"What? No way." Cliff shook his head. "How?"

"Toby. Does he think you like Evie, maybe?"

"No. He knows I don't, I told him. We get along really well, but she's not my type."

"Well, I don't think Toby believes you. Look, you stayed home last night even though you really wanted to come out. And now you can't use your power right, since Toby told you that you suck."

"When you put it like that, it does sound suspicious. But Toby's my friend."

"Is he really? You don't seem to like him much. And you said you've played pranks on him, just like you did to me. Maybe he's more of a grudge keeper than I am. Plus, love makes people do stupid things. If he thinks Evie likes you, maybe he just wants to get rid of the competition. "

Cliff cursed under his breath. "I'm gonna kill that guy. You're totally right.

"Right about what?" Ethan asked, striding back into the room with one of the yoga practitioners from downstairs.

"We think Toby has been pushing Cliff with his bard ability." The woman gasped in surprise, so I explained about Evie, and Toby's crush. "Plus, he's done some stuff like this before, right Cliff?"

"Well, not this extreme. It's always been petty stuff, like ordering me to shave with toothpaste, or telling me to go run ten laps at the gym."

"A bard must never use his powers for their own personal amusement," the woman objected sternly. "This is unacceptable."

"We'll deal with it, Dolores. First, do you think you can help Cliff get back to himself?"

"Yes, of course." She put a hand on Cliff's shoulder and looked down at him kindly. "Why don't you come with me? We'll get you all sorted out."

He stood up, ready to follow, then glanced back at me. "You guys are going to handle Toby?"

"We will. This won't happen again, I promise." Ethan said with an edge to his voice.

Cliff nodded, and walked out with Dolores.

Ethan sank into the chair Cliff had been in and rubbed his hands over his face.

"Well, this sucks."

"How does Gregory's protocol deal with stuff like this? How can you be sure it won't happen again?"

"That's the problem. I can't."

"But you just promised-"

"I know what I said. I just wanted to wipe some of that hopelessness off Cliff's face. It's a first offense, so protocol is for me to talk to Toby, and he'll have to start going to counseling at HQ every week, and working with Dolores one on one several times a week, minimum. Dolores works with speakers who are testing their limits. She has a very strict moral code, and is pretty good at getting others to toe the line."

"How is she going to help Cliff?"

"She's a bard, too. She knows how to unwrap the damage of other speaker's words and reprogram the victim so they can get back to being themselves. It's not always easy, but she's one of the best we have."

I exhaled heavily, feeling relieved. "Well, that's good. I think you should talk to Evie, too."

"How so?"

"Didn't you see her last night? She was practically hanging over Toby's every word. Not that he's not worthy of the attention, but she didn't seem into him before. Now she's all over him? Seems suspicious to me – what if he warped her, too?"

"Good point. I'll call her now."

"Hold up," I said, putting my hand on his arm before he could dial. "I want to hear more about Gregory protocol. What happens if there is a second offense?"

"Depends on the offense," he said with a frown. "Sometimes we attempt further counseling and mentoring. Sometimes we require the offender live at HQ, where they can be watched."

"Other times?"

"They are exiled. Gregory's denies all support for the warper, fiscal and familial. Basically, the warper is shunned. All contact is cut, and they are listed in our database as a criminal offender."

"Wow, that's harsh."

"It's necessary. Most warpers don't stick around to hear whether they have warranted an exile or a reprieve. Either counseling works the first time around, or it doesn't and the warper seeks out like-minded associates. People who approve of the offender's behavior, and even encourage it."

"You mean other warpers."

"Yes."

"Do you think we'll be able to rehabilitate Toby?" I said, concerned. I barely knew him, but I hated to think of anyone I knew becoming like the killers I'd seen.

"Honestly? I don't know. It sounds like he's been abusing his powers for some time already. He may already be addicted to the rush of control, the power of it. Only time will tell."

His voice was heavy, like my heart.

"I should call Dr. Kim and Evie, make sure they know what's going on. Will you be okay?"

"Me? Yeah, sure, I'm good. We did plenty of work today, anyway. I might go check out your shop again, though."

"Great. You get a 30% discount on anything in the store, too, as one of us. Sort of a members' discount."

"Oh, cool, that's awesome. In that case, can I put that statue on hold, do you think?"

"The Anzu? Sure. Just tell Laura I said it's okay, and to put it behind the counter."

"Great, thanks. Is she a starseed, too? She looks so young."

"Her parents are. She's been temping here for years. She graduated college last year and just started working here full time." His phone buzzed and he made a face when he looked at it. "I better go. That's Tag, looking for me. I'll be away for the next few days, we're supposed to be checking out a lead on that new group of warpers."

"Is it dangerous, where you're going?"

"Depends what we find. Hopefully, it'll just be some recon, a quick in and out. Who knows, maybe we won't even find anything. If you need anything, text me. Okay? You can also always come here, everybody here is good people, and there's pretty much always somebody around. Oh – that reminds me. Make sure Laura gives you a key for the back door. The shop is locked up at night but if you take the alley two doors down that will lead you to the back parking lot. Use the key in the red fire door to get into our stairwell." He paused. "Well, that's it then. I better get going."

"Right!" I got up and gave him a quick, awkward hug. "Thanks for everything."

He squeezed me briefly and I felt the barest wisp of movement over my hair. "Anytime, Callie. Stay safe."

"Thanks, you too."

And then he was gone.

Not a ghost disappearing from my life this time. A friend, doing what he had to do. What he'd been doing for years.

Life was strange that way, the way you could suddenly find yourself worrying about someone you'd never known existed, when they'd already been putting themselves in danger for years. Living their life. It hadn't mattered then. But now that you knew them, that act of risk became the scariest, most important thing in your world.

Empathy, most of the time, was a personal, private beast. It reared its head because I knew him. Because he was my friend.

So I prayed he'd stay that way, whole and safe.

Chapter 20

The next forty-eight hours were a blur. Practice, gig, practice, gig. Typical weekend fare, but now, with everything else going on, I was finding it harder to focus. I alternated between feeling blissfully relaxed while I played, to fretting about Cliff's mental state and Ethan's physical safety every time we took a break.

Even Tag and Toby edged their way in there. I couldn't help it. I wanted everyone I knew to be happy and satisfied with their life, it was the way I'd always been. It was probably part of why I'd made such an easy target for manipulative, abusive boyfriends in my youth. I'd outgrown being a victim, but I still had enough concern for everyone to go around.

Sunday afternoon the guys and I were together again at Nick's place, this time for our monthly business meeting where we went over the books, hashed out things we could have done better, gave compliments and critiques. We'd figured out years ago that doing this once a month cut down on angst during our regular practices and kept everyone copacetic. We did a potluck brunch, and usually wrapped up by sharing whatever projects we'd been working on and playing some video games.

This month, my contributions were tequila sunrise mixers and a tropical fruit salad. Jax showed up fresh and salted from a morning surf with an armful of Challah bread, raw honey and jam, and Nick had made breakfast tacos with scrambled eggs and fresh guacamole. The two of them had spent the first half hour of our meeting teasing me about my spotty playing the week before and waxing poetic about how awesome my new boyfriend was.

I made sure to look appropriately offended and abashed, nodding my head in all the right places while reminding myself that I wasn't lying to them. Ethan was a boy, well, a man, but whatever, and he was my friend. Anything else didn't merit closer scrutiny at the moment.

I'd thought about letting them in on my new double life, but what would I tell them? How could they believe me? My reading was still touch and go, and I hadn't had success with anyone that wasn't a reader themselves yet. Maybe someday I would tell them. Someday when I knew it would be safe. Keeping secrets from Nick wore on me especially. He was like an older brother, like family. It didn't feel right. But until I was more comfortable with my new reality, it didn't feel right to put them in the middle of it, either.

So I smiled, and I nodded, and I drank another sunrise. When it got to be too much, I pulled out my laptop and played them the songs I'd been working on. They gave me some good ideas for finishing one, loved the other one, and finally we moved on to listening to Jax's lyrics and Nick's fresh melodies. Some of them would go great together. Some wouldn't. It was all good.

I leaned back on the couch and buried my bare feet under Keeta where she slept at the other end, feeling content as

I watched the boys, my boys, sing together. Nick was running through a song for the second time and Jax was testing out harmonies in his signature low, gritty voice. The melody was tight, and the lyrics were smooth.

"What about if we add something like this?" I asked, and sang over Jax, spiking the verse with a staccato aria.

"Oh, that's good," Jax murmured, following along. I stopped singing and closed my eyes, listening to the song come together.

Yeah. This was good. I smiled and tilted my head back, relaxing into the pillows.

Without meaning to, I felt myself shift, tumbling out of my body and into a bank of fog. The air was cold, leaving a trail of dampness over my skin. I peered around, lost in the whiteness. A mansion materialized out of the mist in the distance, and I stepped forward.

"Get down!" a voice next to me hissed, and I crouched reflexively. I looked to my right and was met with the irate glare of Tag. "What the hell are you doing here?"

I shrugged, not having an answer to give him.

He snorted. "Right. Fine. Look, the fog is clearing, so you need to stick with me, if you're gonna stay." He reached out and his hand passed through me. It was weird, I could feel the air, feel the mist, but not his hand. Maybe I was just imagining what the atmosphere felt like, because my mind expected it? I thought about asking Tag, but had the feeling he wasn't exactly in the mood for a Q&A.

"You're only in a partial travel," he was saying, "so you can't get hurt. Ethan says you're getting better at reading, so maybe you can be of use."

"Okay, I guess?"

"See that house?" he asked. I nodded, but he wasn't watching me, having put his goggles back to his eyes. "Word is, the couple who live here are recruiting warpers. Ethan just left to scout closer for a head-count. We need to get inside, and see if we can get any intel on where the program is being run from, and who is in charge."

"What if we get caught?"

He put his goggles down and gave me a blank stare.

Right. Don't get caught, I thought. Or rather, don't get Tag caught. Because I could shift out at any moment.

"What do I do?" I whispered.

"Keep up, and stay hidden." He took off through the mist, creeping along a bank of boxwoods. Since I was at least a foot shorter than Tag, staying out of sight was easy. All I had to do was make sure I was behind him.

We were within thirty feet of the house when I heard something.

Can't believe she wants me to take her to that new Tarzan movie. She wants to see some blonde giant prancing around naked in a tree, she can go by herself. Like I need to see that. Pass. Wait. What was that?

"Tag," I breathed urgently.

"What?"

"I hear someone. A guard, I think. And he's heard us, or Ethan."

Tag swore. "Alright. I'm on it. Can you warn Ethan?"

"I don't know, I'll try."

The words were no sooner out of my mouth than I was flush against Ethan's back, drawn to him with a thought.

He tensed, ready to turn on me, and I flung a mental warning at him.

It's me, Callie.

He relaxed a fraction and exhaled. I hadn't realized I was holding breath.

There's a guard walking around searching, I think he heard you or Tag.

He reached back and squeezed my hand, pulling me with him, closer to the house. I hadn't even realized it, being more focused on just having found Ethan, but we were right against the south wall, standing by a set of French doors. Silent as a cat, he opened the door and slipped inside, never losing his grip on my hand, even as he deftly pulled the door shut behind us.

I looked around the room, reaching out with my mind, but saw and heard nothing.

Not even when Ethan spun me around and pinned me against the wall among the heavy damask of the draperies. His forearm lay heavy across my chest and kept me in place. It was only then that I realized, despite my partial traveling, I could feel him. As if my body knew what his should feel like, and was filling in the blanks. Like somehow, he made me whole.

"You were supposed to text me, not drop in for a visit," he drawled.

"Trust me, it wasn't a planned trip."

He leaned towards me, forcing me to bend my neck back to look up at him, he was so tall. His eyes gave me no hint of what he was thinking, and it pissed me off. This was so not the time for whatever this was. Just because I hadn't sensed anyone nearby, didn't mean we were safe.

"Get off me," I said quietly. Before I even finished the sentence, he had backed up and folded his arms over his chest.

"Okay, so what do you think?" He asked, suddenly all business, sounding like a teacher. "Are you sensing anyone else? Did the guard hear us?"

"No, nothing." That in itself was odd, and I wondered why the guard was coming up silent now. Maybe he was out of range? I still didn't know how far I could read.

"Good. That's because there isn't anyone else here. That guard you heard, he was the only one I-"

Somewhere above, we heard a door slam and footsteps heavy on wood flooring.

Still, no thoughts filtered down.

"Now what?" I whispered.

Something in his face changed, and suddenly I had an inkling of what he would have been like in the army. What kind of adversary he could be.

I was glad he was on my side.

His eyes had hardened to sharp obsidian, and his mouth became grim.

"Now? We finish the mission."

Chapter 21

I wasn't sure what the mission entailed, exactly, but I stuck close to Ethan as we crept through the house. We encountered two guards, one by the stairs and one coming out of a bathroom on the second landing, but Ethan was able to take both of them down with no trouble, knocking them out.

Each time, neither Ethan nor I sensed their thoughts.

"It's not right. We should be able to read them, at least enough to pick up on their presence."

"Even if they're shielding?" I wondered.

"If they were readers, at least one of them should have picked up on your thoughts."

"Right," I said, feeling stupid. I hadn't remembered to put up my musical ward. "Sorry."

"Don't be. Thoughts or music, it doesn't matter. Either one would have tipped off these guys if they were warpers. I think they are just regular people – but I still should have picked up some static. Normal humans don't usually project much, but everyone has thoughts buzzing around. Even if I can't read them well, I can hear the background noise if I try."

"So then who are these guys?"

"I think a better question is what," he said ominously. "See here?" He pointed to the unconscious man's arm, where Ethan had pushed up the sleeve. A mariner's star was tattooed in black and gold with the words "Non Sibi Sed Patriae" scrolled below. *Not for self, but for country.*

"He's Navy?" I knew the unofficial motto from Doug, who had a tattoo of his own winding around his upper bicep.

"Looks like. But that's not what worries me. This mark, here?" He pointed to a fresh, tiny scar next to the tattoo. The white line was thin and raised, like the kind you get from a razor blade. Or a scalpel. "He's been chipped. With what, though, I don't know."

"What do you mean?"

"Could be a tracker, could be something else. No way to know unless we take the chip."

"Ew, gross."

"Yeah." He pulled a small multi-tool out of his pocket, flicked open a small knife, and gently eased the chip out from under the man's skin. On the tool, he slid open a tiny compartment on the tool's casing, dropped out two pills that were held inside, and replaced them with the chip.

"What are those?"

"Just some field meds, antibiotics. But the case is shielded, so it should keep anyone from tracking the chip." He shook his head, looking down at the soldier with frustration. "This better be important, because there's a good chance we've just cut this mission short. Come on, we're running out of time."

"What exactly are we looking for, anyway?"

"Not sure. An office? A laptop. Anything that'll tell us what is going on here."

We padded down the hallway, checking each fancy bedroom. Finally, at the end of the hall, we found what we were looking for.

The large room was a private study, complete with a huge burl wood desk and creepy old oil paintings of people long buried. Books lined one wall; papers and maps littered the work surface of the table.

Ethan rifled through the papers and let out a stream of curses.

"What is it? Did you find something?"

"Yeah. These addresses are all Gregory buildings. Not just the public banks, but our private safe houses and regional headquarters. See?" He pointed to addresses for Bronzehead Books and the Joshua Tree facility. He reached in his pocket, removed a tiny camera and started taking photos of all the papers, opening drawers and snapping images of more things as he went.

Tag slipped into the room then, and I jumped a little.

"Time to go," he said, ignoring me. "Joey just radioed up, there's a car heading up the driveway."

Ethan put everything away and we ran down the stairs, through the living room, and then, we were out the back door like a band of thieves.

The mist had cleared and we sprinted for cover along the hedges, then made our way safely to the forest. I felt exhilarated, and part of the team. I never would have thought I would enjoy something like this, but it was both scarier and more fun than I ever could have imagined.

I let out a tiny giggle, and clapped a hand over my mouth, surprised.

When I looked up, though, it wasn't Ethan and Tag looking at me in consternation. I hadn't blown their cover.

I was back in the warehouse, and my bandmates were staring at me.

Nick laid his guitar across his knees and leaned forward. "Alright, Cal, what gives?"

"What do you mean?" I asked, flustered.

"You've been totally out of it for the last twenty minutes, just staring at the ceiling. I thought maybe you were resting, at first, but we've been talking to you for a couple minutes now and couldn't get a response. What the hell is going on with you?"

"Yeah, man, if I didn't know you better I'd say you were doing drugs," Jax said.

"Seriously?" I laughed, sitting up. "Come on, guys, I'm just tired."

"No. You're not. You've been acting strange for weeks. What's going on, Callie?" Ethan repeated.

I opened my mouth and hesitated. Maybe it was time to come clean. I couldn't keep my powers a secret forever. And honestly, I didn't like keeping secrets from my friends.

"Come on, we're your mates. You can tell us," Jax encouraged.

"It's not anything like what you're thinking," I promised. "Really."

"Callie, I don't even know what to think," said Nick. "That's the problem. I'm worried about you. You're all over the place lately, and that's just not you."

"I'm fine, I swear. I-"

My phone rang.

"Hold on, let me just get this." I looked at the number, but I didn't recognize it. "It could be Ethan."

I saw a look pass between my friends, and I knew what they were thinking. That maybe I was with another guy who wasn't treating me right. That I was hiding something.

Oh, they had no idea.

But I couldn't ignore the call. What if something had gone wrong with Ethan's mission?

I answered the call. "Hello?"

"Callie, it's Henry Kim."

"Oh, hi Dr. Kim. What's up?" I shrugged nervously at the guys,

"I didn't want to say anything until I knew for sure, but I have some really great news for you. We've found your family."

"What?" The word barely came out of my mouth, not so much a syllable as it was a gush of air and choked emotion.

"Yes, your grandfather. He's flying in now. Actually, he's asked if he can see you tonight, if you have time."

"Are you sure? You have proof?" The guys were watching me, confusion and worry apparent on their faces, and I tried to smile, to reassure them. But I think there was a disconnect between my brain and my body, because it came out as more of a grimace.

"As sure as I can be without a blood test. Which we can run when you get here, if you want. It's up to you."

"Yes. Yes, I think that would be good. I just- Wow. Okay. I'll be there in a few hours."

"Great. I'll get everything ready. Bring a bag, you can stay in the same room you used last week. And Callie?"

"Yeah?" I said, still reeling.

"He's a good man. I know him. Okay? I thought you might like to know that."

My heartbeat slowed to a sprint. "Thanks, Dr. Kim. That does help."

"Anytime," he said kindly, and ended the call.

After, I just stared at the phone for a moment in shock. I had family. I had a grandfather.

In all my years, I'd only spared moments to wonder about my mother, my father. It'd never crossed my mind to think beyond that. To the family extensions that I was missing. Grandparents. Uncles. Aunts. My god, cousins. I might have cousins.

The couch shifted beside me and Nick took my hand. "Callie, are you alright?" Concern laced his voice. "Is that what all this is about? Are you sick?"

"What? No!" I laughed a little too loudly, still not quite in control of my mind or my body.

"But you said 'doctor'," Jax reminded me.

"Oh, right." I giggled, too high. Not my voice. "No." I forced myself to calm down.

"No," I repeated. "Dr. Kim is... someone Ethan knows who's been helping me. He's been looking for my family. And it seems he's found them. Or at least, one of them."

"No way," Nick said. "That's fantastic. Your parents?"

"My grandfather. He's flying in, right now." I jumped up, surprising Keeta, who hopped off the couch and danced around me. "I have to go. I have to pack a bag, and I have to drive out to Joshua Tree."

"Joshua Tree? What's in Joshua Tree?"

"That's where Dr. Kim lives. He knows my grandfather and we're meeting there. Oh, there's too much to explain now. Look, I swear, we'll have a nice, long talk soon, okay?" The guys both looked at me like they were wondering who I was. "I promise, okay? Everything is fine, really. You don't have to worry."

I hugged them both and scooped up my stuff, stuffing everything into my large shoulder bag.

"Really, don't worry. I'll call you in couple days."

And then, I was hurrying out the door, mentally packing my bags already. What did you wear to meet a family you'd never considered having?

Chapter 22

Walking into Joshua Tree headquarters, Keeta stayed glued to my side. I was beyond nervous, and I knew she felt it. Heck, I was pretty sure everyone in the building could feel it. Ever since I'd pulled off the highway, I'd been trying really hard to play "American Idiot" in my head so that the mayhem in my mind wouldn't disturb other readers. For some reason, though, the song wouldn't stay on a loop, and kept morphing into Green Day's saddest song, "September." Which really wasn't helping settle me down.

I felt like a radio in an empty desert, full of static, blips and hisses.

The compound had security at the parking lot that scanned your hand when you pulled in to make sure you were in the starseed database. Ethan had walked me through the process before we left the week before, so getting back in had been easy. I wasn't sure where to find Dr. Kim though.

Keeta followed me up to the room on level four that I'd stayed in before. I dropped my pack down on the bed, and then went down to the office where I'd met with Dr. Kim before. Unfortunately, he wasn't there.

I figured my next best shot was heading back to the common room or the cafeteria. Since it was just about dinnertime, my stomach voted for food.

I passed people in the hall returning to their rooms, but no one I knew. I knew I could have asked one of them if they'd seen Dr. Kim, but meeting an unknown relative just about filled my stranger danger quota for the day.

I smiled but avoided any lingering eye contact, a trick I'd learned early in life to deflect unwanted attention. My golden eyes had drawn stares and comments from a young age, not all of it good.

We rode the elevator back down to the first floor and headed into the cafeteria. Many of the tables were full this time, everybody eating or waiting for their orders to be up. I looked around, saw Evie sitting with Cliff and some other people, waved, and headed over to the kitchen to place my order. This time, I asked for a hearty platter of potato skins with all the fixings and poured myself a huge glass of fresh orange juice before walking over to sit with Cliff and Evie.

"Hey guys, what's up?" I said, sliding into a seat next to Evie.

"Not much, how are you? And you, my snowy beauty? How are you?" The latter questions were addressed in a higher pitch to Keeta, who was now getting her face fluffed and adored by Evie. Out of the corner of her eye, she gave me a look. "Seriously, girl, what is going on with you? Beauty says you are all kinds of riled up. And you're broadcasting some pretty mixed up signals there, too."

Cliff raised his eyebrows, giving me a once over. But, of course, nothing was externally amiss. Unless, of course, you were easily provoked by brown leathers and a white tank top sporting a faded anarchy symbol. I reached down to finger the opal ring hanging just above my neckline, absentmindedly examining the golden flecks that mirrored my own eyes. It had azure and black flashes of luminescence, too, and the darkness drew me in, making me think of Ethan's eyes.

I shook my head, and re-focused on Evie. "Yeah. Today was a bit crazy, even for me. But enough about me, introduce me to your friends."

I swear I did my best to make friends. I really must have been sending out some dissonant signals, though, because after a few minutes the rest of the table had cleared out and Evie leaned towards me.

"Okay, spill. What is going on with you?"

Cliff leaned forward, all ears, and I sighed.

"Kim found my grandfather, and I'm supposed to meet him tonight."

Cliff let out a low whistle, and Evie looked confused. "And that's a bad thing? Was he missing?" she asked.

"No. I was." Evie looked confused. "I was given up for adoption when I was a baby."

That always sounded so much better than "my deadbeat parents abandoned me at a fire station." Though, either way, the result was the same.

"Wow, that's heavy. And he's coming here now?" she asked.

"Yep. He's flying in today. Might even be here already. Oh, shoot, that's my number, hold on." I hopped up to grab my food, snagged a few packets of hot sauce, and flopped back down in my seat.

"Don't you want to meet him?" Evie asked, picking up where we'd left off.

"I think the better question is, why haven't I already? It's not like I've been hiding. Honestly, I'm not sure I want more family. I kind of like the one I have already."

I couldn't help thinking I'd had a good, easy life before the lunar eclipse had triggered the biggest changes of my life. I'd been happy. Fulfilled. I'd loved my lifestyle. I'd accepted who I was. I'd never bothered looking for my family. It was a loose thread I hadn't felt the need to pull.

Now, I felt like someone was knitting a sweater around me, a little too small, a little too tight.

Everything was changing, too much, too fast.

"Well, it sounds like he really wants to meet you. I mean, he's coming here, just to see you. That's got to count for something, right?" asked Cliff, tossing a grape in the air and catching it in his mouth.

"I guess. I mean, yeah." I smeared a generous helping of sour cream over a wedge of potato and took a bite, considering. "I guess I'm just nervous. I don't know anything about him. About my parents. I have so many questions."

I'd spent a lifetime not thinking about it. About them. Pushing my feelings down. Because I'd had a good life. And because if you could give up a kid, then you didn't deserve to be missed.

But now?

Everything had changed.

I shook my head, trying to dislodge the drama like a dog trying to shake off water. It didn't work, so instead, I aimed for changing the subject.

"What about you guys. How've you been?"

Evie and Cliff exchanged glances.

"What?" I asked.

Evie stood up. "I think I need some sugar. Be right back."

"Cliff? What's going on?"

"She's pretty upset about the whole thing with Toby. She's been trying to be calm about it, you know, not letting him know just how pissed she is, cause she doesn't want to set him back any with the rehab work Dolores is doing, but I get how she must feel. I mean, he just made me feel bad about myself. But her? He messed with her feelings, man. Made her like him more than she really did. She feels violated."

"Oh crap, I can't believe I forgot all about that. She must feel terrible. It's practically like date rape."

"Yeah, right? She says she's been emotionally assaulted. And now Dr. Kim wants her to be understanding, but how do you move forward from something like that?"

"I don't know. I mean, if it was me I don't think I could. Is he here?"

"No. We had some meetings that first night here. Then Dolores took him on some retreat to start the rehab."

"Oh. How about you? Are you holding up okay?" I asked, reaching out to put a hand on his arm.

"Me? Yeah, sure," he assured me with a lop-sided smile. "I'm golden. I mean, come on, it's not his fault, right? How could Toby not be threatened by all this awesomeness?"

I laughed. "Totally, you are so rad."

"Oh, mad points for the 90s lingo."

"Thanks. My bassist is a Hawaiian transplant, he's been schooling me in the way."

"What way?" Evie asked, sitting down and spooning a frosting-rich sample of cake into her mouth.

"Callie's rocking some mad twentieth century surfer lingo."

"Hey," I teased, "I'm pretty sure that all the best slang starts in Los Angeles. I'm just paying homage to my Cali peeps."

"Right, okay," Cliff rolled his eyes. "So, when does your granddad get here, anyway?"

"No idea. He could be here already. I tried to find Kim in his office and the lab, but he wasn't there."

"Oh, did you try calling him?"

"No. That would have made too much sense." I said, feeling stupid. I couldn't believe I hadn't thought of that myself. After all, he had called me earlier, so his number had to be in my cell.

"You can always use the PA system next to the stairwell on each floor, kind of old school, I know," Evie said, rolling her eyes. "Hold the button, and you can page anyone throughout the building."

"Really?" I thought back, but couldn't remember any announcements from the last time I'd been here. "I guess that's convenient."

"No one really uses it, unless there's some sort of emergency, like a fire or a lockdown." Seeing the expression on my face, she continued," Don't worry. We don't get many lockdowns."

"I'd be more reassured if you said they never happen."

169

"Sorry. I'm not gonna lie, chica." Her lips puckered like she'd eaten something sour. "No one's immune to becoming a warper. Or being warped."

"Preaching to the choir, gorgeous," Cliff said, laughing it off, though the twinkle was missing from his eyes.

I chewed my lip, not wanting to get into it, and pulled out my phone while Evie and Cliff started bickering in that way that siblings, crushes and gal-pals all have. For a minute, I wondered which tack their relationship was taking, but then I remembered that Evie wasn't really Cliff's type. Besties it was.

I scrolled through my received calls, took a minute to add the latest one to my contacts under "Kim" and wrote out a quick text, letting him know I had arrived.

Then, since I had my phone out, I sent a group message to Kate, Doug and Mel, telling them I was hanging out in Joshua Tree for a few days with a friend. Not exactly a lie. But not the truth, either. At some point, I knew I would have to sit down with Kate and tell her what was going on. She'd know something was up the minute she saw me. She always did. You couldn't have that many kids coming through your home over the years and not develop a strong intuition about these sort of things. Besides, it wouldn't be right to talk to Nick and Jax, and not Kate. Mel and Doug? I didn't think I could tell them. Mel wouldn't appreciate knowing there was some truth behind what she called Kate's "woo-woo" spirituality. The knowledge would shake her core beliefs. And I'd love to tell Doug, but somehow, I didn't think it was a great idea, what with him being in the military and all. I didn't want to force him to split his loyalties or cause any ethical dilemmas.

No.

I'd start with Kate, and the boys in the band, and see how they took it.

I blew a piece of hair out of my mouth and looked up. Now all I had to do was wait for Kim to text me back, meet my grandfather, so that I could have something good to tell everyone.

My phone pinged, and I gave a small start. I glanced down, and saw a message from Kim.

Simple words.

He's here. Come to my quarters on the third floor, apartment 328.

So why did everything feel so complicated?

Chapter 23

I walked to the meeting alone. Evie had begged me to let her take Keeta for a walk, and I didn't have the heart to say no. So I went alone, no ally at my side.

I paused outside Kim's door and took a deep breath.

And then I counted to ten.

And then twenty.

I was about to knock, when the door swung open, practically beckoning me inside. Kim stood to the left, smiling as he held the door open.

"Callie, come in."

"I thought you weren't a Gregor. How'd you know I was out here?" I asked nervously.

"I told him."

A tall, pale man with dark eyes turned away from the windows to face me. His brown hair was salted with gray at the temples, but he hardly seemed old enough to be my grandfather.

"And yet, here I am," the man chuckled, reading my mind again as he came forward. "Joseph Winters. It's nice to meet you."

He held my hand in his and looked into my eyes. Quickly, I notched up my mind shield, keeping the thoughts within private and mine alone.

I searched his features for a sign that we were related, but other than our mutual height and some strong cheekbones, I didn't really see it.

"Calliope," I said, introducing myself and taking my hand back.

"So Henry said." He looked me over from head to toe, not judging, but as if he were searching for something. When he saw my necklace, he blanched visibly.

"Come, why don't we all have a seat," Kim said, pointing to the couch and chairs by the window.

I moved to sit, and Joseph followed slowly, as if lost in thought. He sat across from me, and Kim took a position between us in a chair. Surreptitiously, I watched the man who shared my blood.

He was older, but not as old as I'd been expecting. Somehow though, he'd changed just in the last minute, and looked slightly more worn. Weary. He met my gaze and I shifted uncomfortably, looking away.

I heard a sigh, and then his smooth voice.

"I imagine you are wondering where I have been all your life," he started, and I couldn't help a small disbelieving laugh. Or maybe it was a snort. I don't know. I tried to keep it in, I did, but the abandonment issues were flaring up in a pretty ugly, undeniable way. My heart was constricted, and wide open at the same time. I felt like I was bleeding out.

I didn't say anything, waiting for him to go on.

He didn't. I looked up again, and I saw him frowning at his hands, as if he would find an answer there.

He wouldn't.

"I haven't wondered," I said, taking pity on his sadness. "I never really thought beyond having a mother and a father, and honestly, I haven't thought much about them, either. I figured anyone who didn't want me, didn't deserve being missed."

"But you were wanted," he protested vehemently. "I'm sure you were."

I looked at him doubtfully.

"I mean, you would have been. You are now. I want you." He stood up and started pacing the room. "I didn't know you existed. I had no idea. I swear to you. If I had known... I would have scoured the earth to find you, I swear. Do you believe me?"

"I do," I whispered.

"My son- Your father- You have his eyes, you know."

I shook my head. I didn't know. How could I have?

"He disappeared the year before you were born. He came to me one night, ecstatic, in love. He said that he had met the woman he wanted to spend the rest of his life with. He wouldn't tell me who. But he said that she was in trouble, that he needed to take care of her. He said her father was a dangerous man, a warper, but that she was good, and that together they were going to start a new life. He insisted that the only way they could do that would be to go into seclusion, off grid. He asked for my blessing, and then I never saw him again."

"Did you give it to him? The blessing. Did you give it?"

"Of course. I'm a bit of a hopeless romantic, you see. I loved your grandmother very much, and I had always hoped that Finnegan would find that, too. He promised that he would contact me when he was safe, travel back and let me know he was okay. But then a year later I received notice that his body had been found, on a beach here in California. There was no indication of any family with him, and I never discovered who your mother was. But now..." He trailed off, staring at the chain around my neck.

"Yes?" I wrapped the ring tightly in one hand, like a talisman.

"You think you know who the woman was?" Kim interrupted.

"Yes. That ring, I've seen it before. In the possession of an extremely powerful bard, Ozan Fanai."

A sharp intake of breath accompanied this revelation, and we both looked at Kim, who sat rigid on the edge of his chair. "Are you sure?" he asked.

Joseph nodded and I started to worry at the look on Kim's face. "What? What is it?"

"Fanai is-"

"A warper," Joseph cut him off. "A very powerful, ruthless man. He has consolidated his power to place himself at the right hand of a half dozen rulers in the Middle East. He is the secret power behind them all, and they have no idea. Even thirty years ago, Ozan was powerful. Frightening. But I had no idea his daughter was the woman who my son was in love with."

"So what gives you that idea now?" I asked.

"Your necklace. That ring. The last time I saw it, it was on Fanai's hand. It was kind of hard to miss, since it gave me this." He pointed to a tiny white scar along his chin.

"So? How do you know your son didn't steal it, or maybe someone else?"

"I suppose I don't, not for sure. But I do know Ozan never, ever took off his ring. And my son said your mother had a dangerous father. It all adds up. Why else would your parents have made sure you had it when they gave you up? No, I can only assume that they wanted to leave you some clue to your parentage, or maybe some insurance."

"Some clue," I muttered.

"Don't be flip," he admonished. "That ring is said to amplify the powers of any sun child who wears it. Having it, makes you stronger. In some ways, it is the best protection you could have."

"Assuming I grew up and survived this long. And assuming I had sun powers. But I don't."

"Some children exhibit two abilities. It's more rare, but it often happens," he said.

"I already have two – reading and traveling."

"She travels?" he turned to Kim. "You did not tell me this."

"I didn't want to ruin the surprise." Kim smiled.

"Why is it a surprise?"

"Your father, Finnegan, was a reader. But I travel, like you."

"Don't be modest, Joe." Kim chuckled, and went on to explain. "Your grandfather is famous among travelers, both for his work here on earth, and beyond."

"Really?" I asked, intrigued. "Why?"

My grandfather looked embarrassed, and Kim explained.

"Over the centuries, we've come to realize that many people astral travel during their dreams, and I'm not just talking about starseeds. Of course, most people never realize that they are actually having real experiences. One human researcher, Robert Monroe, worked doing research for decades on this phenomenon and discovered that in addition to traveling, many evolved souls were helping the deceased cross over."

"All in their dreams?"

"Yes. The interesting thing is, it's something that some starseed families have been doing for generations. Since the beginning, really."

"Souls can get stuck in their own illusions of reality as they transition," my grandfather said. "They die, but they don't move on. Many even think they are in heaven. Some souls are so stuck, some don't even know they are dead. It's something our family has worked on since the beginning, helping to clear the earth's atmosphere of these souls, moving them into the light. If we don't, their energy creates stagnation on many levels, and everybody on the planet is affected."

"Problem is, there aren't enough travelers to keep up with the world population anymore. So imagine our excitement when we found out that some humans without the starseed genetics were actually starting to do the work, too." Kim said excitedly.

I nodded, considering. "Huh. That's pretty far out. But it's cool. I get it. But why are you so famous for it?" I asked, looking at my grandfather.

"Let's just say I move quickly on the astral realm," he grinned.

"Pfft, your grandfather can move a hundred souls in under an hour, compared to most people's one or two. Travelers usually need to convince the person to follow, and do the work to help them transition to the other side one at a time. Joseph is like the pied piper, he shows up and souls just want to follow him. He works so fast, he gathers them like a conga line and shuttles them in groups to the Light."

"Wow. That sounds...impressive." My grandfather blushed and I laughed. "So am I supposed to do this, too?"

"I'm just happy to have met you. If you decide you want to train with me, of course, I'd be happy to teach you."

"But Joseph," Kim said.

"No, Henry. Whatever Callie wants to do, or not do, that's up to her. Now cool it."

There was an awkward silence for a moment, which I broke. "So tell me more about our family. About my parents. Where are we from?"

"Well, on my side you're a Cherokee/Irish mix, and your grandmother was British and Scottish with a bit of Italian thrown in just for fun. On your mother's side, I believe you would be mostly Turkish and North African. You look very much like your mother, though as I said you have Finn's eyes. Little Wolf, we used to call him."

His eyes turned glassy, and he took a deep breath.

"I'm sorry. It's just... It's difficult. I haven't talked about Finnegan in a long time. When he died, it was like a piece of me died, too. My wife, your grandmother, she passed away the following year. Finn was our only child, the light of our life. I think the loss was just too great for her." He shook his head, clearing it. "Anyway. Your name, I thought it was Finn's idea of a play on words, since we always had a statue of Cailleach Bheur, Winter Goddess, at our front door. But now, I'm sure it was a clue to your maternal parentage. You know who Calliope is, of course?"

"Yes, the Greek muse of eloquence and poetry."

"Indeed. Her voice was supposed to infuse the listener with ecstatic harmony, rather like an inspirational siren."

The insinuation hit me. "Or like a speaker."

"Yes. I think there can be no doubt who your mother was."

"Do you know what happened to her? Where she is now, or if she's dead?"

"I have no idea. I can only assume that if you were given up, that they had no other alternative. I'm so sorry, Calliope. I wish I had better news."

"That's okay," I said, getting up to hug him. "We've got each other now, right?" I surprised myself with my words, my actions, but I found that I meant them. I felt a kinship with this man, despite the difference in our skin colors and features. I could feel it. We were family.

"Thank you, Calliope."

"Please, call me Callie." I patted him on the back and led him back to the sofa. "So, now what? Are you going to stay here for a while? Where do you live, normally?"

"I have a few homes, one in Virginia, one outside of Dublin, and another small vacation home here in Newport Beach."

"Fancy," I teased.

"Life has treated me well. And now, I'm happy to say I have someone to share it with. Whatever's mine, will be yours someday. My lawyer is already drafting up the papers."

I swallowed, overwhelmed. My most precious belongings were my dog, my drums and my van, in that order. I'd never imagined owning anything of significant value.

He saw the look on my face and chuckled. "Don't worry. I live a quiet life, and I'm not planning on dying anytime soon. Though that does bring up one thing we should talk about."

"Yes?"

"That ring you're wearing." His expression darkened with a scowl. "It's dangerous. Anyone who knew Ozan will know that ring. If they see it, it puts you at risk. Since you don't have sun powers, you should think about not wearing it."

"But I've always worn it." I couldn't imagine taking it off. I couldn't remember a time that I ever had. "Besides, how likely is it that I would meet someone who remembers a ring from almost thirty years ago?"

"Trust me. If I know Ozan, he's still looking for that ring. At least think about wearing it under your shirt?"

"I can do that." I smiled, and tucked the stone against my chest under my white tank top.

"That'll do, I guess," he said, returning my smile.

"Yeah. Plus, if I'm close enough to some warpers for them to recognize the stone, I think the ring is going to be the least of my worries, right?"

He blanched and I giggled. "Jeez, grandpa. Lighten up. You sound like Gandalf. 'Keep it safe. Keep it hidden.' I'll keep it out of sight, okay? I promise."

"Thank you, Callie." He searched my face as if seeking something, or someone, in there. "Thank you."

After that, there really wasn't much to say. We talked a little bit more about my grandmother, my father. But I noticed that as we spoke, the man who had seemed so handsome and vibrant at the start of the evening was starting to look faded and worn. Kim must have noticed it, too, because he shot me a look and gave a rather fake yawn.

It was a good thing Kim was employed as a researcher and teacher. He would have made a terrible spy.

"Well, that's my cue," I said, tucking a piece of hair behind my ear. "I should walk my dog before it gets too late. I'll see you in the morning, maybe?"

"Yes, of course," my grandfather said. "Breakfast at nine? And maybe later we can drive back to the city together, I can show you where I live."

"Sounds perfect. I've got plenty of room in my van for any bags you might have." I hugged him and stood, letting Kim walk me to the door.

"Thanks," Kim said. "Joe had a long day, but he'll be fine in the morning, after he sleeps off some of the jet lag, you'll see."

"I hope so. Thanks, Dr. Kim."

"Please, call me Henry," he insisted.

"Alright. Thank you, Henry."

I shook his hand and he pulled me in for a quick hug.

As long as you're here, you should train more with Marnie." I groaned and he chuckled. "I'll let her know to expect you after breakfast."

Chapter 24

The night was long and slow. I drifted between dreams like a feather on the breeze, never staying long, the hardness of reality always just out of reach.

At some point, I simply settled into darkness. I was still conscious, still lucid in my dream state, but had reached my inner still point, that place where time stretches infinitely before you, rife with possibilities. I don't know how long I stayed there. How long I lingered. But eventually, like a new moon in the night, I rose. Far, far away I saw a pinpoint of light, and I stretched towards it, reaching. Yearning.

For a while, it seemed like I was moving so, so slowly. Too slowly. The point stayed small, far away. But then it began to grow and expand, and I realized that I was traveling with great speed and accuracy, ever towards the light.

And then, when I thought I might become one with light, explode into fire and sparks, I surged into it, within the glare and the white, and flew out the other side.

To...somewhere else. Some-when else.

Carriages drove past. Horse hooves clattered on the sidewalk. Women hurried by wearing bustles and veiled hats, no one noticing the grimy girl huddled under a shop window, wilted flowers spread in a rough wooden box before her, a number and letter "5d" written in chalk on a sign.

Another dream, it seemed, though far outside my normal realm of experience. But then, what was normal lately, I wondered. I hopped across several puddles and knelt before the small child.

"Hello," I said.

"Hullo," she answered.

"You have some very nice flowers."

"Thank you. They're not long for it, I fear," she said with a sad sniff.

"You might be right," I agreed.

Feet came to a stop beside me, and I looked up.

Joseph.

"Hello, Grandfather," I said, standing up. "Imagine seeing you here. Is this a dream?"

"No, it isn't."

"Well, you'd probably say that whether it was or not." I smirked.

"I suppose I would. But I assure you, it's not a dream. I'm here to collect young Patience. I got here just before you, but when I saw you I decided to wait a minute before contact."

I looked at him, and then behind. I noticed he wasn't alone. About five feet away, a small group of men and women waited calmly, observing us with mild interest.

"Are you collecting souls? Wait, is this young girl-"

"Yes. She's been lost here in her own private hell for quite some time, it seems. She doesn't even know she's passed." He put out a hand and smiled down at her. "Come, Patience. It's time to go."

"But I haven't sold all my blooms yet. And mama will be so mad."

"That's alright. You bring them with you, and I promise we'll find a place for all of them."

"Alright," she agreed easily, and placed her hand in his as she scrambled to her feet, the box of posies now tucked under one arm.

He guided her to the others, and then came back to me.

"So that's it then? It's that easy?" I asked.

"For me, yes. Well, usually," he conceded. "Sometimes one must convince them. For most travelers it takes longer. Helping only a few souls move on each night. But as Henry said-"

"You're a legend," I laughed.

"Well, I was going to say I have a knack for it. But have it your way," he said with a twinkle in his eye. "So, what do you think? Want to join me? See how it's done? You found your own way here, so I imagine you might have a knack for it as well. The family business, you might say."

"Sure, why not. I'm always up for helping people." I thought of the degree in social working I'd achieved, and how some of my friends thought I was wasting my abilities on rock and roll, when I could have been helping kids in crisis.

Maybe, I thought, there was a way to have it all. Do it all. Be it all.

Kate had always assured me I could do whatever I wanted. That if someone told me my skin was too brown, that I wasn't smart enough, or good enough, that it wasn't true. That if someone said a girl couldn't do something, then I just needed to prove them wrong. That if a goal seemed too hard, I better work twice as hard and push on through to reach it. Time and again, night after night, when things were hard at school or out in the big, bad world, she would tuck me in and read me stories of amazing women who could do big things. Women who changed the world. Girls who could. And every night, she'd prompt me to repeat with her that "if they can do it, I can do it, too."

I thought of Kate, and I thought of the other lost souls waiting for people like me and Joseph to find them.

I thought of the times I had been lost, and the people who had helped me through.

I looked up at my grandfather and felt a slow smile come over my face.

"You know, I think I would like that very much."

I placed my arm through his and like that, we were gone.

Chapter 25

"That was A.Maz.Ing!" I gushed for the tenth time from behind the wheel of my van.

My grandfather laughed heartily over the speakerphone on the seat next to me. "I'm glad to hear that you are enjoying yourself."

"Are you kidding? I mean, traveling was cool and all, but the work I've been doing with you just seems so important."

Every night since we'd met, I'd been helping him ferry lost souls into the light. It had been the best week ever.

"I feel so, whole. I was happy before, don't get me wrong, but now I feel fulfilled. Like what I'm doing really matters. And I don't even have to give up drumming to do it."

"No, I would never want you to do that. It's clear that music is an important part of who you are. You know, my mother was a song walker, too. You remind me a lot of her."

"Really?"

"Yes, she had the same fire in her, the same big heart. I've had a friend ship out all the family photo albums from my house in Virginia, so you'll be able to see some pictures of her soon. Your father, too."

"That's amazing, Grandfather, I can't wait."

"Me, too. We'll make an evening of it. Now, tell me about your other training. It seems like we've hardly had time to talk, with everything else going on."

"Oh, it's good, you know? I think the work with you has actually helped. I hardly have to think about blocking any more, and I can travel on command now."

"That's good. That's good," he said. "I'm glad it's going well."

My phone beeped, and I picked it up, glancing at the screen.

"I'm going to have to call you back, okay? I've got another call. See you tonight?" I asked.

"Wouldn't miss it." He hung up and I accepted the incoming call.

"Hello?"

"Callie? It's Cliff."

"Hey, Cliff. What's up? I'm on my way to rehearsal, so I have you on speaker. Can you hear me okay?"

"Yeah, it's fine. Listen, something's going on with Toby. Do you think you could meet me later?" His voice sounded tight with tension.

"Yeah, sure. I should be free by five. What's up?"

"I think it's better if we talk about it in person. Where do you guys practice?"

I rattled off the warehouse address on North Robertson in West Hollywood, just as I turned into Nick's parking lot and pulled into a space. I shut off the engine and listened to Cliff.

"Okay. I get off work in a little while, I can meet you there when you finish up."

"Okay," I said, starting to feel a little worried. "You sure you don't want to talk now?"

"No, I gotta get back to work, anyway. The sous chef is giving me the eye. See you in a few."

"Okay, see you." I hung up the phone. Well, there wasn't much I could do for Cliff right now, I thought, and gathered up my things. I was a little on edge, but I knew it was nothing a little music couldn't fix.

I pushed open the door to the warehouse and sniffed the air. A sweet, spicy aroma filled the air, so I knew Nick was here already. He liked to "set the mood," as he put it, and often burned incense. Keeta padded past me, sneezing quietly on her way to her favorite spot, a cool patch of concrete away from the haze of smoke that was sheltered from the worst noise of the speakers. I walked in and spotted Nick putting a new string on his guitar.

"No Jax?" I asked, dropping onto the couch next to him.

"He said he was having lunch with Jenna," he said, and I rolled my eyes. Lunch with Jenna tended to turn into a whole lot more. Jax would probably be late.

"Okay. Well, my friend Cliff is stopping by around five, I promised I'd help him out with something."

"Cliff... Have I met that one?"

"No. He's, um, friends with Ethan and Toby."

Kind of. Sort of.

"Oh yeah?" Nick's voice went up a bit, sharpened by interest. "How is Ethan, anyway?"

"I don't know. I haven't seen him in days. He's on a business trip."

"Doesn't he own a bookstore?"

"Books and collectibles. He's on a buying trip."

"Oh, that's cool." He bought the lie, and I felt like the worst friend in the world. "I guess he has employees, then?" I nodded mutely. "That's great he has people he can trust like that."

I groaned inwardly as he twisted my knife of omission deeper.

"You okay?"

"Oh, sure, just some indigestion." I pounded my chest a few times and smiled weakly.

"I told you, Callie, you have got to stop eating at Taco Sol. Anything that cheap cannot be good for your health."

"But the green chile quesadillas! They are sooo good. You know they are."

He shook his head and snorted, turning his attention back to the guitar.

"What about you and Marnie? You guys were really hitting it off last weekend. Have you called her?"

"I did." He frowned and plucked at the new string, testing its sound.

"And?"

"I don't know. I mean she gave me her number, not the other way around. But every time we talk she has to run off somewhere, and I haven't been able to get her to go on a date yet."

"Mmm. She does take her work pretty seriously, and I know she's been under some extra pressure lately. Don't give up. She definitely likes you."

"Well, maybe you can put in a good word for me?"

"Sure thing, lover boy," I winked.

Jax arrived and we got down to business, practicing and refining new songs. While we played, I wasn't able to let go or travel. I was too consumed with wanting to tell the guys about what was really going on with me. I'd already filled them in on meeting my grandfather, and they were over the moon happy for me. Maybe that was enough for now? The more I was drawn into the world of starseeds and warpers, the more I wondered how safe it would be to tell them. I didn't want to lie to Nick and Jax, but I didn't want to put them in danger, either.

By the end of rehearsal, I was no closer to knowing which was the better decision, but at least my beats were tight. Cliff walked in at five on the dot and leaned against the wall to wait after giving me a small wave. He stood there while we finished the song, and then I called him over.

"Hey guys, this is my friend, Cliff." Everybody shook hands and passed around smiles and jokes, completing the obligatory male-bonding rituals.

"So, you're a friend of Ethan's, huh?" Nick asked.

"Yeah, sure," Cliff said absently checking his phone. "Um, Callie, about that thing?"

"Yeah, sure, no problem. I'm all set. Guys, I'll catch you tomorrow, okay?" We had a wedding gig down in Orange County at 3pm. "The place is called Cactus Grove, right?"

"Yep. I'll text you the address now."

My phone pinged, and I checked the text. "Got it. Oooh. Swanky." I put the phone away, whistled for Keeta, and followed Cliff outside.

"Okay, so what gives? Why all the cloak and dagger?"

"Sorry. I know, I hate drama. Just, I wasn't sure who to talk to. Evie's already really mad, and everybody at HQ takes things so seriously, and I just, I don't want to cause trouble but-"

"Dude, spill it."

"Right." He took a deep breath and exhaled loudly. "Sorry. It's probably no big deal. Really. I'm probably totally wrong. But if I'm right-"

"Cliff!"

"Right. The thing is...I'm afraid that Toby is joining the warpers."

Chapter 26

I sagged against the van.

"You're kidding."

"I wish I was. I know he can be kind of an ass sometimes, but Toby and I, we came up in this together. We got our powers at the same time. For any differences we had, I thought we were friends."

"What about the extra training and counseling he was supposed to be getting? You're saying none of it helped?"

"I don't know." Cliff took his cap in one hand and dragged his other hand through the mess underneath. "I thought it would. But Evie's been so mad at him, and the longer she refuses to go near him, the angrier he's gotten. It's like, he's blaming her rejection on everyone else."

"But it's his own fault! You can't warp someone into liking you."

"I know. I talked to him about it, and he seemed to get it. But that was last week. People have been talking about him behind his back, and saying some pretty nasty stuff to his face. I guess Evie spilled the beans to a few of her friends, and word spread. Now no one trusts him, and he feels betrayed."

"Seriously? Sounds like he just needs to suck it up and do the time."

"Apparently Toby disagrees. He's lost his shot at Evie and he's talking about defecting. Says that over there, they appreciate men with talent."

"Ugh, please. You're making me sick. What about his parents? Has anyone tried talking to them? I mean, aren't they all law and order-ly?"

"They are. I think they've been the hardest of all on him. Told him if he doesn't straighten out he can find another place to live."

"Ouch." A shiver ran down my spine, a sign of the dropping evening temperature as much as anything else. I let down my hair to help keep the breeze off my neck.

"I know."

"So what's your plan? I'm assuming you have one?"

"Kind of. I figured we could both go over and talk to him. He thinks you're pretty cool, and you're new, so he might still trust you. I figured maybe we can talk him down."

"And if we can't?"

"I don't know. Knock him out? Take him hostage until he sees the light?"

I laughed, then saw he was serious. "Cliff, I'm not kidnapping anyone."

"Not kidnapping. Just, keeping him safe."

"No, Cliff."

"Fine," he huffed. "His parents are at some big gala tonight, they won't be home until late. But if we can't make headway, maybe they'll be able to help us talk some sense into him."

"Okay," I said doubtfully. "Sounds like a plan."

I turned and called Keeta away from the fence she'd been investigating, and opened the doors on the van. She hopped in, and I gestured for Cliff to do the same.

"Okay, where to?"

He called out directions, and the closer we got to Toby's, the more tense we both became. As we got closer, a Green Day song on the radio reminded me that I should probably be shielding my thoughts, just in case. As far as I knew, Toby was strictly a child of the sun, but it was better not to take any chances.

Because as much as I wanted to help keep Toby out of the clutches of the warpers, I totally got where Evie was coming from. The idea of some guy tricking me into liking him using a sneaky mind trick was about as abhorrent and disgusting as being drugged and date raped. I couldn't completely decide if it was equal to or worse than being roofied, but I kept coming back to the thought that it had to be far, far worse. Because you weren't just taking someone's body. You were taking their free will. You were stealing their mind. I wasn't sure there could be any worse violation.

Finally, we were there. Rush hour traffic had not been unkind, despite the relatively short distance.

I pulled up in front of a nicely landscaped home in Brentwood that somehow managed to be fancy yet understated at the same time. Maybe it was the curved roof over the stone facing, or maybe it was the lack of columns where most of the other houses on the streets had them, but Toby's home looked both cozy and well-appointed.

"Ready?" I asked.

"As I'll ever be." He reached for the door and paused. "Hey, thanks for doing this, by the way. I know you barely know me, or Toby, but I really...Well, thanks."

"Aw, that's so cute, you think I'm doing this for you? Nah. I just like to collect favors." I cackled and winked.

"Dude, you've got one seriously weird sense of humor, you know that?" He chuckled, and I giggled.

"Sorry. Stress makes me do weird things."

"No, problem. In case you haven't noticed, I have my own issues with social norms."

"Okay then. I guess this is it."

"Yep." We opened our doors at the same time, and walked across the lawn together to ring the doorbell. Keeta whined from the seat Cliff had just vacated, not happy to have been left behind. I shushed her, and she quieted but stared balefully at us from the open window.

Cliff pressed the button for the bell and we waited. And waited. I was just about to say we should give up, go home, when the door swung open and Toby was there. He pushed his glasses up on his nose and frowned at us.

"What are you guys doing here? This isn't a good time. I'm busy." As if to prove it, he glanced at his phone and shot off a text before ramming it back in his shirt pocket.

"I know just how busy you are, Tobs," Cliff said, pushing his way inside past our ungracious host. Toby moved aside and I followed Cliff into the hall.

"By all means, come on in," Toby complained.

"Thanks," I said, looking around. "Great place you have here."

"Yeah? Well, it's not mine. And I won't be here much longer." He walked away and we trailed behind him. I gave Cliff a look, and he shrugged. Toby led us downstairs, into a basement apartment. Several computers lined one wall, and a TV hung in the corner nearby. Otherwise, it was a straight up man-cave. Well, if the man in question was a comic-book reading teen. Video game posters and Marvel action figures were the primary décor, and the lighting consisted of two lava lamps and an angled desk light. Tiny windows at the top of the walls would let in a small amount of light during the day, but right now they were mostly dark, like the sky outside.

Toby sat down at his desk and spun around in his chair, sweeping a hand towards a small couch.

"Well, go on, sit. Can't say I'm not hospitable." We did as he asked and looked at each other. Suddenly, I realized that I hadn't mastered building a wall against the influence of a person like Toby. What if he turned on us? Was there anything we could do? By the look on Cliff's face, I imagined his thoughts were running in the same direction.

"Now, now, no need to look so concerned, you two," Toby giggled. "I promise, I have no intention to harm either of you. But tell me. What is this, an intervention? Some sort of last ditch effort to beg me to stay?"

"Yes," Cliff nodded eagerly. "You're a good guy, Toby. Everybody knows that. People just need some time. You don't have to leave."

Toby laughed, a sad, sharp sound. "I am ninety-nine percent sure that isn't true, friend. There's nothing for me here anymore. Even my own family is fed up with me. Do you know they told me to move out tonight? My mom said she can't look at me anymore, and that it's time I grew up. She kicked me out. Me!"

"There's other options, Toby," I said. "You could stay at the Bronzehead. Or HQ."

"Please. Most people in those places would sooner kill me than share a meal. No. I'm done with all that."

Footsteps above made the ceiling creak, and I tensed.

"Expecting someone, Tobs?" Cliff asked lightly.

"Don't call me that," Toby snarled. "You think you're such a charmer, always the funny one. Well, we'll see who gets the last laugh."

"Cliff, we'd better go," I said, having a very bad feeling. I started to rise, but a command from Toby forced my legs to buckle and my body to bend back into a seated position.

"Sit. You're my guests now."

Chapter 27

I tried to rise, but I couldn't. Cliff struggled next to me, and I knew he was in the same bind.

Toby had used the power of speech against us. Never had I felt so violated, or so angry.

Quickly, I checked to make sure that my necklace was hidden inside my shirt. It was, but when Toby turned towards the stairs I tucked it inside my bra, making sure it would stay out of sight. Maybe it couldn't do me any good as a traveler or reader, but I still felt like I gained something from its touch against my skin. A sense of protection. Of family.

That last thought made me think of Joseph.

Toby glanced at me. "Don't get any ideas, you. I heard Tag and Evie talking about how you can pull Ethan to you. Well, as of now, you have no power to do that. Do you hear me? You can't contact him or travel to him. You are powerless. Both of you."

I snarled at his tone. I may not have been able to reach Ethan, anyway, since I had so little control over the tug. But the idea of this scrawny jerk telling me what to do didn't sit well with me.

"Callie," Cliff whispered as Toby went up the stairs, "I can't glam. He really did take away our powers!"

"Shh," I said, trying to reassure him, even as I saw that his hair had reverted to a sparse, thin covering on his head. "He can't actually do that, not permanently anyway."

Well, I didn't think he could, anyway.

"It's just the power of suggestion. Marnie says most bards can't hold a command for more than a couple hours. So as soon as it wears off, we're good."

In fact, I thought to myself, if I could go to sleep, I had a feeling the command wouldn't hold. The subconscious mind worked differently from our waking, logical brain. So all I had to do was get to sleep, travel to Joseph to send for help, and survive long enough to get rescued.

No big deal.

I took some calming breaths and worked really hard to convince myself of that.

And it was working, too.

Right up until the moment that Toby walked back down into the room, followed by three men.

Dressed in casual civilian clothes, they didn't look so different from the rest of us. Near our ages, each was in fine physical shape. Each had short, military style shorn hair. None smiled.

All three were familiar.

All three were murderers.

I gasped, surprised, and then tried to school my features back to looking bored. Never let them see you scared, I thought. It worked in grade school. It worked on stage. If nothing else, maybe some false bravado would help Cliff stay calm.

He didn't need to know that the three men who had just walked into the room had killed General Kipner with their minds, squeezing him like a ripe tomato till he bled from the onslaught of their singular, unified intention. I knew I sure as hell would have been happier not knowing.

I lifted my chin and glared at Toby. "Nice new friends you've got there, care to introduce us?"

"Sure," Toby smiled at me sweetly. "Calliope Winters, meet Cy, Roger and Marcus."

"Marco," the swarthy, dark-eyed one said gruffly.

"Sorry, Marco," Toby ducked his head, looking nervous for the first time. "So, as I was about to tell you earlier, you guys arrived just in time. The boys here were about to take me somewhere my kind of talent is really appreciated."

He paused, tapping his chin as if in thought.

"You know, I bet your talents would be appreciated, too. What do you say, boys? Up for a few more recruits?"

"Like hell!" I swore, just as Cliff yelled, "Wait just a minute!" and Roger nodded.

"I think the Admiral will be excited to have more new recruits," he agreed with just a hint of pleasure in his voice. "Toby, you're all packed?"

"Yep, ready to go." He picked up a computer bag and a backpack that had been sitting on the floor and nodded.

"That's it?" Roger sounded surprised.

Toby sneered. "I'm leaving as much of this life behind as I can."

Roger gave him an assessing look that seemed to end with approval. "Good. Then let's go. I trust you can keep these two under control? We didn't bring any restraints."

"Oh, don't worry. You won't need them." He sniggered and turned to us, speaking roughly. "Come on. Up. Walk outside and do whatever these three tell you to do. Don't bother trying to resist, you'll just give yourselves a headache."

Of their own volition, our legs began to move, taking us up the stairs, through the house and out the door. Trying to stop myself didn't just hurt my head, it made my heart pound and my joints scream in pain. My pulse raced and skipped, as if it couldn't decide which way it wanted to beat. I knew there were ways to combat speakers, but I hadn't learned any of them yet. I'd been so proud to learn how to keep my thoughts from broadcasting, I'd forgotten to ask how to keep my thoughts my own.

Outside, Keeta barked happily to see me returning, but when I walked to the SUV parked in front of my van, her barks turned frantic. No doubt, she could smell the fear rolling off Cliff and me. Or, as Evie had told me, Keeta had a natural canine ability to read basic thoughts and intentions. Too bad I couldn't tell her to run for help.

"Shut that dog up," Roger said to Marco, who started to walk toward the van. Images of Kipner's final moments flooded my brain, and maybe some of it broadcasted despite Toby's command, because Keeta went wild. Feeling hopeful, I thought as hard as I could of Ethan's face and the Bronzehead, not so far away.

Keeta had always taken her job guarding the van very seriously. So seriously, I'd never worried about rolling up the windows far enough to keep her in. I'd known she would never jump out willingly.

Now, she backed up a bit from the window, almost as if she was retreating, and then suddenly she burst through the opening in a flash of white and fur. She ignored the man, and started for me. Again, I concentrated on the images of Ethan. The Bronzehead. Of us, running. She paused mid-stride, the barest moment of uncertainty in her eyes.

She did hear me.

Hope lit me from within, and I yelled, "Run, Keeta! Find Ethan!" And then she was gone, all my hope contained in the ferocity of one small, tamed white wolf and I was doubling over, a blow to my stomach taking my breath away, before everything went black.

Chapter 28

When I woke, I was chained to a chair in a plain, over-lit concrete room. The walls had been newly painted a creamy gray – I could tell, because the fumes were still noxious.

I was alone in the room. No Cliff. No Keeta. Though that didn't mean they weren't nearby. The room had no windows, unless you counted a dark pane of one-way glass, or another tiny pane high in the fire door behind me. I had no idea where I was, except that the men who had killed Kipner definitely seemed to be in the military, or working with it. I was still wearing my own clothes, so that was something. The idea of Toby or the three musketeers disrobing me was enough to give me a permanent case of the heebie-jeebies.

I tested the chained cuffs holding my arms behind me, linking me to the chair, and noticed a small flesh-colored bandage on my left arm as I twisted to try and get a better view. The Band-Aid distracted me for a moment. First of all, no way was it one of mine. Mine were all rainbow flying unicorns and superhero Amazons. Flesh-colored bandages only blended in on white people, and I'd hated them since I was a little girl. Second, who put it on me, and why? I sincerely hoped I had fallen on a rock back at Toby's and gotten a scratch, because the alternative left me cold. I wasn't a fan of shots, especially when they contained mystery medications.

I closed my eyes and tried projecting from my body to reach Cliff, Ethan, Joseph, anybody, but my consciousness stayed securely rooted in my body. Wherever I was, I must not have been out long enough for Toby's commands to wear off.

That's okay, I thought. I got nothing but time. And I tried again. And again. I was not going to give up. It just wasn't in my genes. Or at least, I didn't think it was.

I don't know how long I'd been sitting there trying, but my arms and butt were starting to go numb when I heard the whisper-click of a door opening. I opened my eyes and peered at the woman entering the room. Dressed in a naval officer's uniform with the single star and thin stripes of a low-ranking lieutenant, heels clicking like a death knell across the floor, she came to sit at the table.

"Ms. Winters," she began. "I am Lieutenant Kroksky. I apologize for any rough treatment you may have received, but I want to assure you that we have only your best interests in mind."

I snorted. "You have to be kidding, right?"

She ignored my outburst and opened a file, placing it before her. "I understand you are a traveler and a reader. Is that correct?"

I stared her in the eyes, assessing. "My brother is a lawyer, you know. What you've done is illegal."

"Really, you think so? I see nothing in your file indicating that you have any known family. According to the papers

I have here you are being detained as a danger to national security, having threatened a new recruit in a classified military operation. I can hold you here as long as I deem necessary for interrogation."

"I don't know anything that could possibly help you." I tried taking another tack. "I'm just a drummer in a band."

"You can play it that way if you like. It doesn't matter. Either way, we will be running some tests on you over the next few days. Assuming you are what we think you are, you will be joining our program."

"I don't think so," I growled.

She leaned forward and looked at me, smiling. "This isn't optional, sweetheart. You will cooperate, one way, or another."

I looked away, refusing to engage with her any further.

"Oh, and don't bother trying to use your abilities while you're here, either. We've given you a little gift of our own, something to block your powers until we decide you are ready to cooperate."

She laughed and stood, her heels clacking annoyingly towards the door. I heard the door open, and then she paused. My curiosity got the better of me and I turned, watching her. Her eyes glinted coldly, unblinking like a snake.

"Think of it as your patriotic duty, Ms. Winters. A chance to serve your country."

She put a strange emphasis on the word "serve," making me think she would be just as happy to enslave me as to recruit me. So, having the feeling it would annoy her, I went with a good, long eye roll. Never underestimate the power of an eye roll to infuriate and provoke.

She left and I sat quietly, waiting for the next act in the performance. I'd watched enough crime dramas to know that making the prisoner wait was part of the game. And, of course, someone had to be watching me through the one-way glass. Too bad my hands were cuffed. Since I couldn't give them the finger, I settled for mouthing a few choice curses at them with a wink.

And then I reached for my powers again, and came up with a whole handful of nothing. Whatever they'd given me, I would bet it had been in that shot. The spot on my arm was starting to ache, though that could have just been my mind rebelling against the invasion.

Before I could think about it too much, the door opened again and two armed soldiers entered the room. Both avoided eye contact with me as I was unchained and ordered out into the hallway.

"Boy, you guys are all business, huh? You do this often, kidnap girls against their will, violate their constitutional rights?"

I looked back at the men to see if they would answer and all I got was a "Keep moving."

"Well, at least you're well-trained lap dogs," I muttered. "Where's my friend, Cliff Collet? You know, the other US citizen you are unlawfully detaining?"

That time, all I got for my impertinence was a shove with the point of a gun. Nice. Gentlemanly. Remind me to take that "My Brother is in the Navy" sticker off my van.

I thought about pulling the lawyer card, but didn't actually want to get Doug involved in this if I could help it. Instead, I focused on where we were going. The halls were a maze of white, lit with glaring fluorescent overhead fixtures. After six turns, I found it hard to keep track of where we'd been. Everything looked the same. Finally, we came to a door guarded by two men. Neither of them would look at me, while one of my escorts slid a card for access and I was led roughly down another white hallway. This one was a little different, though. Doors lined the hall, each one numbered, each accessible by key card. Every door had a small video monitor next to it at eye level, and instantly I knew what was behind door number 25.

My cell.

Sure enough, the soldier inserted his card into the slot above the handle on the door, waited for it to turn green and then removed his card, opening the door.

He didn't give me the card, so any hope I had that I wasn't a complete prisoner abandoned me.

I couldn't even think of anything to say. No protest. No mockery. I'd gone numb with the shock of my current reality. Nothing I could have said at the moment would have made a difference, anyway. These were simple soldiers, doing their job. Who knew what they had even been told? They probably thought I was some sort of government terrorist.

Certainly, they showed me no compassion as a hand took my shoulder and shoved me inside, slamming the door closed behind me.

Well, damn.

The room had a small shower and bathroom facilities, a bed, and a desk with a chair. No window. No clock. I couldn't even control the overhead light, meaning that it would no doubt turn itself off at some point when they deemed it was time for me to sleep. Or maybe not. Maybe they would go for sleep deprivation, all the better to weaken my resolve, my grip on reality. Fantastic.

"What have you gotten yourself into, Calliope?" I whispered.

Resolved to remain strong, I decided to work off some of my fear doing calisthenics. When that got old, I sat on the bed and started to think.

While I was exercising, I'd visually searched the room for the camera feed, but seen nothing. My best guess was that it was in the overhead vent, or the light fixture. The idea that someone was monitoring my every move, that I couldn't even shower or pee in private, made me feel sick. I hoped I wouldn't be here long enough to get used to the invasion of privacy. I spent the next half hour using the sheet of my bed to create a makeshift curtain from the shower stall to the desk, hiding the toilet from any overhead voyeurs.

Then, and only then, did I go to the bathroom. I was just finishing up when I heard two knocks on the door, the briefest of warnings before the door opened.

"Calliope Winters?" The voice carried clearly through the thin sheet of fabric.

"Do you mind? Peeing here."

"Your presence has been requested. Come out, or we'll have to come in."

"Jeez, fine." I muttered. I stood up and flushed the toilet, ducking as I left the little sanctuary I had created. Immediately, my arms were grabbed tightly and I was steered out the door.

"Where are you taking me?" I asked with as much bravery as I could muster.

"You'll see. Now keep quiet," the guard snarled and walked faster, dragging me with him as the other man marched at my side.

Honestly, my faith in the nation's finest was fast deteriorating.

Again, we walked through unmarked corridors that all looked the same to me, until we entered a laboratory of some sort. People were walking around in white coats, monitoring men and women strapped into chairs. It wasn't so different from Dr. Kim's lab, until you noticed the armed guards in each corner, and the fact that half the subjects were restrained.

My escort pushed me roughly into a seat.

"Hey!" I yelled. "You can't do this, I'm an American citizen!"

I struggled, but he just ignored me, deflecting every move I made while he strapped me down and left without a word. No one in the lab even seemed to register the disturbance. The sense of defeat was infuriating. I hated feeling helpless. Being trapped.

I rallied against the emotion, examining my restraints, looking for a way out. There had to be one. I just had to think.

A man walked over, not even looking at me as he read from his chart.

"Calliope Winters, age 28, reader, traveler." He taped some wires to my head, my chest, my inner arms.

"What are you doing?" I asked. "You can't do this. It's all a mistake, see? I don't know who you people are, but I don't belong here."

He looked up at me, no emotion in his eyes. "I suggest you relax, luv. The more you relax, the easier this will go for you."

And then he winked and jabbed a needle in my arm and walked away.

"Ow! Hey!" I called after him, then stared at the needle, eyes following the tube up to where it was attached to a bag filled with a light green liquid.

Helpless, I watched the liquid drip down, second by second. I looked around the room again, really taking it in. Men and women in chairs. All hooked up to bags of medicine, if you could call it that. All unconscious. Oh no.

I struggled again, trying to dislodge the needle, but all I earned was pain at the insertion site as it wiggled slightly under my skin. A feeling of fatigue began to wash over me.

No.

I tried to travel, again, for the umpteenth time in one day, and nothing happened. Whatever they had given before, I still had no control over my powers.

I thrashed futilely in my seat. One of the men in white coats walked by, laughing at me like you would a toddler trying to escape their crib, and I glared at him. He winked, and turned up the radio that had been playing quietly. The crooning of Three Dog Night, singing about old-fashioned love songs, clashed with the ugliness of my current reality. For a moment, I stopped thrashing, incredulous. Was I in some alternate reality?

Exhaustion began to set in, making my limbs feel heavy. Unable to help myself, I began to hum along with the music. I heard some of the doctors behind me, talking about a solar eclipse that was set to end within the hour.

"We should be getting some fresh subjects, soon."

"I'm just interested to see which of our tests this time around have paid off. It's such a pain having to wait for something so arbitrary for validation."

"I know, it hardly seems scientific, does it?"

The voices faded, and the music played on.

The music played, and my eyelids drooped closed. I could feel my consciousness fading, but I tried to hold on, grabbing on to the song like a lifeline.

Holding on, and trying to pull myself awake. The thread was tenuous, but I did it, and then I was doing more than just staying awake. I was traveling on the song, soaring on the waves of sound, leaving my bound body and flying high into the sky.

Chapter 29

I flew out of the room, down the hallway, pulled towards freedom in an un-erring way. My astral body knew where to go, and it showed me how to navigate the maze of white cement. There were many checkpoints, locked doors, and confusing turns, but I passed through each without issue. I thought about finding Cliff, and my body naturally turned in a new direction towards where he must be.

But no. Who knew how long I would be able to maintain this journey. It was a miracle I had been able to harness the song at all, an aberration that I had been able to overcome their drugs and burst free. I needed to use my time wisely. I needed to see where we were being held, and get help.

Finally, I escaped out into the light of day. The building cast a strange shadow on the ground, shaped wrong, I thought.

I looked up, and saw the sun was indeed mid-eclipse, its cropped rays casting half-eaten shadows here on earth, millions of miles away.

It was so beautiful. Something in me yearned to fly up, into the sky, towards the sun. It didn't matter that my body was being held prisoner, along with countless others. The sun called to me, and it took every fiber of my conscious resistance to stay the course. To look away, look around. The building we were in was long and low, no more than two stories of concrete in the desert. Other buildings stood nearby. It was a base. I was on a base.

I flew up, seeking a better vantage, and saw buildings sprawling over a vast area. The one I had been in was off to one side, distanced from the others by some tennis and basketball courts. I wondered how often the doctors and soldiers I'd met played there, laughing off the things they'd seen and done during the day.

Memorizing the lab's position within the base, I flew upwards, looking for the base entrance. The place was huge, like a small city. Finally, I saw the main road leading out, the gatehouses keeping the place secure. I flew towards them, and read the sign. Naval Air Weapons Station. China Lake.

I'd heard of the base before. I'd dated a conspiracy theorist nut who had talked about it being a secret base working with alien tech. I'd stopped dating him when he took me on a romantic weekend to Area 51.

Not my idea of fun back then. I'd thought he was crazy, and I'd been bored out of my mind lying on a blanket in the desert watching him scan the night sky for aliens.

Now?

Well, he may not have had it right, but he'd clearly been on to something. He just hadn't realized how close he really was to the real alien.

Me.

Oh, if he could see me now. I thought of how he could smile, and again, my thoughts started to pull me the wrong way, and I remembered to focus. To do what I needed to do.

Find Ethan.

This time, the single thought was all I needed. I flew faster than a beam of light across the sky, too fast to even take note of what I was passing or where I was, and then I was descending in an arc, down through clouds, down through mist and air, down through matter and stone and dust. Thank heavens I wasn't made of matter myself, or I would have been a wreck by now.

But I wasn't. I was light.

I was energy.

I was starseed.

Homing in on Ethan's energy like a moth to a flame, I shimmered through every conceivable obstacle without a care and arrived in a conference room at the Bronzehead. Keeta barked as I appeared next to her and I reached for her, wanting to stroke her soft fur. Unfortunately, I couldn't, and as she tried to jump on she passed through, landing with a frustrated yelp. Ethan looked up from where he'd been pacing, and everyone at the table did, too.

"Callie!" he exclaimed.

"Hey, guys. Hey, baby!" I knelt down next to Keeta, so happy that she had made it to safety. Evie, Joseph, Dolores and Tag looked on from their seats. "Good girl."

"What's going on?" Joseph asked, standing and coming over to me. "Are you okay?"

Evie spoke up. "Keeta told me you'd been taken, along with Cliff. But that was about all she could tell us."

"Yeah, Cliff knew Toby was turning, so he asked me to try and talk him down." I laughed humorlessly. "You can see how well that turned out. He warped us both when we showed up, held us prisoner until his new friends showed up."

"Who took you, Callie? Where are you?"

"The Navy has us, at China Lake base. They're doing some kind of experiment on me, on all of us. There's a ton of people there, prisoners. And they blocked my powers."

"How did you get here, then?"

"I don't know. They had music playing in the lab, where they're injecting us with something, some kind of chemical experiment. I traveled on the song."

"I told you, you were a song walker." Ethan said softly, warmly, pride shining in his eyes.

"Yeah, well, I don't know if I'll be able to do it again. And I don't know what they're doing to me, or to Cliff. Please, you've got to come find us. I don't know how long we have."

"Have they threatened you?"

"Only a little. But I don't want to become like them. What if that's what they're doing? What if they're making me like them? Warping me?"

"Shh," Ethan tried to comfort me. "They won't. They can't. We're coming to get you. Okay? Just hold on."

"I am. I will. I-" A sharp pain exploded in my forearm, and I gasped, looking down. My arm looked fine, but the pain persisted, waning to a low, throbbing.

The room began to fade, along with the people, the lights, Keeta. A spiraling sensation took hold of me, and I spun into darkness, into light, into darkness, and then I felt heavy. Weighted.

Slowly, I opened my eyes, and found myself back in my body, back in the chair in the lab at China Lake. My vision was blurry, and I blinked.

"Welcome back, luv," the man who had winked at me before said, patting my arm with antiseptic where the IV drip had been inserted.

"What've you done to me?" I slurred.

"Nothing you'll notice. Not yet. Just laid a bit of prepwork for tomorrow's act."

"Whaddyou mean?"

"Don't worry, luv. Today we just took a bit of bloodwork to determine your powers, and gave you a cocktail that will make your body more receptive to some of our other modifications. You'll see, soon enough."

My brain wasn't working well, but I knew I didn't want to be modified, whatever that meant. I tried to break free, again, but had no better luck that I did the first time.

The man laughed and gave me a little wink, something I was really starting to hate.

He walked away and left me to stew, plotting all the ways I would love to mess him up.

I must have spent the better part of an hour going over ways to string him up, box him senseless, stake him over mounds of fire ants. You get the idea.

It passed the time.

I'd just about run out of inventive revenge scenarios when more guards came into the room, maybe ten of them, and began removing people from their chairs. Two by two, they dragged other patients away. Some people walked away on their own. Not prisoners, I guessed, but willing test subjects. Voluntary warpers, like Toby, or maybe fellow sailors who had signed up to become better soldiers.

The thought turned my stomach, and I looked away.

"Your turn, luv." Mr. Winkie had returned. He unstrapped me, and I rubbed feeling back into my wrists. I looked around, saw no one was watching us, and started to pull one hand back, ready to cold cock him.

"Nuh-uh. Not so fast." He laughed, backing up a step. "Sit still."

I froze, and his grin widened.

"Perfect. Now up you go, that's right. Stand up." I did as he instructed, unable to resist.

Dammit. Another bard, I thought. I was beginning to think it was my least favorite power.

"Good. Alright. Here we go." He linked an arm through mine. "Mind your manners. Can't hurt your doctor, now, can you? No," he cackled, "you can't! You have to treat him like your best friend. Don't you?"

I ground my teeth, refusing to give him the satisfaction of an answer or a plea. More than anything, I wanted to yank my arm out of his, but I couldn't. Arm in arm, we walked through the hall, the bard humming a happy tune, me, fuming. He'd pay for this. He would. At the moment, all my ire with the warpers, with Toby, with our US Navy, all of it focused in like a laser on this guy. If I could have burned him with my gaze, I would have.

Not for the first time in my life, I wished I had elemental powers. Real magic. But no. I had no magic, only my psychic gifts, and at the moment, they weren't working too well. I couldn't read him at all, so whatever edge the music in the lab had temporarily given me, I'd burnt out after that one trip to the Bronzehead.

The doctor walked me through a couple of security points before we came to the door I recognized as housing the hall of cells I'd come from. He chatted with the guards for a moment, all of them laughing at something I didn't understand, and then we walked towards my room.

"I still don't understand," I said lamely. "What do you people want with me?"

"Go ahead and play dumb, Calliope. I get it. You don't see things our way yet. But you will, trust me. And then? Then, we can talk."

"Do you at least have a name?" I asked. The better to hex you with, I thought silently.

"Xavier Oxley," he said, stopping in front of my door. "It's been a pleasure, really." His eyes roamed over my body, lingering too long in all the wrong places.

Again, I wanted to punch him, and I swore to myself that one day I would. Outwardly, I simply bared my teeth at him in a feral smile.

"Wonderful. Well, if you want to get me out of here, maybe we could go grab a bite to eat? Take in a movie?"

He laughed, a hard, brash sound.

"I like you, Calliope, I really do. Now, why don't you lean in here and give me a little something to remember you by." He pointed to his cheek and I found myself compelled to kiss the cold, smooth skin. Bile rose in the back of my throat and I swallowed.

"I will get you for this," I whispered, before rocking back on my heels.

"I'm sure you will try," he chuckled. "Now, in you go."

He swiped his key card and the bolt on the door clicked open.

"Stay out of trouble, and I'll see you again in the morning," he said as I stepped inside my room.

"I can't wait. Do I at least get fed while I'm here?"

"Ah, yes, of course. You slept most of the night away, and today. You missed breakfast. Dinner will be served in a couple of hours. In your room, of course."

"What a shame, I'll really miss your face. Not."

He laughed. "You really are divine, luv. Till tomorrow then."

He slammed the door on me, and I swear I could hear him humming as he walked away, the arrogant bastard.

Chapter 30

Back in my room, free of the numbing stricture of Oxley's control, I shook out my arms. Trying to dislodge the shivers that ran through me, the disgust his warping cast over my skin. I was going to need a shower.

Looking around, I noticed that someone had come in and cleaned. A fresh change of clothes lay folded on the bed, which had been stripped down so that now there remained only a fleece blanket and a bottom sheet.

The shelter I had erected around the shower and toilet had been removed, taken away, and the theft made my heart hurt. Still, I refused to normalize my conditions. I would persist in my resistance.

I picked up the clean clothes, then dragged the blanket off the bed and gathered it in my arms, crossing the room to make another fort of privacy. Not knowing if someone would be sent to force me to take it down, or if I would be allowed this gesture of decency, I quickly showered and peed. I pulled on the serviceable underwear and sports bra, the basic cotton drawstring pants they had left me, worn soft with repeated washings and wearings by who knew how many other prisoners. I put the sweatshirt aside on the desk, opting only for the tank top they'd given me. I made sure my necklace was still hidden, nestled inside my bra where no one could see it.

I was sitting on the bed, running my fingers through my hair and really wishing they had given me a brush or a hair dryer when I heard the tell-tale clunk of my door lock releasing and the door opened. Two guards entered the room, one with a gun trained on me, the other carrying a tray of food and drink to the table.

"Such service," I drawled. "Thanks, boys."

They ignored me, of course. A girl could start to think she'd lost her charm pretty quickly in a place like this.

They were already retreating from the room, refusing to even make eye contact with me. I wondered, were they warpers, too, or simple enlisted? How much did they know about what was going on here?

I sighed. Not that they would ever answer any of my questions, anyway. They were just leaving when I called, "Feel free to let the door hit you on the way out!"

The rear guard, the one with the gun, stumbled and bumped into the door, making me giggle. The other soldier glared at me, and slammed the door shut on my laughter.

Jeez, I thought. It wasn't my fault his friend couldn't walk.

I walked over to the desk and contemplated the food. Was it medicated? I thought about the shots and procedures they'd already done on my body without my permission. The warpers weren't shy about using their powers, or their drugs on people. Why hide something in food, when they had no qualms about doing it in the open?

Having rationalized feeding my hunger, I sat down at the desk and dug in. The food wasn't great – your typical military high carb, low nutrient fare – but it was edible and I didn't detect any strange tastes or odors. I washed the salty pasta and bread down with the water they'd given me, then went to the sink for a refill and drank that, too, suddenly realizing how thirsty I was.

I took a third glass back with me to the bed, and sat down in a lotus position, leaning against the wall. I held the cup in my hands, gazing into the water, looking for inner peace. I tried to send out threads of consciousness into the building, to see if I could pick up anything in the other rooms, connect with anyone else telepathically, but all I got was radio silence.

Whatever they'd done to my abilities, they still seemed to be on the fritz.

The lights dimmed, and I guessed this must be some sort of a warning for lights out. Quickly, I swiped the sweatshirt off the desk, pulled it over my head, and lay down on the bed. I didn't know if the room would be plunged into complete darkness, or what. I shouldn't have worried. The lights stayed dim for a while, probably ten minutes, and then they faded out, leaving me in the dark. Once they'd been off for a few minutes, my eyes acclimated to the low light, and I realized that a sliver of white was shining along the bottom of the door, the bright lights of the hallway leaking into the room. It was just enough illumination to find the toilet in the middle of the night if I wanted to.

Feeling more secure, like a child with a nightlight, I relaxed. Breathed in. Breathed out. All I had to do now was wait. I knew my friends wouldn't leave us here long. They would find a way to get us out. I just had to believe that, and do my best to find out as much as I could in the meantime. The best way to do that was probably to cooperate. Pretend I wanted to be a warper. However, I was reluctant to do anything that might make them move up the timetable for my conversion. It terrified me, not knowing which needle, medicine or experiment might be the last one needed to corrupt my mind and my power.

I thought of my other friends, Nick and Jax, and wondered how mad they were at me, whether they were looking for me. I'd missed a wedding. I never missed a gig. And I always called if I had to beg off rehearsal. It was rule number one when you were in a band. You always showed up. You never missed a show.

If I knew Nick, he'd have shown up at the apartment, and probably called Kate. So that was another person who was probably worrying about my whereabouts. I'd have a lot of explaining to do once I got out of here. I actually welcomed the thought, looking forward to coming clean with my friends and family. At least, telling them as much as I could. I would have to be careful. I didn't want to put them in danger. If the warpers knew who I was, would they come after my people?

Maybe everyone would be better off if I just disappeared after this, went east with Joseph. I thought about it, and felt sick. No. What I wanted most of all was to be free again. Being a prisoner did not sit well with me. I wanted to play my drums, live my life. No one had ever dictated the path of my life to me. I wasn't going to allow that to change now.

But first, I had to get out. I thought about how nice it would be to breathe fresh air again. To see the sun.

At that thought, the ring against my chest seemed to warm, and I reached into my shirt, holding it carefully in my hand, shielding it from view. I didn't know if the cameras worked on low-UV settings, but I wasn't going to take any chances.

The ring had definitely warmed. No. Not the ring.

The stone.

I curled up on my side and brought my hands to my face. Peeked within.

It was like looking into a tiny nebula, a galaxy in my hands. The opalescent flecks and spots that normally shimmered in the light now gleamed brightly, stars in a stone. It was beautiful.

And new.

I'd never seen the stone do that before. I thought about its supposed connection to the sun, the way it was supposed to amplify powers for sun children. There had been an eclipse that day. Had that triggered some sort of a response in the stone?

As if in reply, the stone brightened, grew warmer.

Why now, I wondered. I'd seen other solar eclipses. Had I been that oblivious, that I hadn't noticed the stone reacting? Or had something else changed?

I thought about the soldier, tripping on his way out. The way I had *told* him to let the door hit him on the way out.

Could I have-?

But no. It had to be a coincidence. I'd been told in no uncertain terms that no one ever had more than two powers. Why should I be the one to break that rule?

But what if the stone made it possible? What if-?

Or maybe it was something to do with the drugs they'd been giving me?

The idea that somehow the warpers had already succeeded in making me like them made my lips pucker. I would not be like them. I wouldn't. It had to be the stone.

Or maybe I was just imagining things. Probably, that soldier had just tripped all on his own. Surely it had nothing to do with me.

After the terrible things I had seen warpers do, the last thing I wanted was the power to tell people what to do. No. Even if I had the power, I wasn't sure I'd be able to bring myself to use it. Refusing to think about it anymore, I tucked the piece of stone back inside my shirt, and let myself drift off to sleep.

Chapter 31

The lights came on, dim at first, coaxing me into wakefulness, and then brighter, making sleep an impossible notion. Assuming that the breakfast brigade would be coming through soon, I quickly used the toilet and brushed my teeth. The night before, I had hand-washed my faded Hammerbox t-shirt and underthings when I showered, so I pulled them on, along with my soft brown leather pants.

Borrowed clothes were fine for sleeping in, but if I was going to stand up to Oxley again today, I knew I'd feel stronger in my own clothes.

I had just finished when the door clicked open and a different set of guards strolled in with my tray of food. I really loved how they always bothered to knock before entering. Though I supposed there wasn't much point when they could already watch whatever I was doing on camera.

Gross.

I remembered that I still needed to test my possible solar ability. I'd thought about how to do it, since if I did have new powers, I didn't actually want to alert the warpers to it.

As the first soldier turned with the empty dinner tray, I said casually, "Hop to it! Don't want to be late for your other duties."

He looked at me strangely, but added a little bounce to his step. Encouraged, I looked at the other soldier, standing by the door. As they passed through, I gave the same command as the night before.

"Do *let the door hit you* on the way out!"

The second soldier careened into the first, and sent them both crashing into the door. A burst of laughter escaped from me, and I quickly covered it with a cough.

"Wow, are you guys okay?" I asked with fake concern. They looked at me, confused, and gave me some sheepish smiles before leaving.

As far as anyone knew here, I was just a traveler and a reader. For now, my secret was still safe.

But I knew what I needed to know.

Somehow, a third power had activated in me last night. Like my mother's father, Ozan Fanai, I was a speaker.

All that was left to be seen was how strong my voice could be.

I sat down at the table and fueled up with a surprisingly good breakfast of scrambled eggs, English muffins, and sausages. Orange juice and creamed coffee on the side. While I ate, I ran through some ideas of how I could get off-base. The more people I had to mind control, the more chances there would be for my new power to fail. I had no I idea what the limits I had, or if this was even a

227

permanent ability. If I'd gain the bard power through something they had done to me when I was passed out, who knew how long it would last. I needed to get out, and I needed to do it quickly and cleanly. In order to find Cliff and get through all the access points, I would need the help of someone with special clearance, which brought me back to Oxley.

I would only have one shot at this. If I couldn't warp Oxley with my voice, then he would know what I was, and I was sure that they would take extra precautions to block my abilities.

I was still confused about how I had even been able to use them so far. All I could think was that something about the stone acted as an amplifier, negating the effects of whatever chemicals they had pumped me with.

I had just committed a loose plan of escape to mind when the door clicked open behind me. I turned, and was greeted by the now welcome sight of Oxley leaning against the doorframe.

"Ready to face the day?"

I stood and smiled warmly, surprising him, and walked past him into the hall. A quick glance around confirmed what I'd suspected. Oxley was too confident. He'd come without an escort, which meant I had one less person to bend to my will.

"Had a change of heart, have you, luv?" he asked, leering at me.

"Oh, yes. You know," I said, trailing a finger down his chest and staring him in the eyes, "I would love it if you would just *call me Callie*. Can you do that?"

"Of course, luv. I mean Callie." He frowned, as if the words felt wrong in his mouth.

"Perfect." I laid a finger on his lips. "Now, I want you to listen carefully, and not interrupt." I peered at him closely to see if my suggestions were taking. His jaw worked soundlessly, and then he closed it, eyes narrowing. "Great. You are going to take me to my friend Cliff, and then you are going to help us get off this base. You will do nothing to alert anyone or anything to the fact that we are escaping at any time. Understand?"

"Yes," he said in a strangled voice.

"Awesomesauce. Now how about you get me out of here. Where are they keeping Cliff?"

"He's down the hall, third door on the right." He coughed, as if trying to clear the words he'd said from his throat.

"Perfect, take me there and open his door."

I marched him down the hall, being careful to link arms as we had last night in case we were being watched. I watched him slide the card through the sensor and heard the click of the bolt sliding open. For the first time, it sounded like freedom. Oxley opened the door and I stood back, careful to stand as if I was the one being controlled. Cliff was lying on the bed, an arm over his eyes, still wearing his clothes from yesterday.

"You want me, you're going to have to come and get me," he muttered.

"Done," I said with a smile.

He dropped his arm and peered at me, squinting in the bright light.

"Callie? What's going on?"

"You're being jailbroke, that's what's going on. Now get your butt out here, you goon." He hopped off the bed, a smile on his face, while Oxley glared at us both. Uh-oh.

"Cliff, don't act so happy, okay? Pretend you're still a prisoner. And you, Oxley, put that sick smile of yours back on your face and try to look like you're still in charge. You *want* to help us, okay?"

Cliff slowed down, looking at the two of us in confusion.

"What's happening, Callie?" A look of fear came over his face. "How are you doing this? Are you with them now?"

"No! Of course not," I said, lowering my voice to whisper to Cliff so Oxley wouldn't hear. "Somehow, last night's solar eclipse activated the power of the speaker in me. My mother's dad could do it, but we thought I wouldn't ever be able to since I already had two powers, but lucky you, and lucky me, because here we are."

"But how isn't it blocked?"

"I don't know. Some of my other powers are still kind of working, too. Not reliably, but... Maybe since this one is new? Or it's something to do with something my father gave me," I said enigmatically, not wanting to spill the beans about my necklace in front of Oxley. "Listen, we can talk all about it later, okay? We need to get the hell out of here."

"Sounds good to me. What about Toby?"

"What about Toby?" I scoffed. "He's chosen his side. He can rot here, for all I care."

"Okay," Cliff said reluctantly. "I guess you're right. I don't know why I always stick up for that guy, anyway."

"You're a people pleaser. That's okay. But you need to stand up for yourself, too, you know?"

"Yeah, I know," he sighed.

"Alright, enough small talk, let's get out of here. Oxley? If you'll lead the way out of the building in the most inconspicuous way possible?" I walked back to Oxley and slid my arm through his, giving it a small squeeze. "You know, I think I'm starting to like this guy after all," I laughed, looking back at Cliff. "Remember to look like Oxley's making you do this, okay? No smiling, just follow along with your eyes down and look pissed."

"I can do that, I've had some practice lately." He grinned and then wiped the smile off his face, doing as I told him, looking exceedingly underwhelmed with his current situation.

"Tell me about it," I agreed. And then I faced forward and pretended to look angry as Oxley led us through the security checkpoint at the end of the hall. These guards acted as uninterested as all the others I'd seen. "Don't ask, don't tell" was clearly a mandate here.

When we had rounded another corner, Cliff spoke up.

"Callie, do you know what they're doing here? Yesterday they had me doing cardio for over an hour. What's the story with this guy?"

"This guy," I said, "is some kind of doctor. Yesterday he gave me some drugs that knocked me out. I still don't know what for. How about you enlighten us, Oxley?"

He growled at me, but had to comply. "Our work here is to advance the human race. Take the best of what you have to offer, enhance it, distill it, and feed it back to our own people to make us like you, but stronger. Right now, your kind is a threat to humanity. People worry about corruption in politics, but they have no idea. All it takes is just one of you to pull the strings. Did you know there is a man in the Middle East who puppets ten countries?"

"I believe I've heard something about that, yes." I murmured. Apparently, Ozan had been busy, even without the benefit of my ring. "But you have to know that isn't the norm. The United States government has been working with starseeds for generations. Since the beginning. We've always worked together, keeping warpers from taking over. Now, you're working with them?"

"With them? Honey, I am them. I'm not just in this for the science. The power I've gained makes everything worth it. If someone's going to be controlling the masses, it better be me."

"I guess today's really not your day then. Is there any way to reverse the process you're working on? How does it all work? Tell me."

He gritted his teeth, but the words came out anyway. "We've been testing your kind for almost a decade. We decoded the DNA differences between natural-born 'starseeds' and the rest of us. Turns out, we're not so different."

"I could have told you that."

"You have more natural crystallization in your bone structure, yet your pineal gland is more resistant to calcification."

"So?" asked Cliff.

"So, you are better at harnessing the energy around you, and within you. You guys are like lightning rods. Did you know that everyone produces measurable units of light? No? Well, starseeds produce up to five times as much. The innate abilities that all humans have, the light, the extra electrical impulses, everything gets heightened when you throw your DNA into the mix. All we have to do is mix up a little cocktail, made from your blood, and let nature take its course."

"And can it be reversed?" I demanded.

Oxley's face darkened with anger. "For now, yes. I've been working on a permanent solution, but we still need to find something to stabilize the reaction. For some reason, humans burn through the energy too quickly. We are stronger when we get amped up, but it doesn't last."

"What do you mean?"

He sighed, and I could actually feel the last of his mental resistance fading away. "We have to get regular infusions of DNA every five to seven days, depending on our individual metabolism and hormone cycle."

"Good to know. Thanks for being so helpful. There's something I don't understand, still. Why did you guys go after Kipner?"

"Like you said. You guys have been working with our government since before there even was a United States of America. Kipner was part of the old guard. There's a new game in town. Sometimes, change is rough," Oxley said, shrugging. "Disagreements occurred. Kipner found out what we were doing, called Kroksky and threatened to go to Nialls, shut us down. He didn't see the beauty of our plan."

"So Kroksky had Kipner taken out?" I asked.

"Oh no," he laughed. "Kroksky doesn't have that kind of power. Admiral Sherwood gave that order. Apparently, he's had it in for Kipner for a while, some kind of payback for embarrassing him at the White House years back."

"Great," I muttered. And now we were escaping. Making ourselves targets of some madman's ire. Wonderful.

"Well, this is it," he said, stopping at a door.

"This is what?" I asked.

"The door to freedom. You walk out here, you're as good as free."

"I don't think so. You're going to make sure we get all the way off-base safely, personally."

"I thought you might say that. Okay. Fine, let's go."

He opened the door, leading us out into a small garden area. A couple other scientists were standing around, smoking. Oxley nodded at them and walked us by without stopping to say hello.

"Won't they think that was odd?"

"No. I'm not much for socializing."

"No, I mean us, walking with you."

"Oh, that. No, I come outside with test subjects all the time."

He sounded oddly wistful, I wondered what reason he could have for bringing subjects outside the lab. Away from the cameras. Then, I remembered the kiss he'd made me give him, and decided I didn't really want to know.

We walked around the building, making our way towards a parking lot. I didn't ask Oxley any more questions, using the silence to think. Had I covered all the angles? Could he be tricking us, even now? I really hoped not, since the idea of being at his beck and call ever again pretty much made want to vomit.

We had almost made it to the lot, when I recognized the no-nonsense heels of Lieutenant Kroksky clicking across the pavement towards us.

"Oxley," she smirked. "I see you're taking some new recruits under your wing."

"Oh, yes," I gushed, not giving him a chance to answer. "Oxley is sooo wonderful, dontcha think?" I ran my hands through his hair and hung on his shoulder. I pretended to nuzzle his ear, whispering instead, "you will not betray us.

You will get us off this base with your complete protection."

"Indeed. I had no idea you swung both ways, Ox. Intriguing." Kroksky looked us over, and for a moment I feared she might invite herself along for the ride.

Cliff blushed at my side and I gripped his hand. "Oh, no, Oxie brought this one for me. I told him I've always had this certain fantasy, you know?" I winked at her and somehow managed to keep a straight face.

"Right, baby?" I breathed in his ear. "Tell her."

"Oh, uh, yeah." Oxley coughed. "Yes. You know I aim to please."

I giggled. "Please don't tell anyone, Lieutenant. I'd hate for anyone to think Oxie is giving me special treatment. Maybe you could just *forget you even ever saw us*?"

"Of course," she said, a confused look coming over her face. "I can do that."

"Great, great." I nodded. "It'll be like *you never met us at all*. Bye!" I gave her my best Valley Girl wave and dragged Oxley and Cliff away.

"Well played," Oxley muttered.

"Oh yes." I laughed. "I aim to please."

Chapter 32

"Where to, Master?" Oxley inquired in a voice laced with sarcasm. We'd just climbed into his Porsche Panamera, so new you could still smell the leather conditioner.

"Well, gee, when you put it so nicely... How about you take us to the nearest truck stop?"

"Fine. Don't think you can escape us so easily, though. We'll have people on your trail within the hour." He put the car in gear and backed slowly out of the parking spot.

"Mmm. You see, I've been thinking about that," Cliff said, leaning forward from his spot in the back. "Why not have Huxley here-"

"Oxley," the doctor growled.

"Huxley," Cliff repeated, "can drop us off, then go back and destroy every record he can find of us ever being there. While he's at it, he can destroy all the research in the labs, too."

"Ohhh, Cliff, I love the way you think!" I cheered. "Yes, that's perfect."

"Now, wait a minute! That research represents years of hard work. We've-"

"Broken the laws of nature," I finished drily for him. "Created super soldiers without morals. Hurt countless people, and violated the rights of citizens? Yeah, we know how hard you've worked. And for nothing, right?"

I ran my hand along the door, caressing the natural wood grain interior as we drove through the base at a snail's pace.

"No, I think we all know what your motives are. Greed and power. Apparently, some lust, too. Well, I think Cliff has had a brilliant idea. After you leave us, you *will* destroy our files, and then you will destroy all the work at the lab. Your research files, the DNA samples, the formulas you are using to augment people, the power blocker, destroy everything."

"I'll be fired. Or worse." His voice shook with fear.

"Aw. That's really terrible. How about this... Do it anyway. Make it look like an accident if you can. Erase the files, start a fire in the lab, whatever. I don't care how you do it. But you *will* do whatever needs to be done."

"Callie," Cliff said, sounding worried. "Are you sure?"

"Yes. You heard what he does with the patients here. Whatever happens to him, he deserves it, trust me. And you know it, too, don't you, Oxie baby?"

Oxley swallowed.

"Great. Now-"

"Callie, look!"

"What?" I looked ahead and saw a shining gold Oldsmobile 442 rolling towards us down the road. "Is that-?"

"Who else drives a car like that?" Cliff answered, sounding giddy.

"Oxley, stop the car!" He did as I ordered and pulled over. Cliff jumped out on his side and flagged down the Olds. I reached for the door handle and then paused. "We're going to leave now. You will return to the building we just left, delete all our files and your research, everything you have access to, and then you will destroy the labs and the formulas your people have been working on. You're going to do all this, but you are going to forget you ever met me or Cliff. You'll never remember doing any of these things I've just told you to do, and you will deny doing them for as long as you live. Good luck!"

I jumped out of the car and ran to Cliff, who was already opening the back door of the Olds and climbing in. Three pairs of eyes watched us incredulously as we scooted across the leather interior, shouting, "Go! Go! Go!" Once we were moving again, Cliff and I collapsed against each other laughing.

Dolores was the first one to recover, pushing Cliff off her shoulder.

"I thought you guys needed rescuing? Who was that guy in the Porsche?"

Even as we pulled a U-turn, Oxley was turning, too. I smiled, knowing things had turned out better than I could have hoped for.

"It's all Callie, man. She saved both of us," Cliff said, trying to regain his breath.

Tag turned around in his seat, looking at us, and Ethan glanced in the rearview mirror.

"How so?" Tag asked.

"Callie?" Cliff asked, and I knew he was giving me a chance to keep my new powers to myself. I squeezed his hand gratefully, and started to explain. "Last night, when I traveled to Ethan, that was a fluke, right? They gave us something so our powers wouldn't work, you know? I haven't been able to travel at all other than that, or do any reading. I still can't. But something else happened when I traveled – I got a new power during the solar eclipse."

"What?" Ethan asked, swerving just a little as his eyes flicked to mine in the mirror again.

"Isn't it rad?" Cliff crowed. "Callie's got bard powers! And she's wicked powerful, too. Outspoke that prick doctor back there."

"Back up," Tag said, holding up his hand. "Are you saying a new power activated, and it's working even though your other powers aren't?"

"Yeah." I couldn't help beaming at him. I was pretty happy about how things had worked out, not being experimented on and all.

"But that's not possible. Ethan, I thought you said she's a reader, too?"

"She is," Ethan said at the same time I answered, "I am."

"But-"

"Look, Tag, pipe down, okay?" Ethan snapped. "We still have to get off base. Dolores, you're up."

We pulled up to the guard shack and Ethan rolled down his window.

"Finished already, Major?" a young seaman smiled down at Ethan.

"Yes," Dolores said, leaning over Ethan's shoulder. "We had a wonderful tour, thank you for allowing the five of us to visit your fine facility. It's so important for the army and navy to work together, don't you think?"

"The five of-? Oh, yes, of course. I do."

"Wonderful. Now, remember, we're planning a big surprise for the Admiral next month, so just forget you even saw us, okay?"

"Will do," the boy said, saluting, a glassy look coming over his eyes.

"Perfect. Take care, now, you hear? Maybe it's time you asked for a transfer to a new division." Dolores smiled and blew him a kiss as he motioned for his friend inside to open the gate, and Ethan drove on through.

I exhaled, and took an equally deep breath in. I'd been holding my breath, without even realizing it, and the fresh influx of air was a balm to my nerves. Within minutes, we'd hopped onto 395 and were racing south towards Los Angeles.

Cliff told everyone what I had said to Oxley, how he was supposed to be destroying the records at the lab, and Ethan visibly relaxed behind the wheel. Still, he wanted to get us back to Joshua Tree right away for some testing.

"Ugh," I groaned. "No more tests. Like, ever."

"Ethan's right, honey," Dolores said, leaning past Cliff. "We need to see if we can analyze what they gave you guys, find out how they blocked your powers. It's the only chance we have of coming up with something to counteract it."

"Plus, we need to find out how long it takes to break down, make sure it gets out of your system completely. I promise, just a few blood samples and you're done, okay?" Ethan pleaded. "We need to know what we're up against before we try to break anyone else out of the program."

"I'm in," Cliff said. "Anything to make sure no one else ever feels this way."

"Fine," I huffed. "Joshua Tree it is. Maybe the tests will show how I got this third power, too."

"What do you mean?" Cliff asked.

"Well, I dunno. I mean, was it the meds I was on? Do they open people up more to developing their gifts? Or was it something else?" I didn't mention the necklace, specifically, but I couldn't help holding it in my hand as I talked, like a ward against evil.

"Good point," Tag said pragmatically. "Besides, your homes might be compromised. We need to arrange sweeps for any locations you are known to frequent."

"But, after today no one who matters will remember we were even at China Lake," I protested, feeling sick at the thought that even casual acquaintances of mine might be in danger.

"Toby will," Cliff said, looking out the window with a frown.

"Right. Good old Toby."

"Look, let's just focus on one thing at a time, okay? Tag, text Evie and have her meet us at HQ with Keeta."

"Oh my God, my van!" I hadn't thought about it at all since we'd been taken. But it had been parked for two nights now in front of Toby's house. What if someone had had it towed? I'd left everything in the car with Keeta – my phone, my purse, my keys. I moaned. The band's gear.

Oh no. They really were going to kill me. As if missing the wedding gig wasn't bad enough.

"Crap, that's right. Do you think it's still there?" Cliff's question echoed my own thoughts.

"I don't know," I groaned. "I hope so."

"We'll find it, Callie, don't worry. It's just a van. Everything that matters, is right here. You guys are safe. That's all that matters."

Ethan's eyes met mine in the mirror as he tried to reassure me.

"I know, I know. It's just. The band gear, my purse... Everything was in there. I even left the windows open, that's how Keeta was able to get out."

"It's going to be okay," he repeated, and for the first time in days, I heard him, not just with my ears, but in my head. *I'm not going to let anything happen to you. Trust me. We've got this,* his voice whispered in my brain. *I've got you.*

"Okay," I whispered back, out loud, and reached for a smile. "Okay."

Chapter 33

"I still don't see why we can't go back and save the other prisoners at China Lake," Cliff said stubbornly, clenching one hand on his leg.

He was sitting in a chair that I had vacated only minutes before, getting blood drawn for the lab to analyze. Hopefully, they would be able to figure out what the Navy had been using to dampen our powers. I knew the effects of the injections were already starting to wear off, but it was worth a try.

I nodded, completely in agreement with Cliff. "Right. Tell me again how we're doing the right thing?"

I stared Nialls MacGloughlin in the eye from my side of the round table. Never in my life would I have imagined that I would have cause to meet the head of Homeland Security, much less be confronting him. But here I was. Practically threatening mutiny to one of the President of the United States top advisors.

My phone pinged, and I ignored it. By the time we had gotten back to headquarters, someone had already retrieved my van and driven it back. My purse had been waiting for me here, along with Henry, Joseph and Nialls. Amazingly, everything was still inside. Toby's parents lived in a ridiculously safe neighborhood. Or maybe most thieves figured a beat-to-hell van like mine couldn't possibly have anything inside worth stealing.

Nialls sighed, looking at Henry for support. Henry just shrugged and put his hands up, leaving any explanations solely up to Nialls. Joseph sat with his arms folded, no emotion showing on his face. Apparently, he wasn't taking sides at the moment.

"Look. Right now, according to what you both have told us, the people at China Lake have no idea they have been compromised. My own intel tells me that a large fire was just put out in at the lab, but that no one was hurt and that it's been deemed a chemical accident. No foul play is suspected. Assuming your inside man did everything he was told, the computer records will have been cleared as well. The only person likely to notice or care that you are missing is this man, Toby Fickman, and he just landed at Dulles Airport in Washington, DC. With any luck, he has moved on to bigger and better pastures-"

"Yeah, where he can frolic with other warpers," Cliff mumbled.

"-and he has more important things to think about than the two of you," Nialls finished, ignoring Cliff.

"So? That doesn't change anything. We've only delayed the inevitable. The warpers are still holding people against their will."

"Yes. And we will save them soon. I promise. But right now we have the element of surprise on our side. If we break everyone out right now, we'll tip our hand."

"Let's just say we agree with you," Ethan said, leaning forward and putting his hand on my thigh under the table to cut off any pending disagreement. "What is the plan moving forward?"

I held my breath, and not just because I was waiting for Nialls' answer. Ethan's hand on my leg was red-hot, reminding me that my feelings toward him weren't entirely platonic. Flames rose through my body, licking at my skin, and I made a conscious effort to play Green Day as loud as possible to drown out any other thoughts I might be having.

Joseph cleared his throat. I realized that Nialls was talking, and tried desperately to listen, leaning back in my chair and pretending to feel much more relaxed than I was. Seeing my reaction, Ethan squeezed my thigh and removed his hand, giving his full attention to Nialls.

"-clear that there is a greater conspiracy going on. We don't know if it's confined to a small group within the Navy, or if it goes deeper. I wish that Kipner hadn't taken matters into his own hands, maybe he'd still be here today. But the fact that Sherwood had him taken out before he could report to me tells me that for the moment, at least, the other side is feeling pretty secure. Which means they're more likely to make mistakes."

"So we just sit back and wait for them to mess up?" I scoffed.

"No, of course not. I have everyone and everything connected to Admiral Sherwood and China Lake under surveillance, as of today. We're going to find out who else is connected to these warpers, and who's really pulling the strings."

"You don't think it's Sherwood?" Cliff asked.

"It's possible. But I've known Rodney a long time, and I don't think he would have come to this on his own. Experimenting on unwilling starseeds, American civilians? No. It's just not like him. I think someone got to him. Changed him, maybe even warped him. We need to find out who."

"And what about Toby?" Cliff asked. I knew he still hoped for Toby's redemption, why, I wasn't sure. I guess he was just a better person than me, or more of an optimist. As far as I was concerned, Toby was a lost cause.

"He's being tailed, too. Right now he's traveling with three men." He flipped his phone around, showing me a grainy surveillance image. Even with the blurriness, I could tell who they were.

"Those are the guys who kidnapped us, the same ones who killed Kipner!"

"I suspected as much. We've identified them all as former Navy Seals. Given the natural and enhanced abilities of these men, we are keeping a close watch on their movements, as well."

"I hope you've got multiple eyes on them. Four people, it's easy to lose one in a crowd," Tag said in a low voice.

"Trust me, my people know how to do their jobs."

"Well, what about us? I can't just sit around doing nothing while people are being hurt. What can we do?" I asked.

"Besides sit tight? There is one thing. Just before you arrived, I received a message from my IT specialist back in Washington. She traced the paper trail for the research at China Lake, but it came to a dead end. Sherwood has used several legal loopholes to cover the project from oversight."

"So?" asked Cliff.

"So," Nialls said, looking at me, "the lead attorney on the matter is Doug Rice."

The world fell away, and I stared back into his eyes. Without even meaning to, I read Niall's mind perfectly clearly. I stood up, angrily pushing my chair back and slamming my hands on the table.

"No. I won't do it."

"What's her problem?" Tag asked, looking at me.

"Rice is Callie's foster brother," Henry said quietly.

Tag whistled.

"Look, Ms. Winters," Nialls went on, ignoring the others. "You don't have to do anything extreme. If you don't want to gather intel for us, then just bring him in. In my experience, a connection like yours will have more weight than my own as Secretary. He'll have been told that what he is doing is for the good of the country. It's up to you to make him see that it isn't. That's all."

"You won't hurt him?"

"Why would we? We just need to know what he knows. I don't really care how it's done, so long as you get results."

"But, won't we be putting him in danger? Compromising him? If Kroksky got her hands on him-"

"We won't let that happen." Ethan looked up at me, the promise in his eyes.

"Funny. I think I've heard that before," I said sourly, and he winced. Right after I said it, I wished I could take the words back. It wasn't his fault Cliff and I had been taken.

I opened my mouth to apologize, and then shut it. Now wasn't the time.

"This is very simple, Ms. Winters. Either you bring him in, or we do. You have forty-eight hours. Dismissed."

Nialls shut his ledger and stood, everyone else following suit.

"But what am I supposed to tell him?" I asked, not ready to give in yet.

"The truth, Ms. Winters," Nialls answered, his hand on the door. "I suggest you start with that, and hope he follows your lead."

He left the room, Henry on his heels.

Joseph walked around the table. "Ethan, Tag? I want one of you with Callie at all times. I'm going to call some of my friends in Virginia, see what they've heard on their end."

"Really, you, too? You think I need protecting from my own brother?" I ignored Tag as he snorted and walked out.

"I hope not," Joseph looked at me with a kind smile and pity in his eyes. "Hopefully your brother is not as connected to the warpers as Nialls believes. But if he is..."

I straightened defiantly. "He isn't."

"I hope you are right. I'm just glad you are safe now." My grandfather drew me into a quick hug and then left the room.

I sank back into my chair with a groan, burying my head in my hands.

"Dammit, Doug. What have you gotten yourself into?" I whispered. A hand landed on my knee and I jumped, opening my eyes.

"Sorry, didn't mean to scare you." Ethan's dark eyes roamed my face, taking in every detail.

"No, I'm sorry. I thought everyone had left."

"It's okay. You have a right to be upset," he shrugged. "I can't imagine how it must feel, to have to come out to your family this way. Not growing up knowing who and what you are, that's bad enough, but having to worry about your brother on top of it... Are you two close?"

"I thought we were. Now? I wonder. We've always gotten along, but Doug isn't exactly the warm and fuzzy type."

"Ah. I know how that can be." I knew he must be thinking of his own brother, the one that had joined the warpers. At least I had the luxury, for the moment, of not having to believe Doug knew who he was really working with.

I moaned in frustration. "And the band. I was going to come clean with them before, and I didn't. Now I've missed a gig. I didn't want to bring them into all this, but I don't think I have a choice, look." I held up my phone, showing him the unanswered texts. Nick, Kate, Jax, even Mel. Everyone had been texting me. "What am I supposed to tell them?"

"I don't know. It's your call. I know you thought you could keep this part of your life separate from the rest, but maybe that's not the best thing. Maybe you need to come clean. I'm starting to think maybe we all do."

"What do you mean?"

"Maybe the warpers wouldn't have been able to gain traction if there wasn't so much fear and mystery around us. If people knew about us, maybe they'd be better protected."

"You think? I don't know. Like you told me before, people are scared of what they don't understand. What if they wanted to study us? Segregate us?"

"What if they did? Maybe they'd be right. More and more starseeds seem to be awakening with every eclipse. Maybe the warpers don't have it completely wrong. Maybe it's time to find a way to share what we have with everyone. Awaken all of humanity's latent powers."

"Maybe. Or maybe that would start another war of the worlds."

He laughed. "You're probably right. I just...Sometimes I get so tired of fighting. I'd like to see a world where everyone was safe. Where you are safe."

His hand still on my leg, he swung my chair around to face his, bringing us knee to knee.

"Ethan, I-"

"I mean it, Callie. When you and Cliff were gone, it was all I could think of."

"That's funny," I tried to joke, "not being turned was all I could think of."

"Don't joke, Callie. I'm serious. When you projected to the Bronzehead, I don't think I've ever been so relieved. Or so frustrated. If I could have, I would have teleported you out of there right then."

"You and me both," I smiled, and his gaze fell on my lips. "Ethan-"

"I know what you're going to say. Don't."

I said it anyway.

"It's not the right time." I reached up to put a hand on his shoulder, to hold him off, but somehow my hand ended up fisting around his shirt, bringing him closer instead.

"Screw time," he said, and brought his lips to mine, his mouth moving firmly against my own. It felt so right, so good. Passion bloomed within me, and I had an insane urge to lay him out on the table right there, right then, and have my way with him.

"Oh God," I breathed, tearing myself away from him. "We can't."

"Why not?" he asked, a gleam in his eye. He telegraphed an image to me, exactly what I had been imagining a moment before, and I flushed.

"You saw that?"

"Mmhmm." He pulled me close and nuzzled my ear. "I saw everything."

I moaned, half with passion, half with frustration. This time, I did push him away.

"We're supposed to just be friends."

"Says who?" he grinned.

"Says me. I'm not ready for this. It's too much. Everything's happening too fast."

He leaned back, appraising me with an easy, confident smile.

"Okay. So we'll take it slow."

Suddenly an image appeared in my head, unbidden, of what a slow night with Ethan would be like.

"Slower than that," I laughed, swatting him to hide my interest.

"Fine." He held up his hands in surrender and stood, eyes flicking to the clock on the wall. "I'm going to go work off some of this sudden excess energy I've got. How about you text your people, set up some times to talk, and let me know when you are ready to go?"

"To go?" I eyed him warily.

"Yeah. To go. To LA, to bed, wherever, whenever." He shrugged and leaned down, his next words whispered and sending shivers down my spine. "It's your call, Callie."

Chapter 34

I know. I know. I said I'd take it slow. But damn, how was I supposed to resist that?

Moments after Ethan whispered in my ear, I was yanking him by his hand out the door, down the halls, back to my room.

So much for texting my family. Some things just had to wait.

Apparently, my needs weren't one of them.

I was lying on the bed in a post-coital daze a half hour later when my phone pinged, again. I groaned, and Keeta jumped up from the floor where I'd ordered her earlier, now sniffing my face excitedly. I patted her and she leaped up onto the bed, making herself comfortable by squeezing in between Ethan's warm body and my own.

He scooted over to make room, leaning up on one arm while he petted the dog on her belly. A ray of light reflected gold and copper off his hair from the afternoon sun in the western sky.

"I think someone's jealous," he grinned. Keeta thumped her tail.

"I think you're right." I leaned over and gave her a kiss on her cold, wet nose, and then pulled Ethan closer for one on the lips.

Again, my phone pinged, and then it rang. I sighed, sitting up. "I should have called them before. Crap. It's Kate."

I answered the phone. "Hi, Kate."

"Callie? Oh, Callie! Where have you been? Nick called looking for you yesterday morning, he said you left rehearsal with some guy, and then you never showed up for the Cho wedding? What's going on? Are you okay? Are you hurt? Do you need me to come get you?"

"Whoa, slow down, Kate, breathe! I'm fine, I swear. I just...um, well, look something did happen, but nothing like you're thinking, I promise. I can explain everything, okay?"

"Okay," she said, "go ahead. I can't wait to hear what you've been doing that has kept you so busy you can't call me, or your bandmates."

"I'll tell you everything. I'm just, um, I'm driving right now, okay? I probably shouldn't stay on the phone. I have some time tonight, how about I come over for dinner?"

"Well, I-"

"Invite Dougie and Mel, too, okay? I haven't seen them in a while."

"Okay, I'll call them. But Callie, can't you just-"

"Oh, crap, Kate, there's a cop, gotta go!" I hung up quickly before she could press me for any more information.

I hung up, and looked over at Ethan, who was watching me with a huge grin on his face.

"What?"

He started cracking up, and I had to join him, even though I wasn't sure why he was laughing.

"You're a jerk," I said, finally.

"That was just so, classic. I haven't watched a girl lie to her parents since I was in high school and... Well, never mind, you don't need to know. But seriously, you suck at lying, you know that, right?"

"Shut up," I said with a smile. Then, I sobered up. "Damn. How am I going to tell her? All of them? Mel is going to totally freak out. She doesn't like anything that doesn't fit neatly into a Home Living magazine."

"Do you want some moral support?"

"You want to meet my family?" I asked, surprised. "Isn't that a bit, I don't know, fast?"

His eyes trailed over my body, and he gave me a devilish grin. "I thought maybe we were done moving slow."

I snorted. "This was a momentary lapse in judgment. I'm still not sure I think this, whatever this is, is a great idea."

"You seemed to think it was pretty great a few minutes ago," he said, feigning innocence.

I coughed. "Right. Well. Anyways," I stood up and pulled on some clothes as quickly as I could. "Maybe reinforcements aren't a bad idea. I'll bring Cliff."

"Excuse me?" He said, sitting up. His eyes narrowed. "Cliff? You're supposed to have a full-time detail on you, and that's going to be me."

I didn't argue, knowing that having Ethan around would make me feel better, safer. But I still wanted Cliff to come, too.

"Fine. But Cliff's coming, too, assuming he's free. I think I'm going to need some proof to back up my story, and who better to show off than a grammer?"

Ethan grimaced. "Can't you just read their minds? Maybe use some of your new speaker powers?"

"Are you kidding? I don't want to scare them. And mind-reading is such a party trick, they might not buy it. But a grammer..."

"We could bring Tag, he's a lifter."

"Seriously? Tag, at a family dinner? Thank you, but no. I don't think anyone's ready for that." The idea of Tag's scowl at the dinner table wasn't appealing in the slightest. And knowing Mel, she'd probably fawn all over him. Yuck.

"He's not that bad. He just takes a while to warm up to new people."

"If you say so." I pulled on a thin cardigan that I found at the bottom of my huge purse, and put my Elvis shades on top of my head. "You hungry? 'Cause I could really go for some grub right about now."

"Don't you still have some people to call?" he asked, drawing his shirt back over his head, a worn surf tee that made me think of Jax.

I looked away, checking my hair in the mirror. I let out a small squeak of dismay. Why hadn't anyone told me I looked like Diana Ross circa 1982? My hair had completely gone wild, between the lack of a blow dryer and the incredibly hot, definitely not slow, sex.

"Huh?" I asked absently, digging around in my purse and finding a ball-point pen that would have to do. Quickly, I wound up my hair on top of my head and secured it in a bun stabbing the pen through its center, pulling a couple strands loose to frame my face, so that now I resembled more of a punk-rock geisha than someone coming off a walk of shame.

"Jax? Nick? Your bandmates? I thought you said you were going to talk to them, too?"

"Ugh, do I have to?" I groaned, throwing myself down on the bed beside him.

"Well, you have to tell them something. Why not the truth?" he said, gently running a finger along my jaw.

"I know. You're right. I know you're right."

"Why not look at it like a test run? If all goes well, you won't be so nervous with your family. And if it doesn't, well, you'll know what not to say."

"Gee, thanks. That was super motivational. You should write a book or something," I mocked.

"I know, right? Now how 'bout it?"

"Fine," I grumbled, reaching for my phone. I flicked through the texts, reading them, one after the other.

- Dude, where r u???

- Everything okay? What's your ETA?

- Hello? Callie?

- Dammit Callie, pick up your phone.

- Can't believe u bailed on us. Papa Cho uber pissed.

- Pick up gf, ur freaking us out.

- Callie?

Those were just from the wedding. The texts from today were longer. More ranting. More worrying. More anger. The Cho family had been new A-list clients. Missing their gig had surely cost Molten Requiem some stellar referrals.

There was even one from Tommy, saying he'd heard from a friend that there'd been some drama at the Cho wedding, and reminding me that if we needed better representation he was still willing to take us on.

I swore. Nick really was going to kill me.

"That bad?" Ethan asked, pulling on his pants.

"Worse." I nodded, waiting for the phone to ring. Waiting for Nick to answer.

"Holy Hell, Callie. Where have you been?" Nick's voice came over the line, anxious and rough. I swallowed. I'd dialed the number, but I didn't really know what to say. "Callie? Say something. Are you in trouble?"

"No!" I exclaimed, sorry that I had worried him even more. "No, I'm here. I'm fine. Really. Just, some stuff happened and-"

"Are you freaking kidding me?" he yelled over the phone. "You're fine? Fine? Do you have any idea what Jax and I have been doing today? Where we've been?"

"Well, no, I-"

"First, we called Kate. I didn't want to worry her, but we thought maybe something had happened with the family. Of course, you know the answer to that one. Then, we thought maybe you had an accident, and we started calling all the hospitals. Finally, we decided you must have gone on some kind of romantic getaway, and forgot to inform us. But neither of us could remember the name of your guy's bookshop, so we didn't know how to find you.

Jesus, Callie. What were you thinking, just disappearing like that?"

"I swear, Nick, if I could have called you sooner, I would have. I didn't have my phone, and where I was, there really wasn't anything I could do. Listen, I can't talk now, how about I come over with some pizza and we can talk it all through, okay? I can be at the warehouse in two hours."

"I don't know. Honestly, Jax and I are pretty pissed. We had to call Jax's old drummer, Guillermo, to play the wedding with us, and now we owe their band three joint gigs. Maybe it's better if we don't see each other for a few days."

"Come on, Nick. They're not so bad. Frank won't mind having them play with us a few nights. Plus, we've got that huge show coming up next week," I reminded him. "We need to practice."

"Yeah, so? What do you care," he said sullenly.

"I care. I do. Look, I will tell you everything, okay? Just, give me a chance, okay?"

"Fine," he huffed. He still sounded mad, but I knew he'd already worked through the worst of it. Nick's temper ran fast and hot, and he couldn't sustain the burn for long.

"Great. I'll see you soon." I hung up and looked at Ethan where he was petting Keeta by the door.

"Guess we're leaving?" he asked.

"Yeah, let's go find Cliff. We'll order the pizzas when we get closer to the city," I said. Keeta thumped her tail against mine and looked up at me. "Don't worry, we'll get you some sausage, too."

We walked down the hall, knocking on Cliff's door.

"Yeah?" his groggy voice called.

"It's Callie, can we talk?"

"Just a minute," he said, sounding tired. I heard feet shuffling to the door and then it opened. Cliff stared at us, blinking owlishly. He ran a hand through his hair, which had reappeared in the last hour, a sign of his glammer powers returning. "What's up?"

"I need your help. Can you come with us to LA for dinner? I promise there is pizza involved."

"Oh, gee, well, then... Why am I coming, exactly?"

"I have to talk to some people about what's going on, and someone who can demonstrate an active power will go a long way towards making all this craziness more believable. We'll be making two stops – one with my band, that's the pizza, and then dinner later with my family."

"You want me to meet your Navy Jag brother?" he asked warily.

"Yeah," I sighed. "It would be a big help. Please?"

"Yeah, all right. I need to pick up my car anyways. Besides, I owe you. You wouldn't even be in this mess if I hadn't asked you to tag along to Toby's. When do we leave?"

"Now?"

He looked sadly at his rumpled bed, where he'd obviously been settling in for a nap. "Alright. I'm in."

He slipped on his sneakers and grabbed his things. "Can we stop at the cafeteria first, grab some fruit or something to go?"

"Yeah, I'm pretty hungry, myself," I smiled to myself, thinking of just how I'd worked up an appetite recently.

"Awesome. Let's do this thing." Cliff walked off towards the elevator and Ethan walked with me, running a hand down my back, a casual gesture that sent happy shivers down my whole body.

"Stop that," I whispered.

"Stop what?"

"You know what. We don't have time for that."

He laughed, a low, deep rumble that I felt in my heart. "Honey, I can wait."

Chapter 35

Cliff hadn't been kidding about not sleeping well the night before. He'd passed out in the back of Ethan's car, Keeta sharing the nap and resting along his body. He didn't even wake when we picked up the food, although Keeta scented the air eagerly.

Crossing the lot at Nick's after we'd parked, I saw Jax and Nick's cars so I knew they were both here.

I shot off a quick text to Kate, letting her know I'd be bringing a couple friends for dinner, and then steeled myself to enter the warehouse, cradling the bag of Keeta's sausage in front of me like a shield.

Now or never. Now or never. Now or never. The phrase played on repeat through my brain, like a mantra.

"You can do this," Ethan said encouragingly, waiting by the door.

I nodded at him, trying to believe, trying to agree, that it was all going to be okay.

And yanked open the door.

"Hey guys," I sang out, trying for a happy note. "Pizza's here!"

Jax and Nick, shooting aliens on the Xbox, barely spared me a glance. I went over and sat in the chair by the couch, and Cliff followed, sitting across from me on the other spare chair. Ethan plopped the pizzas down on the coffee table and stood by me. I watched my bandmates ignoring me, and sighed. This was going to be just as hard as I thought. Well, at least Keeta could enjoy herself. I opened the bag in my hands and placed the aluminum container of cooked ground sausage on the floor for the dog, where she happily set to polishing it off.

I sat back to wait for the boys to finish their off-world mission.

"Mind if I-?" Cliff pointed at the pizzas and I shrugged.

"Knock yourself out," I said.

He grabbed a slice. After watching him for a moment, I decided to have one, too. God, I loved pizza.

I offered a slice to Ethan and he just shook his head, barely taking his eyes off my friends. It was unnerving. All his military training had come to the fore, as he stood stock still, legs shoulder width apart, arms crossed over his chest, immobile like a guard on duty. I had a feeling that he could stand like that for hours. Not just could. Would.

I polished off my slice and decided enough was enough.

"Alright, pause the damn game, will you?"

Nick focused on the screen, talking to me while he blasted the helmet off a 6-armed Martian. "We're listening. Talk. Explain to us what you were doing that was so important you couldn't even text us back. Better yet, explain to me why you feel like you needed to bring backup today. You guys in some kind of cult or something? Cause I can tell you right now, I've resisted Scientology this long, I'm not gonna join now."

Okay, so he was pissed. Really, really pissed. I couldn't remember the last time he'd strung so many words together at once.

"Gee, Nick, don't hold back, okay? Jax? How about you? You feel the same way?"

Jax didn't deign to speak, just shot me a glare out of the corner of his eye and continued running down a tunnel after Nick towards the mother ship.

Well, hell, I thought. Let's all hop aboard the crazy train.

"Okay fine. Here goes nothing." I took a deep breath. "The truth is, I would have called you if I could, but I couldn't."

"No service at the ashram?" Nick asked, and Jax snorted.

"I wasn't at an ashram. I was at the China Lake Naval Base. In a cell."

"I'm sorry, did you just say you were in a cell?" Nick paused the game and looked at me.

"Hey!" Jax protested and tossed his controller on the table in disgust. "I was about to kill that guy."

"Focus, Jax. Callie's about to tell us why she was in a naval jail."

"Not a jail. A secret test facility."

"And you were there because?" Nick asked skeptically.

I looked at Cliff and Ethan, and they both nodded. *Tell them*, I heard in my head, though I wasn't sure which of them had thought it.

"Because they wanted to study me. And Cliff. They took both of us, right after practice two days ago."

"And why would they do that?"

"Because of this," Cliff said. Suddenly, the television was gone, and the Mona Lisa was hanging on the wall where the screen had been. Long, red velvet brocade curtains hung on either side of the painting.

"What the hell? How did you do that?" Jax exclaimed.

A large bird swooped into the room, looking suspiciously like Dumbledore's pet phoenix, and settled onto my shoulder. Even though I knew it wasn't real, the weight of it was tangible. The mind was an interesting thing. Or maybe the hologram had properties beyond what I had been told. It didn't really matter. Right now, watching my friends' eyes widen, I felt sick. They were afraid. I could see it. I could feel it. And it was because of me.

"Cliff, stop. Drop the glamour."

The bird dissolved into nothing, and the TV reappeared.

"Callie?" Nick's voice shook. "Want to tell us what's going on? Are you guys witches, or something?"

Cliff laughed, and I gave him a look. Instantly, he schooled his face into a more somber look.

"No. Not witches. Or magicians. We're just people, like you. Just, a little more, too." I paused, and decided now wasn't really the time to go into the whole alien DNA thing. "Some families have powers that have run in their lines for thousands of years. I guess what you would call psychic abilities. Cliff can make people see things that aren't there, like a hologram, or a glamour. Ethan can read minds, and astral travel. A few weeks ago, I found out I can, too. That's how I met Ethan, and then Cliff."

"And those other people that came to our show?"

I nodded. "All of them, yeah. You remember that guy, Toby? Well, he's the one who turned us in to the Navy."

"I thought he seemed kind of off," Jax murmured.

"Were you ever planning to tell us? About your powers, I mean?"

"Of course! I was going to tell you last week. Then they found my grandfather and I-"

"Your grandfather, he's one of these people, too? People with...abilities? You said it travels in families." Nick asked.

"Yes." I nodded.

"Okay, so let's just say we believe you." Jax sat forward, putting his hands on his knees. "The Navy? You want to explain what happened there?"

"I think the less you know about that, probably the better," Ethan answered for me. "But suffice it to say that they are interested in our abilities."

"Hey, I heard about that. The government has all kinds of secret psyops programs. Remember, I was telling you about how the CIA dosed all those people with LSD?" Jax elbowed Nick, who hadn't moved. "Nick?"

"Yeah, I remember," Nick murmured. He blinked. "So that's it? The Navy is after you or something?"

"Something like that, yeah," I agreed. "But we're working on it. I'm doing everything I can to keep you guys safe, I swear."

"We all are," Ethan agreed.

"And you?" Nick came to life, staring hard at Ethan with a gleam in his eyes. "What are you doing to keep her safe? I'm assuming you really do care for her?"

"I do. But you should know as well as anyone, Callie can take care of herself." He brought his hand down on my shoulder and gave it a gentle squeeze.

"Okay." Nick took a deep breath. "Okay. Then you know what I'm thinking?"

"Yes. And I couldn't agree more."

"Okay then. Well, I guess there's just one more question then." Nick looked at me. I looked between him and Ethan, wondering what they'd just agreed upon.

"Yeah? Shoot," I said, feeling nervous. I could think of a million more questions I would have, if I were in his shoes, and I wondered which one it would be.

"Okay. What time is practice tomorrow?"

I laughed – a short, happy sound of surprise.

"Seriously? Anytime you want."

"Great. Well, why don't we finish these off," he smiled, pointing at the pizzas, "and play your new friends some tunes?"

"Sounds like you're playing my song," I grinned.

Chapter 36

Hugs. I'd been getting a lot of them in the last few hours. First, when it was time to leave the warehouse, Nick and Jax had practically suffocated me in an exuberant group hug. Then, on the doorstep of my childhood, a crushing embrace from Kate. The only mother I'd ever known.

The only mother I ever would know.

And as it turns out, she didn't know me at all.

I waited for her to let go, knowing that for Kate a long hug was like a conversation. If you didn't let her finish it the first time, she'd just keep coming after you.

After another twenty or thirty seconds, she stepped back, gripping my arms, and looked me hard in the eyes.

"Now. Tell me what you've gotten yourself into."

"I-"

I faltered, and looked to my friends for help. But what could they say? Cliff shuffled his feet and Ethan just gave me an encouraging chin nod.

"Um...Well, I," I started.

The familiar sound of a motorcycle roaring up the house broke the tension. Doug parked neatly and dismounted, leaving his helmet hanging on the handlebars of the black and chrome Harley. A rare sight in jeans and a fitted white tee, Doug jogged up the steps of the porch.

"Hi Kate, Callie." He leaned down to kiss us both on the cheek.

"Doug, darling. It's so good to see you. Calliope was just about to introduce me to her new friends. Right, dear?"

"Right," I smiled brightly. "Kate, this is Cliff Collet. Cliff, Kate Bess. And this, Kate, is Ethan Hale. Ethan, meet Kate."

Kate tucked a stray piece of blonde hair behind her ear and shook both their hands. "Please, won't you come in? I hope you boys like fish," she said, leading the way inside. "I found an amazing deal on some wild Alaskan salmon this morning, and made a divine cherry-lime ceviche."

I looked around. The tell-tale signs of teen living were evident in the shoes and hoodies by the door, but the house was quiet.

"No Terry and Evelyn?" Kate's two latest fosters were on the verge of aging out of the system, and weren't around much. Evelyn preferred to spend most of her time out with friends, and Terry was a bookworm who studied every night at the library, always getting extra credit on one project or another.

"Not tonight. I swear, it's almost as if I live alone," Kate laughed, but I could hear the undercurrent of sadness in her voice. Kate had few flaws or weaknesses, but being alone was up near the top of the list, along with a strange addiction to pork rinds and an aversion to dating. Pretty much anything that could possibly lead to marriage was off the table, since a string of bad relationships had turned her off romance forever. It wasn't something she liked to talk about, but I knew enough to get that it wasn't an aversion she was likely to ever grow out of. She'd spent the last few decades building an amazing career, and caring for kids in need. If there was still a small space to fill in her heart, it wasn't for lack of trying.

"Terry and Evelyn?" Ethan whispered as we walked down the hall.

"Other fosters," I whispered back, removing his hand from my waist. I looked behind us, and Doug quirked an eyebrow at me. Caught red handed, I thought.

Ethan snorted, trying not to laugh, and I knew I'd broadcasted. Again. Damn. Was I ever going to get a handle on that?

Marnie said I just had to practice, that eventually I'd be shielded all the time, so practice I would. I blasted some Green Day at Ethan, and he grinned. "You know," he said, leaning down close to my ear, "I'm starting to think that might be our song."

"What's that, dear?" Kate turned.

"Nothing, ma'am," Ethan said, turning up the southern charm. "Just commenting on how nicely you all get along. My own brothers and I fight like cats and dogs."

"Ah. Well, boys will be boys, I always say. So long as you all still love each other at the end of the day."

"Yes, ma'am," he said, his easy smile slipping slightly. "You couldn't be more right."

Even without trying to read him, I knew he was thinking of his oldest brother, the warper.

Kate led us into the dining room, where the table was simply set with bright blue dishes and emerald green glasses. Everything in Kate's home was bright and bold, easy and welcoming. Except the foster rooms – those, she allowed the kids to decorate however they wanted. Every new foster was given a paint roller and ride to the local hardware store their first day in so they could pick out their own paint colors. Mel and I had painted our room hot pink with black trim. Doug's room had been a cool, crisp gray with a hint of blue.

Once we'd all sat down at the table, Kate passed around a light salad topped with cherry tomatoes, corn and feta.

"So, I can't remember the last time Callie brought friends home for dinner. Tell us about yourselves, Evan, Cliff."

"Ethan, ma'am. I grew up in Maryland, did a tour of service with the army right out of school, and decided I liked it out here when I was passing through. Been here for close to ten years now."

"Really? What do you do now?"

"I run a small bookshop and retreat center called the Bronzehead."

I watched Doug for any reaction, but caught none. Either he had become a better actor in his twenties, or he didn't know about the small starseed facility.

"The Bronzehead? Isn't that the esoteric place down near Antoine's? That's a nice shop."

"You've been there?" I asked, surprised. Though I shouldn't have been. Kate seemed to know everyone and everything, and she'd always had a spiritual bent.

"Well sure. I've found some amazing antique jewelry there. In fact, you know that pair of earrings Nikki wore for the AMAs last year? I got them from the Bronzehead. Amber and peridot, set in gold and copper. They set off her eyes perfectly." Her eyes took on a faraway look, remembering. "Who does your buying?"

"Oh, I do, mostly. I have some dealers who know what I like, they keep an eye out for me."

"Good to know. I'll have to add your name to my list of buyers. Do you have a card?"

"I sure do." He drew out his wallet and handed her a card from the worn leather tri-fold. I eyed Kate suspiciously, wondering if this maneuvering was purely business on her part, or a covert way of keeping an eye on me.

"Wonderful, thank you, Ethan." She placed the card on the table in front of her. "Perhaps now it will be easier to get in touch with Callie, the next time she decides to disappear."

I sputtered, having just taken a rather large swig of water. "Kate!"

"What?" she asked, blinking innocently at me.

"Nothing," I said, getting up and clearing plates from the table. I so was not ready for this. Telling the guys was one thing. Spilling my secret to family? I'd never be able to take it back.

I leaned over the counter, bracing my hands on the cold marble, trying to get a grip. Trying to breathe.

This was it. After today, my life could never, ever go back to normal.

The door behind me creaked open, and I waited for Kate to ask me what was wrong. Instead, muscled thighs pressed into mine, and warm hands came down on my own, strong arms braced against me.

"You okay?" Ethan nuzzled my ear.

"Mmm, I am now," I murmured, before coming to my senses. "Ethan, come on. You can't do this here."

"Why not?" he asked, running his hands up my bare arms.

"Because...because, I," I paused, unable to think clearly, and unable to provide a good reason. Then I remembered. "Because, you are not here as a boyfriend. You are here as backup, remember? Now cut it out and help me," I said, without heat.

"I thought I was," he said, still not moving away.

I groaned. "No, really. Not. Helping." I ducked under his arm and spun away, picking up the bowl of fresh ceviche. "You want to help? Grab those bowls."

I flounced out of the kitchen, leaving Ethan to bring in the clean plates. Kate smiled up at me as I set down the bowl.

"Everything okay? You look... flushed." She noted with a sly smile.

I rolled my eyes and sat down in my seat with a huff. Doug laughed. "Some things never change," he said.

"Oh yeah?" Cliff asked, passing him one of the bowls.

"Oh, yeah," Doug chuckled. "Callie's always been the wild one in the family. I remember the last guy she brought home-"

I aimed a small kick at his shin and he smirked at me.

"Let's just say, Callie has some special skills."

Cliff's eyes went wide. "You mean, you know?"

"Well, sure. No one is better at delivering a shock than Cal." Doug spooned a healthy serving of the fish salad into his bowl and leaning conspiratorially towards Cliff, who looked oddly flushed. "But I guess you've figured that out on your own."

"Oh, um, sure," Cliff blanched, and glanced at me. Doug ate, oblivious, but Kate looked back and forth between us.

"Okay," she said, laying her fork down. "That's it. I think I've been patient enough. I was going to do the polite thing and wait for dessert, but I've had it. Callie, what in the sam-hill is going on with you?"

"Uh-oh, you're in for it," Doug stage-whispered.

I kicked him again, harder this time, and he laughed, rubbing his shin. Kate shot laser beams out her eyes at me, a trick only the best of moms can master.

"Sorry," I said. "He's just so...argh!"

"Calliope Winters," she warned.

"Right." I closed my eyes for a moment and took a deep breath. "Honestly, I'm not sure where to begin."

"Why don't you try at the beginning? That's usually a good place to start," she said, trying not to crack a smile.

"Right. You're right. Well," I began, and I launched into a recap of everything that had happened, starting with that night at the Hammer, the blood moon and my first flight. My first meeting with Ethan. I couldn't help smiling at him when I told that part, heat traveling through my body as he returned my look. Kate never interrupted me once. No one did. I left out the part about Kipner, and the mansion mission I'd crashed with Tag and Ethan, not sure how much Doug should really know. Kate looked most affected when I described meeting my grandfather.

"So, you have family?"

They were the first words she'd said since I started.

"Yes. A grandfather, at any rate. My father is dead, and no one really knows who my mother is. That's all I really know, so far." It was only a tiny lie. Because, really, we didn't know. Not for sure. We might never know. I had no plans to reach out to Ozan any time soon for a family reunion, that was for sure.

"Wow. That's just. Wow." Kate sat back in her chair, stunned. "So is that where you were? With your grandfather? Did you feel like you had to hide him from us? Why didn't you tell me right away? You know, he's welcome here, of course."

"Kate!" I interrupted her sharply, then softened my tone. "It's not like that. I wanted to tell you, I did. I planned on telling you. All of you." I looked at Doug, who was looking at me like I'd grown two heads, and might suddenly use one of them to snap off his own. "I wasn't keeping him from you."

"It was my fault," Cliff said quietly.

"You?" Doug looked at him, shocked. No. Not shocked. As if he'd been betrayed, somehow, which was silly since they'd only just met.

"Yes, me. See, the thing is, all these things Callie can do, these things we can do, sometimes people use them the wrong way, you know?" Kate swallowed, looking at Ethan and Cliff with new eyes. "Not us, no!" Cliff protested, seeing the look.

"No, our friend, Toby," I said scathingly. "He decided he'd rather use his powers to control people, and when we tried to talk him out of it, he turned on us."

"But I don't understand," Kate said. "How could he control people? I mean astral travel, mind reading, these aren't exactly sinister talents.

"No," said Cliff. "They're not. But this can be."

Suddenly, the windows crashed in, glass flying everywhere, and the lights flickered out. Kate screamed, and then the lights came back on, and the windows were whole, undamaged.

"What the-"

"You're a grammer!" Doug jumped up, pointing at Cliff.

"I am," Cliff admitted, at the same time I blurted, "So you do know!"

If Doug was physically capable of ever admitting he was wrong, I swear he would have looked guilty at that moment. Instead, he shrugged. "And your friend Toby, what is he?"

"A speaker," I said.

"Speaker? Grammer? What are you guys talking about? What the hell just happened? Doug? What's going on?"

"Yeah, Doug, why don't you tell us what's going on? Since it was your damn friends who kidnapped me and dosed me up with who knows what for two days."

Doug's eyes went wide and he set his mouth in a line.

"You've been to China Lake?"

I ignored him, choosing to answer the only mother I had ever had, instead.

"You want to know what's going on? The Navy is working with some of the most dangerous people in the world to develop super soldiers. They're messing with people like me, like Cliff, trying to figure out how to distort the powers we have, and how to enhance their own people. And they're killing people, Kate. Killing people!" I aimed that last part at Doug, watched him collapse back into his chair.

"Dammit, Callie. This is bad. Real bad. I knew they were doing some psy-research out at China Lake, but I didn't know... Well, I didn't know. I swear, I didn't."

"Hmphf," was my only answer. What can I say? Old sibling habits live on, well into adulthood. Do any of us ever really grow up?

"Okay, kids, that's enough. Doug, I'm glad you aren't knowingly involved in harming people. But Callie, please explain. What did your friend just do? And what about this other guy, the one that tried to hurt you?"

"Ah, right. Well, there are five main groups of powers. Some are more passive, like traveling, or reading. Some people, like Cliff, can project false realities, making people see things that aren't really there."

"Like this," Cliff interrupted. He whipped off his hat and revealed a mostly hairless head. Then, dark hair shimmered back into place. "We're called grammers, short for hologram, though I prefer the term glammer.

"Oh," Kate exclaimed, putting a hand to her chest in surprise. "Right, like putting on a glamour, I get it."

"Exactly," I nodded. "Some people can move things around, telekinetically, we call them lifters. And some people, like Toby, can make people do whatever they say."

"Most people call them bards, or speakers."

"Bards? I hadn't heard that one before," Doug said, interest keen in his voice.

"Well, get used to it, bro, 'cause you're looking at one."

"What?" He said, shocked. You're a speaker?"

"Yep. So watch it, or I'll make you eat sand," I teased, wiggling my eyebrows. Unfortunately, my joke fell flat. Damn. So much for comedic timing.

"Crap, Callie. That's serious. If Sherwood found out..." his voice trailed off.

"Well, he won't, will he?" Ethan said, his voice nearing a low growl laced with menace.

"No," Doug said, straightening. "Not from me. Never from me. Really, Callie. Family is... you guys are the only real family I ever had. Blood comes first."

"But we're not. Blood, I mean."

"Yes, we are." Doug reached over and held my hand. "We are," he repeated.

"I'm glad you said that," I beamed up at him. "Because I think I need your help."

I proceeded to tell him the full story of what had happened to Cliff and me, and how we had escaped. The more I told, the grimmer his expression became. Occasionally, Kate would gasp. In the end, I didn't think Doug's eyebrows could possibly get any closer together, or his lips any thinner.

"This is bad," was all he said.

"Like, how bad?" Cliff asked lightly. "Titanic or Hamlet?"

"What's the difference," I asked.

"Not everybody dies in Titanic," Doug said slowly, staring at Cliff.

"What about Horatio?" asked Kate, referring to the one major character that lives on at the end of Hamlet.

"Doesn't count," dismissed Doug, "he just lives on to tell the story."

"Really? I always thought Horatio was Hamlet's schoolboy crush," said Cliff off-handedly.

"Really?" Doug asked, a gleam in his eye.

"Really," Cliff said.

Oh. My. God. For the first time in, I don't know, ever, sparks were flying off of Doug, and they weren't the angry kind.

"Huh," Doug grunted, and gave a small smile. "Fine then, I guess Hamlet."

Cliff grinned, until Kate's voice cut through the flirtation like glass.

"Forgive me, but I think we're getting off track. Is Callie in danger? Doug? Just how dangerous are these people you're involved with?"

Doug fidgeted. "I'm not sure. I didn't know the full extent of what was going on at China Lake, like I said. I do know that Admiral Sherwood isn't someone to mess around with. The guy takes confrontation personally, he's a total sociopath. How he's been allowed to get so far ahead in the ranks I'll never know. But if they don't know you were there, then you should be okay. As far as I know, they still think the fire was a fluke, the data losses, too."

"Can you find out more? Without anyone getting suspicious? I don't want you to get in trouble. But any information you can give us would be a really big help," I said.

"We'd especially like to know who else might be behind the project, Washington connections, that sort of thing," Ethan added.

"Right. I'll see what I can find out." Doug answered us, but his eyes were on Cliff.

Definite sparkage.

Oh wow.

Apparently bringing Doug over to our side was going to be easier than I thought, and it had as much to do with me as the handsome young glammer sitting across the table.

Chapter 37

Five nights later I was under the lights, already sweating and blinded by the glare. I couldn't see into the darkness. Beyond the lights, there was nothing.

A thousand people were screaming, banging their feet, yelling in joy.

For us.

Well, okay, maybe not entirely for us. Molten Requiem was about to open for a huge band, and the quicker we finished our set, the quicker they would get to see the band they came for. They knew it. We knew it. The Rooks knew it.

Still. Now was our shot. Our day in the sun. One solid set, and we'd have at least a thousand new fans. Video-taking, twitter-pating fans. In a couple hours, with any luck, our faces would be plastered all over social media.

Maybe not entirely famous, but our bookings would get bigger. Better. Maybe I'd make more money and have more time to spend with my new friends, the people who had come to be another aspect of family for me.

I hit the drums, and rattled some brass. Slowly, I built up a boot-stomping beat, and then Jax joined in, playing his bass almost as well as he played the girls in the crowd. His smile was as bright as the stage lights. I grinned back at him and flew into the song, giving Nick his opening, which he took with confidence. Guitar riffed over the speakers and Nick's smooth, sexy voice slammed out lyrics.

Our lyrics. Our songs. Tonight we wouldn't be playing any covers. Tonight, the music was all us. Our hearts. Our souls. Our beats.

I felt the urge to fly on the song, and resisted. Tonight, I needed to be all here. Fully present.

All in.

That last thought almost made me miss a beat, because it wasn't my own.

I glanced to the side, and saw Cliff, Marnie, Kate and Mel, all standing off-stage, dancing among the curtains. Even Tag was bobbing his head.

Only Ethan stood still, watching me with a smile.

All in? I thought.

All in. He shrugged. *Why not? I want you, Callie.*

Didn't your mother ever tell you, you gotta earn the things you want? I teased.

Oh, I'm working on it. He gave me a smile that burned me, in all the best places, in all the right ways.

I rolled my eyes. Have we figured out what that chip was for, yet?

No, and we're not going to, not unless we get our hands on another one. The lab says the chip fried itself after we removed it from the guard. Next time, the lab wants us to bring it back in a live host.

Great. Because that's not creepy at all. Any news on Toby? I asked.

He shook his head, his dark eyes clearly troubled. *No. He's vanished. Wherever he is, we're afraid we'll hear about it soon enough. Word is, the warpers are planning some sort of attack, something to make people afraid, something to make them more susceptible to group mind control.*

Can they do that?

He nodded. That was all I needed to know. Really, what else was there?

The warpers were determined to get power, any way they could.

It was okay. We were determined to stop them. To remain uncorrupted and uncorrupting. Our ancestors had been protecting humanity for thousands of years. Allowing man to evolve at its own pace. Keeping minds free. No masters. No slaves.

Now, it was my turn.

Every act of free will was an act of defiance, an act of intent.

Every song a ray of light shot into the darkness.

Every moment of happiness, a battle won.

This time, like all the times before, we would prevail. Humanity would rise, and love would win.

And to prove it, for the first time ever, I did something I'd sworn I would never do. Jax and Nick raised their voices in chorus, and mine joined them. Exhorting the audience to remain free. Setting their minds to become only their own. All programming removed. All suggestions deleted. Any vulnerabilities, gone.

One mind at a time, I would defuse the warpers. One song at a time, one show at a time.

We had this. I had this.

It was the birth of a new world below the stage tonight, but there was no big bang, only the quiet lifting of a thousand hearts and minds, easing into freedom.

A Starseed Compendium

of Characters and Terms

Amelia – Callie's landlady at Hillhurst and Los Feliz.

Bronzehead Books – Don't be deceived by the cozy atmosphere of the metaphysical bookstore on the first floor. The Bronzehead is also a hideout and training center for starseeds.

Calliope Winters – AKA Callie. Drummer in Molten Requiem, an LA alternative/punk rock band. 28 years old. Tall, dark and curvy with light golden eyes. Telepath, Astral Traveler, and a Speaker.

China Lake – A Naval Base in the desert lands of California.

Cliff Collet – Always wears a backwards baseball cap over his thick dark hair. Prep cook in Malibu. Writes screenplays. Grammer/Glammer.

Doctor Xavier Oxley – Naval contractor working at China Lake. British type, says "luv" a lot.

Dolores – Speaker. Helps deprogram the mind controlled. Vehement about moral speaking.

Doug Rice – Callie's foster brother. 6'4" with dark flawless black skin and chiseled face. Navy JAG lawyer. Prefers dating men.

Ethan Hale – tall and built, a surfer type with golden coppery brown hair and dark brown eyes. Owns Bronzehead Books. Astral Traveler. Scouts and reads.

Evie Garcia – Friendly Latina girl with short hair. Reader who talks to animals.

Finnegan Winters – Callie's father. Reader.

General John Kipner – Imposing white-haired US Army General.

Grammers – AKA Glammers. Starseeds with the ability to glamour appearance and create illusions. Solar.

Gregors – Watcher organization that oversees the training and well-being of starseeds. Run jointly by humans and starseeds.

Gregory Bank – Huge multinational investment bank. Front for the Gregors.

Griffith Park – Iconic Los Angeles park with extensive hiking trails and hills. Home of famous observatory to the stars and a dog-lover's paradise.

HAARP – The High Frequency Active Auroral Research Program was an ionospheric research program jointly funded by the U.S. Air Force, the U.S. Navy, the University of Alaska Fairbanks, and the Defense Advanced Research Projects Agency. Officially decommissioned in 2015.

Henry Kim – Korean/Asian Doctor and trainer with the Gregors.

Ilana Fanai – Callie's birth mother. Speaker.

Jax – Bassist for band. Brown eyes, raw husky voice, Surfer bod. Oahu (Hawaii) transplant. Chick magnet.

Joseph Winters – AKA Joe, Callie's grandfather. Native American/Irish heritage. Dark hair and eyes. Astral Traveler.

Joshua Tree Headquarters – AKA HQ. Massive training facility and headquarters of Los Angeles area starseeds.

Kate Bess – Callie's foster mom, professional personal stylist. Short, wavy blonde hair and cornflower blue eyes.

Keeta – Callie's dog. White Husky/Samoyed mix with blue eyes. Female. Her name means "snow."

Laura – A young, nicely rounded woman. Works at Bronzehead Books.

Lifters – Starseeds with the power of telekinesis. Solar.

Marnie – Reader and trainer. Mid- to late-thirties with military bearing.

Melissa – Callie's foster sister. Stewardess with red hair and OCD. 3 years older than Callie.

Nick – Lead singer/guitarist for Molten Requiem. Gorgeous blue Irish eyes.

Ozan Fanai – Callie's grandfather. Turkish/Egyptian. The power speaker behind at least six governments.

Readers – Starseeds with the power of telepathy. Lunar.

Speakers – AKA Bards. Starseeds with the power to control minds mind through speech. Solar.

Starseeds – AKA Star Children. Hybrid beings born of humans and The Nommo (ancient alien visitors to Earth).

Starseeds – Children of the Nommo, human/alien hybrids with psychic powers.

Tag Kerry – Tall military guy with short hair. Gruff. Telekinetic.

The Hammer – Molten Requiem's regular gig every Thursday night. Frank is the owner, Jody is a bartender.

The Nommo – Alien race that traveled to earth and interbred with humans thousands of years ago, creating the star children or starseeds. Their offspring are aligned with the sun or the moon, awakening with abilities after their 28th birthday when exposed to lunar or solar eclipse events.

The Satellite – Silver Lake Bar where Molten Requiem plays regularly. Bartender is named Ed.

Toby Meehan – a thin, wiry man with glasses. Speaker. Works in IT, lives at home with parents. His mom's a hostage negotiator with the LAPD. Dad is a top-shelf corporate lawyer."

Tommy Fein – Callie's abusive ex. Smarmy talent agent and possessive scumbag.

Travelers – AKA Walkers or Journeyers. Starseeds with the ability to astral travel and navigate dreams. Lunar.

Warpers – Starseeds who use their abilities negatively for personal gain and/or entertainment, regardless of who it hurts. Anyone can become a warper – when we twist the mind and lives of others, our own becomes warped.

About the Author

Ellis Logan lives a quiet life in New England, obsessing daily over superheros and the gods of old. She spends her days corralling wild children and communing with fairies. When everyone is settled down and the owls begin to sing, you'll find her typing away and munching on dark chocolate while unseen spirits whisper stories in her ear.

Did you enjoy this book?
Please consider leaving a review on
Amazon and **Goodreads**!

Want more?
*The story continues in **Dream Tracker**.*

Follow Ellis on Facebook and Twitter at
EllisLoganBooks

and

Join Ellis's mailing list at EllisLogan.com
to stay tuned for new releases, giveaways
and more!